The Second Time Around
Tabor Heights, Year 1, Book 1

Michelle L. Levigne

M☧ Zion Ridge Press
Books Off the Beaten Path

www.MtZionRidgePress.com

Mt Zion Ridge Press
295 Gum Springs Rd, NW
Georgetown, TN 37366

https://www.mtzionridgepress.com

Published in the United States of America
Publication Date: May 15, 2023

Editor-In-Chief: Michelle Levigne
Executive Editor: Tamera Lynn Kraft

Dedication and Acknowledgement

Dedicated to the theater staff and my fellow students at
Northwestern College (1981-1983).

Some of the references and geography in Tabor Heights, Ohio and
Butler Williams University are loosely based on Orange City, Iowa, and
Northwestern College, along with the towns of Troy and Berea, Ohio.

TABOR HEIGHTS

Welcome to Tabor Heights:
A friendly little town on Ohio's North Coast, where sweet romance is
always in the air.

Here you'll be able to explore the lives of the members of the congregation
of Tabor Christian Church in the space of two years. The stories overlap,
and there's no one right place to start.

Just like any small town, you come in, you meet someone, you hear their
story and get to know them, and they introduce you to their friends, tell
you something about them, and you learn those stories. As you get to
know these new friends, they introduce you to other people, and tell you
about other interesting stories in town.

It's the same way with Tabor Heights. Start with the story that interests
you the most, and then branch out.

Settle back and enjoy your visit.
Welcome!

Year One

The Second Time Around
Detours
Common Grounds
White Roses
The Family Way
Forgiven
Firesong
Behind The Scenes
The Mission
Accidental Hearts

A Quiet Place

Year Two

Cooking Up Trouble
The Wrath Of Bubbles
Invitation To A Wedding
Truck Stop Angel
A Box Of Promises
Wheels
The Teddy Bear Dancer

Chapter One

Butler-Williams University
Tabor Heights, Ohio
Monday, August 28

Dr. Daniel Morgan didn't believe in ghosts, so he didn't have an explanation for the vision that settled into the second seat, far left row, of his freshman theater history class on the first day of the fall semester. Fortunately, the auburn-haired freshman girl with Lynette Teague's face was one of the first into the room, so Daniel didn't stand there with his last two years at Northwestern University flashing through his mind while his new students sat and fidgeted and stared. He yanked himself back to the present, avoided looking at that part of the room, and pushed his heartbreak back into his memories for the duration of the first day lecture.

And the next three classes.

He retreated to his cramped, book-lined office in the basement of the theater arts building and sat with his feet propped up on his desk, staring at the toes of his new sneakers—always a new pair for the start of the school year—trying to figure out what he felt.

"Morgan?" Bekka Sanderson, his student assistant, hung against the frame of his doorway, looking just as drained by the first-day-of-classes mayhem as he felt. Her belt-length straight brown hair had escaped the twistee that restrained it when she met him with his coffee and bagel at 7am and helped him finish assembling the syllabi for all his classes. "You okay?" The fact that she called him *Morgan* rather than *Dr. Morgan Sir* meant there were no emergencies or bombs ready to drop on him.

For that, he breathed a sigh of thankfulness to God.

"I just realized that it's been more than twenty years since I was in those kids' shoes." Daniel let his feet drop down to the cement floor. Bekka knew everything and everyone in the entire Humanities Department at Butler-Williams. What were the chances she would know the name of the girl in his first period class, with Lynette Teague's face and hair?

"Bekka?" an unfamiliar female voice called from out in the euphemistically labeled lobby of the theater department's office. It was more prop storage room and workspace than an area to lounge and served as an auxiliary costume department for big productions.

"In here." Bekka turned and gestured. "Don't go scaring me, Morgan.

The General is the one who gives us the 'I'm getting too old for this' routine just before auditions for the Christmas play. I'm the one who's too old to be playing psychologist for the whole department."

"You're *my* Gal Friday. Tell the General and Joel Randolph to keep their grimy —" Daniel stopped short as the girl from the first period class peered over Bekka's shoulder. He swallowed hard and put on his friendliest smile. "Hello. I hope you're not here to drop my class after one day."

The freshman girl laughed. He was relieved when that wasn't Lynette's musical laugh. Her hair, hanging nearly to the pocket of her shirt, was curlier than Lynette's straight auburn, a little darker, and her nose wasn't the tiny, up-tilted button that demanded kissing and always turned red with the first hint of autumn chill. "No way. It was the best part of the day."

"Because I was the only professor who didn't take roll call, you mean?"

"Uh... yeah." She shrugged, grinning, and that wasn't Lynette's smile. For which he thanked God again. "I'm Kat Tyler."

"Nice to meet you, Kat. Who's your advisor?"

"Dr. Defiore."

"You have to call him the General — you're part of the theater gang now," Bekka said.

"You just missed him," Daniel added.

"I'm not here to see him," Kat said, and tipped her head in Bekka's direction.

"We're hitting the cafeteria for dinner. The food is fantastic at the beginning of the year," Bekka said. "Besides, you know how my grandparents are at the start of the term. I don't need another lecture over dinner on how I should be studying accounting, when I have homework for every single class already. We'd better run. See you tomorrow."

"Bright and early. Double chocolate muffin this time," Daniel added.

"*Seig heil.*" Bekka saluted, two fingers off her eyebrow, and left with Kat, both girls laughing.

Daniel held onto his smile until he heard the wheeze of the ancient pneumatic door leading to the stairwell. Then he slouched in his chair and raked his fingers through his hair. He definitely felt old today.

~~~~~

"I was back at Northwestern for a few seconds there," Daniel said an hour later, looking out over the backyard of his cousin Al's house where his children, Chad and Candy, enjoyed their last chance to use their pool. "And it hit me that our kid would be a college freshman by now, and I don't even know if Lynette had a boy or a girl. Or if she even had our baby at all." He exhaled slowly, marveling at the sensation of a heavy weight
~~~~~

lifting off him, just admitting what had taken all day to become clear in his mind and heart.

"I can only imagine how much a shock it was, seeing that girl walk in." Abby, Al's sister, reached across the picnic table and squeezed both of Daniel's hands. "You were in love, you were willing to marry her and give up a promising future in theater to do what's right, and her rich old aristocrat mother used her stable of lawyers to send you away and lock you out of her life. You're not the kind of guy to just walk away from a responsibility or a wound like that."

"After you and your folks whacked some sense into my head, and God fixed my heart, yeah." He summoned up a smile and wondered what happened to his acting skills.

Nineteen years ago, when his world had been yanked out from under his feet, he wouldn't have survived without his relatives. He had been basically abandoned in his early teens—his mother choosing military service over motherhood, his father vanishing somewhere on the other side of the world. The Morgan branch of the family in Tabor Heights had taken him home and made him feel not only welcome but wanted. Daniel hadn't thought much of their faith and their belief in an unseen God. Then the mother of his child refused to marry him and used the threat of high-powered lawyers and restraining orders to push him out of their lives. He didn't have anything or anyone else to turn to but the 'Bible thumper' relatives he had hoped to escape when he pursued his theater career. Daniel had learned about the Bible and the God he had ignored as a teen, and found his sanity and peace there.

His aunt and uncle had retired and bought a custom RV to go exploring the continental U.S., while his widowed cousin, Al, raised his son and daughter with the assistance of his sister, Abby. Morgan knew he spoiled Chad and Candy in part to make up for not being able to raise his own child—wherever he or she was. He hadn't been conscious of the lack of Lynette and their baby for several years now. Being part of the theater department at Butler-Williams University kept him busy. All his students were his children. He had been content and too busy to think of what he didn't have, until that girl walked into his classroom that morning, with Lynnette Teague's face.

"I think I'd better have a talk with Pastor Glenn," Daniel muttered.

"Duh." Abby squeezed his hands a little harder and released him, finishing with a shooing gesture. "How come we always make our last resort what should be our first step?"

Daniel leaned over the table as he stood up, kissed his cousin's cheek, then called good-byes to the children. He knew better than to get within ten feet of that pool while the children were having that much loud fun. He also knew better than to keep gnawing on his life that might have been and sent up a few prayers on the short drive to Tabor Christian Church in the center of town. He knew it wasn't luck that he caught Pastor Glenn coming out of the church office, half an hour after office hours had ended for the day. His misery must have showed on his face, because the senior minister gestured at the picnic table set up outside the back door of the church and welcomed him with a smile.

~~~~~

Lynette Tyler drove to her daughter's dormitory room that evening with supplies for the cube refrigerator she had found at the wholesale outlet the week before. Maybe she was spoiling Kat, but it felt good to support her daughter in this bid for independence. She remembered how it had felt, starting classes at Northwestern and living in the dormitories when she could very well have commuted from her mother's elegant home on the stylish side of town. Her mother had encouraged her, and Lynette swore she would support Kat, no matter how much she missed her daughter and—yes, desperately—needed her company. The fact that her husband, Mike, didn't want Kat living on campus was reason enough to encourage their daughter.

"My daughter," Lynette reminded herself as she pulled into the conveniently marked visitor parking space along the side of the dormitory building.

What was it about Mike insisting on calling Kat "my little girl" every chance he got that irritated her more and more with every passing month? Besides the fact that Kat was so adamant about reminding people that Mike was her stepfather? She had been ten years old when Mike married Lynette and adopted her, and she hadn't had any choice in the matter. Kat was currently saving up her money to take legal action and get rid of Mike's name. Lynette seriously considered giving Kat the rest of the money for her birthday, mostly because it would irritate her husband.

Lynette wished she hadn't agreed to let Mike adopt Kat. She wished she hadn't agreed to marry Mike when it was so clear that Kat didn't like him from the very beginning.

"You've made your bed—now lie in it," she muttered.

Sighing, she picked up the bags of groceries and opened the car door. Nineteen years ago, she had run away from her problems and made choices she thought were wise. Running away and using her mother's power and influence hadn't given her the results she wanted. Older and wiser—but certainly not happier—she was determined not to run away anymore.

Why wouldn't Mike embarrass them both with a loud, noisy affair, and give her an excuse to end their marriage?

"Mom?" Kat laughed and ran the last dozen yards down the sidewalk. "Gee, I think I see you more now than I did all summer." The
~~~~~

older girl who had been walking with her down the sidewalk took her time catching up with them.

"I brought supplies. I dimly remember the cafeteria food being good only for the first month of school, then the cooks get bored and the quality goes downhill fast." Lynette fought not to wrap her arms tight around her daughter and beg her to let her sleep over in the dormitory. Or even move in.

Kat introduced her friend, Bekka Sanderson, another theater student, as the three climbed the stairs to her room on the third floor. From her hundred-miles-an-hour chatter and glowing face, her first day of classes had been a success. Lynette just laughed when Kat wailed about auditions for the Christmas production starting in one week.

"That's the way it is in theater, honey. Always thinking and living months in advance."

"Mom was a theater student at Northwestern," Kat explained to Bekka as they reached her dormitory room.

"When? Morgan studied there, too." Bekka took two of the grocery bags from Kat so she could unlock her door.

"Really? Cool. Mom, Dr. Morgan concentrates on writing for theater and Bekka is his student assistant, and I really think I should transfer over to him next year, after I get all my basics out of the way."

"Dr. Morgan?" Lynette swore the floor rolled underneath her and she grabbed for the doorframe. She was vaguely grateful Kat had taken the rest of the bags from her and stepped into the room. "Umm, what's this Dr. Morgan like? We had all your interviews with Dr. Defiore. I'd hate to, umm, think of all that time wasted."

"The General usually gets all the freshmen," Bekka said. "Then about a week into the school year, he has his usual panic over the Christmas production getting started, and hands over the ones who have shown any interest at all in writing or tech to Morgan or Boss."

"Boss?"

"Mr. Randolph, the theater tech teacher. He runs Homespun Theater." She stepped over to a desk built into the wall that had to be Kat's because of the stack of books and bound screenplays and the open notebook computer hiding the surface. After a moment of looking, she picked up a spiral-bound booklet and flipped it open. "The incoming theater student survival manual. Morgan's idea," she added with a grin, and held out the booklet for Lynette to see the color photo filling the page. Three older men in jeans and blue BWU sweatshirts, jammed onto a bench made for two, held the "hear no evil, see no evil, speak no evil" pose.

In the middle, with his hands over his ears and his mouth wide in Kat's familiar laughing grin, sat Daniel Morgan. Her Daniel Morgan. The same wavy, dark hair, the formerly heavy, shoulder-length mane cut conservatively short now. The same big, chocolate brown eyes and thick lashes and square jaw. A little heavier than when she had known him in school, with lines from years and experience around his mouth and eyes, but very clearly the man who had won her heart during freshman orientation and filled her head with dreams of stardom on Broadway at his side... and gave her Kat.

"Ahh... I'm guessing you have a lot of fun with your professors,' Lynette offered, knowing she had to say something.

What she wanted to do was grab Kat and drag her out of the dormitory, out of Tabor Heights, back home to Stoughton—and for good measure, throw her on the first plane back to Chicago and let her live with her Granny Teague like her daughter had begged for the last three years.

Lynette knew she couldn't do that. Not without raising a lot of questions. Not without breaking her vow to stop running away from her problems.

Avoiding wasn't the same as running, was it? Because she knew right here and now, she could never risk running into Dr. Daniel Morgan—why had he become a theater professor, when he could have become a star?—at any of Kat's performances on the BWU stage. It would take tricky maneuvering and a quick mind for excuses and hasty exits. She had become adept at maneuvering, in the last four years of marriage to Mike Tyler, keeping him from ruining the catering business they had built together and destroying their standing with the elite of Northeast Ohio. If she could keep the world from knowing what an immature jerk Mike had turned into, she could avoid running into Kat's father and having that particular secret exposed to the world.

It was going to be a long four years while Kat attended Butler-Williams University.

Lynette wished she knew how to pray. She had stopped attending church when the self-righteous upper crust members of her mother's home church shunned her for being an unwed mother. She had stopped turning to God for help when all her prayers didn't bring Daniel back into her life after Kat was born, and she realized what a mess she had made of their lives. It was a little late to get back into God's good graces now, but Lynette couldn't help wishing... and maybe that was a prayer in and of itself.

~~~~~

Over the next few months, Daniel lost track of the times he came into the basement of the theater building to find Kat Tyler keeping Bekka company as she worked on his projects. It irritated him that something so trivial as a physical resemblance to a woman in his past bothered him. How was he going to shove Lynette Teague's memory back into the closet when the girl wouldn't stay away? The only way to get over his nagging
~~~~~

personal problem was to get to know Kat, so she became a distinct person, not just a haunting face in the classroom. Fortunately, a close friendship took root between Bekka and Kat. Bekka was in the Singles class Daniel co-taught at Tabor Christian Church. She had been his student assistant three years now, and knew he liked to hear about the new students so he could help them without putting them through the third degree himself.

Kat's parents lived in Stoughton and ran Chef Michael's Catering. Her mother had a business degree and ran the office, as well as being deeply involved in the community. That left Michael to handle the menus and public relations. The Tylers were wealthy, counted among the elite in Stoughton, and Michael liked to throw his money around and flaunt his connections and influence. Daniel had a good idea just what kind of a person Michael Tyler was, because the man had made it a point to regularly call the heads of every department and sub-department at the university to remind them his business was there to cater for every function they might have. For some reason, he seemed to think he was entitled to an exclusive contract with the university now that his daughter was a student there. He wasn't above pointing out to particularly stubborn potential customers — such as the General — that he was close friends with prominent residents of Stoughton, such as Judge Foggerty of the Tabor Heights Municipal Court. That was the worst thing Michael Tyler could have done, because the judge had no friends or admirers at Butler-Williams University.

None of the Tyler family went to church. Daniel silently cheered every time he heard Bekka invite Kat to join her on Sunday or to come to one of the social events Tabor Christian put together for the students at BWU. He didn't think Kat went to any, but there was time.

Friday, December 15

Lynette attended the Christmas production by herself, much to her relief. Mike decided to boycott all productions at BWU because no one had seen the wisdom of signing a contract with Chef Michael's Catering for all their events. He had grumbled about transferring Kat to another university, as if that would convince the administration to re-consider the contract. The only problem was that Kat's tuition was paid for by scholarships and the very generous trust fund her grandmother had set up for her at birth. Mike knew better than to even try to influence Kat's education in any way — and Lynette chuckled every time she heard him grumble because it was one more area where he didn't get his way.

She enjoyed the production, despite the fact that Kat didn't get a role on stage. Lynette came in late and barely made it to her seat in the balcony before the lights went down. She didn't get to look at the program until the intermission. Dr. Daniel Morgan was listed as not only the co-author of the production, but Faculty Stage Manager. Lynette knew enough from her few short years in the theater department that those words meant he was there to advise and watch the students run around like headless chickens until someone had the brains to ask for help.

She wanted to get up right that moment and flee the theater, but she and Kat had plans to go out for dinner after the production. How could she explain to her daughter that she lived in mortal fear of running into a man she had loved and sent away nineteen years ago?

The only thing Lynette could be grateful for was that Kat hadn't insisted she come behind stage to meet everyone after the production. That would have led to disaster. She waited for her daughter in the lobby, watching the smiling crowds exit the auditorium, the children laughing and sucking on the candy canes that had been handed out to everyone, and she tried to be invisible. Failing that, Lynette sat in the deepest shadow she could find and held utterly still, and hoped every handsome, dark-haired man who walked by was too tired to notice her.

"There you are!" a familiar, laughing, baritone voice called when the lobby traffic had dwindled to a trickle.

Lynette closed her eyes, her heart stuttering, and then couldn't resist the horrified fascination and curiosity. She opened her eyes and followed the sound of that voice, totally unprepared to meet her doom.

Daniel Morgan, dressed in jeans and a blue plaid flannel shirt just like in their college days, strolled across the lobby toward Lynette's shadowed seat. He smiled, lines forming around his eyes and mouth, and the laughter in his eyes wiped away the weariness that proved he had given his all to tonight's production. Just like he had in college. She realized she could breathe after all. Taking a deep breath, swallowing, she braced herself to stand. Nothing in the world could convince her to stay seated and let him tower over her at this first meeting in nearly twenty years.

"How'd you like it?" he said, holding out both hands.

Lynette opened her mouth—and it stayed open in surprise as a boy and girl darted past her from the bench on the other side of the shadowy nook where she had parked. Her intense concentration on being invisible had made her almost deaf and blind to their presence. She stared, not quite able to comprehend her narrow escape, and watched the little girl, maybe ten years old, leap into Daniel's arms. The boy was a head shorter than her, maybe eight or nine years old. They were definitely brother and sister, with the same dark curls and square chins and chocolate-colored eyes. They looked like Daniel.

The boy laughed and wrapped both arms around Daniel's waist, and both children laughed when he pretended to stagger under the little girl's weight. They talked at the same time, calling out the things they had liked about the Christmas production—the elves running up and down the aisles, the actors dressed as angels and stars that dropped down from the ceiling, the live ponies that pulled a miniature Santa's sleigh, and of course the candy canes and the hard wrapped candy that Santa and the elves tossed into the audience by the handfuls.

"It was great, just like you said," the woman who had been with the children said, sauntering across the floor to join them. She had short, dark curly hair, just like the children. Her tall, lanky figure and easy stride stirred up a few flickers of jealousy among Lynette's shock and relief. "These greedy gluttons want to know if there are any leftover candy canes."

"You do?" Daniel jounced the girl, pretending to drop her. She screamed and flung her arms around his neck, laughing the entire time, and he pretended to strangle. "Well, come on backstage and we'll see what the good faeries have for you."

"I'll get you for this," the woman said.

"What'd I do now?"

"Giving the kids sugar? At this time of night?" She slapped his shoulder. The children just laughed more.

"I'll make it up to you," Daniel said, and released one arm from holding the girl to wrap around the woman's waist.

Lynette gasped and felt as if something wrapped around her throat. She knew it was ridiculous to feel this way, because Daniel obviously hadn't seen her there in the shadows, but his gesture had felt like a slap in her face. How many times had he laughed and said those same words to her, as he put his arm around her waist?

"How?" the woman demanded, falling into step with him with the ease of long practice.

"I'll take the kids shopping tomorrow. I'm pretty sure there's somebody they haven't done their shopping for yet." He waggled his eyebrows at her, and she just rolled her eyes and shook her head, grinning.

The children cheered, just as the foursome reached the open door leading into the stairwell, and their voices echoed back. Daniel and the woman exchanged grins.

"Abby Morgan! Is that you?" A woman in a dark green, sparkly evening dress scurried across the nearly deserted lobby on high heels Lynette would never have dared wear. "I need to talk to you about summer camp. You are coming to Patmos with the kids this summer, aren't you? And giving flying lessons like last year?" She hooked her arm through the woman's arm, effectively disengaging her from Daniel's grasp. In a few more seconds, all five had disappeared down the stairwell, the echoes distorting what anyone said.

Lynette closed her eyes and unclenched her hands, forcing herself to breathe. She told herself to be grateful for the near disaster. She had learned something useful, and maybe even comforting. After all, if Daniel Morgan was married and had children of his own, he wouldn't try to take her daughter away from her if he ever found out about Kat.

Daniel was married. Lynette played with the concept in her mind, gingerly, like she would examine a broken tooth with the tip of her tongue.

Well, why not? He had obviously wanted to marry her and take responsibility for their baby. He hadn't backed off in relief and given up the first time she said no to his proposal, had he? And why wouldn't he want children of his own? It certainly looked like he loved those children and got along well with them. Lynette couldn't think of many men who would so easily offer to take children that young Christmas shopping, unless they enjoyed being with the children.

Daniel Morgan was married. Lynette told herself she should be relieved.

Chapter Two

Sunday, December 31

As soon as exams were over, Kat took a plane for Chicago to spend the holidays with her grandmother. Lynette soon wished she had gone with her daughter, because Mike pouted and whined and moped over the fact that Kat didn't come home between semesters.

"That settles it. This summer, she's just gotta work for me. I'll make her my personal assistant." Mike rubbed his hands together, and Lynette swore he muffled a cackle. "I miss my little girl. If she won't stay home where she belongs—"

"School rules don't allow freshmen to live anywhere except on campus," Lynette said for the hundredth time. She wished she had retreated to her craft room, instead of settling down in the TV room to catch the news and pretend she enjoyed spending time with her husband.

"Well, she'll move home in the spring, and I'll make sure she never wants to leave home again."

Lynette shuddered. What would it take for Mike to realize that Kat didn't even like him, much less love him like he seemed to think she should?

When Lynette and Mike flew to Chicago to spend the week from Christmas to New Year's with her mother, Kat had a full roster of activities lined up with her childhood friends that kept her out of the house most of the time. Lynette understood, but Mike grumbled about not seeing Kat until even Mrs. Teague scolded him to stop being so selfish.

Lynette wasn't surprised that on New Year's Eve, before their guests arrived for her mother's traditional party, Mike informed Kat of the plans he had made for her summer as if they were a done deal.

"I'm taking summer classes, and taking over as Morgan's student assistant," Kat said with a calm certainty that told Lynette her daughter wasn't making this up. She had this planned and had probably already signed up for the specific classes she wanted and reserved her room in the dormitories.

"Who is Morgan?" Mrs. Teague said, while Mike's eyes bugged, his face got red, and his mouth worked like a grounded fish.

Lynette couldn't breathe. Any moment now, her mother would turn to her and say, "Do you mean to tell me Kathryn's father is her teacher?" and all her maneuvering and fear and silence over the last four months would be ruined.

And maybe it would be for the best.

"My new student advisor. At least, he will be in the fall. It makes more sense for him to be my advisor, because I'm going to focus on writing, not acting." Kat gave Mike a sideways glance and sidled toward the doorway of the front parlor, where they always waited to greet arriving guests. "Granny, do you mind if I take off with Scooter and Link instead of hanging around? There's a big marathon at their rec center to raise funds for the women's shelter."

"That sounds like an admirable way to bring in the New Year," her grandmother said, her smile warming. She held out her arms and Kat came to hug and kiss her good-bye. The girl fled the room before Mike could get his breath back.

"But I want Kat to work for me this summer. We agreed—"

"No, Mike," Lynette said, sighing. "You told me what you wanted, but you never asked Kat what she wanted."

"But I'm her father! She should do what I tell her. I love her."

"Michael, if you're going to be a wet blanket, kindly avoid my guests this evening," Mrs. Teague said. She levered herself out of her throne-like rocking chair and beckoned for Patricia, the housekeeper, who hovered in the doorway, waiting for last-minute directions.

Lynette breathed a sigh of relief and ignored Mike's mutters of complaint. Another disaster avoided. How many more near misses could she take before the truth came spilling out? She was only halfway through the first year of Kat's studies at BWU. Three-and-a-half years of this misery to go.

~~~~~

In the spring, Amy Whittier, a blonde, energetic sophomore, teamed up with Bekka and Kat. The three girls spent hours together, going to Stay-a-While to sit and drink coffee and talk, and attended campus movies together or spent hours in the library doing research for each other. They dubbed themselves the Musketeers, even before Dr. Holwood, the head of the Humanities Department, gave them the label. Daniel would often look out his office door to see Amy and Kat helping Bekka with her duties. Kat was Bekka's assistant and in training to take over her job. Campus rules only allowed a student to be any professor's assistant for four years total, and Bekka had reached the end of her allowed term.

Dr. Holwood had a special place in his heart for Amy, a struggling poet, who was somewhat acerbic and elitist when it came to poetry. Her boyfriend, Joe Kriegan, was a struggling musician and a part-time student. Amy constantly fought with him over the idea that good poetry didn't need music to make it complete. Dr. Holwood asked for prayers for all his students, when the faculty members who attended Tabor Christian got
~~~~~

together. Amy's name came up quite often.

Kat took Daniel's concentrated survey of scriptwriting course that summer. Her insistence that soap operas did not count as 'real' screenwriting, and her shock and dismay when she learned he had sold several scripts to five daytime dramas shattered that last lingering, nagging similarity to Lynette Teague. Lynette had thought everything he did was golden. She didn't fight with him about anything he chose to do — until she told him she was pregnant, and he immediately set about dismantling his career plans so they could get married and raise their child. Her plan was for him to graduate, become a star in Hollywood, and come back for them. When he refused to abandon them, she left town, and her mother slapped him with threats of restraining orders and other legal action that would ensure he couldn't act in community theater, much less pursue a career on screen. Even cheesy homemade commercials for two-bit cable stations wouldn't take him, once those lawyers got through with him.

Working with Kat instead of Bekka was an adjustment — he understood the struggles Bekka went through with her grandparents who had raised her, and who periodically tried to quash her literary career and involvement in drama. In the past, they had even tried to enlist the deacons at Tabor Christian to convince Bekka that Christians had no business being involved in theater. They hadn't been happy to learn that Daniel was a member of their church, and had been for eight years at that time, and the deacons were not only comfortable with the idea of an actor and writer involved in church activities, but several wanted him to run a drama camp some summer.

Their latest tactic was to charge Bekka room and board as long as she insisted on following her "frivolous" course of study at Butler-Williams in writing and theater. So Bekka worked three part-time jobs, proofread papers for other students, and earned a tidy sum each year by selling short stories and commissioned articles. Her grandparents insisted that the only sensible and proper life for her was to become an accountant or some other "respectable" profession, until she found a man to marry — then she would quit working, stay home, and raise their great-grandchildren.

Daniel had counseled Bekka through five years of this struggle, and admired her determination and her quiet, respectful brand of rebellion. The Sandersons hadn't come storming into his office in more than two years, demanding he advise Bekka to give up her literary dreams and obey them "like a good Christian girl should."

Tuesday, October 1

Kat had problems.

Bekka had told Daniel that her home life wasn't too comfortable, that Michael Tyler was a loudmouth, leering jerk, and Kat took summer classes so she could stay on campus year-round and not go home—but Kat didn't confide in Daniel. He had to guess when something troubled her and learned even before she was his student assistant that she froze up when adults, men in particular, showed too much interest in her activities, her schedule, and her feelings. By the end of September, Daniel learned to pick up a few signals to indicate when Kat was having a bad day, but he left it to Bekka to act as intermediary when he wanted to help.

So he wasn't too surprised when Kat danced into his office that morning and announced she, Amy and Bekka were moving in together.

"Too many wild parties in the dorm, huh? They're kicking you out?" He sat back and put both feet up on the only clear corner of his desk.

"Hardly." Kat tucked a strand of hair behind her ear and hugged herself before coming to rest against the doorframe. "Bekka's grandparents are moving to Florida. Can you believe they actually think she'll drop classes just like that and go to Florida with them just because they say so?"

"Yeah, unfortunately, I do." Daniel shook his head and muffled a grin.

So that was the reason for the sour looks the Sandersons had been aiming his way over the last three Sundays. They probably thought he had encouraged Bekka to resist their most recent and extreme endeavor to control her life. Why she hadn't moved out of their house years ago, he couldn't quite understand—except that Bekka did love her grandparents, and she knew they loved her despite their stiff-necked, narrow-minded, demanding ways. They were all the family she had in the world, and she had obviously reasoned that putting up with their disapproval wasn't too high a price to pay for keeping their family together. He understood, because even if he didn't get along so well with them, he would have felt the same way about the Tabor Heights Morgans. They were the reason he had applied to teach at Butler-Williams University in the first place.

"Amy wants to be closer to campus now that she got the job at the library, and I have been dying to get my own place—I mean, Granny gave me access to my trust fund when I graduated high school and I have more than enough money—but I hate being alone." She shrugged and grinned but couldn't hide that momentary glimmer of darkness, and what Daniel thought might be genuine fear in her eyes. "So Bekka found a place at the Tower, across the street from the police station. It is going to be so great."

"Congratulations. I hope I won't have to come bail you out of jail for wild parties too often."

"Come on, Morgan!" Kat giggled and turned to leave. "Do you really think with Bekka living with us, we'd ever have wild parties? That's the great thing. Nobody would dare invade or bring drugs or anything to our parties, because of Bekka."

"That's true," he muttered, and pulled his feet down off the desk to get to work.

He did have a thick stack of essays on Greek drama to grade. Daniel was pleased that Kat welcomed the influence Bekka would have on their living arrangements. And even more pleased that Bekka's reputation as a straight-shooter, wholesome and clean-living, came across as a positive. He just wished he could get that point across to the Sandersons and other legalists at Tabor Christian, like Arthur Montgomery. He wholesale condemned anything connected with theater, film, art and fiction as unworthy of "real" Christians.

Monday, October 7

"It's going to be so great," Kat bubbled, the afternoon after signing the lease for the apartment.

She managed to chatter and work as she helped Daniel dig through his library to find four books he wanted for his lectures the next day.

"Privacy. No more fighting over the washer and dryer in the basement of the dorm. No more worrying about guys walking through at the worst possible time. No more fighting ten other girls for one shower. And finding other people's junk in the bathroom and wishing the cleaning crew would get their butts in gear. No more being enslaved to the cafeteria menu. Ugh!" She giggled. "I can pack myself a lunch or come home for meals, instead of spending tons at the cafeteria."

"So you can spend more money at Stay-A-While?" Daniel said with a grin. He was delighted when Kat wrinkled up her nose at him and pretended to swat at him with a workbook.

"Hey, the whole coffee house experience is part of going to college. That's what Mom says, anyway." She let out a tiny cry of triumph and tugged out the long-lost book from under a stack of others tucked behind another stack. "Especially for the theater crowd. It's like a requirement or something."

"I thought your mother got her degree in business."

"Oh, Mom started out in theater at Northwestern."

"She did?" Daniel shook off the chill that raced down his back, the momentary sensation of falling. His mouth worked when he hadn't meant to speak. "The one in Illinois, right? That's where I got my BA. What year?"

"Gee, I'd have to think back. It was only two years. She had to quit when she had me." Kat's smile faded and Daniel fought an urge to wrap an arm around her and offer comfort.

Touching wasn't allowed between advisors and students. He was careful about such things, and always kept his door open enough that someone could look inside when he had students in his office.

"Mom met my father at Northwestern. He died before they could get married," she finally said.

"I thought your father—"

"Mike Tyler is not my father! He met Mom when I was eight." Fury—and something else—flashed in Kat's eyes and made her voice tight. She visibly fought to unclench her fists before she dug her fingers through the precious, fragile, out-of-print paperback she held. "My dad is dead, and he was a theater major. Mom even says I got my writing talent from him." She forced a smile and a shrug. "So, have we got everything?"

"One more and we're done."

Daniel let out a long, silent sigh and concentrated on his relaxation exercises. It had been a false alarm, just a coincidence that Kat's mother had been at Northwestern. He tried to think back to any stories he had heard about any theater majors who had died before he was a student, then decided it wasn't worth pursuing. Obviously, the whole subject of her parents' romance, especially her real father's death, was painful. He wouldn't do her any favors by asking questions.

"Mom is so great in business. The manager type, you know?" Kat continued as she knelt and dug through a shelf. Daniel fought not to let his surprise show on his face. It wasn't like her to continue talking about something when she got that hurting look. "I think she'd be happier in theater, but their business keeps her really busy. She's smart. Really smart." She sighed. "But she can't see past the jerk. I don't understand why she had to marry Mike. We were doing just fine on our own."

"Maybe she was lonely," Daniel offered.

"I'd never be that lonely." She shuddered and continued working. "We're having a housewarming, the day after we move in," she continued after a few moments of working silence. "Can you come?"

"I don't know. Those wild student parties could ruin my reputation."

Kat groaned and rolled her eyes, but she grinned. Anybody who knew Bekka would know the rules. No alcohol. No loud music past 10pm. No drugs. Bekka believed in good clean fun with fully functioning minds and bodies. Daniel was proud of Bekka, for her reputation and the respect she earned on campus without being a Pharisee. She wasn't a leader, but she was someone other students sought out for advice. He was glad Bekka had taken Kat and Amy under her wing, even if it did interfere with her writing life. How she managed three part-time jobs, two classes each semester, and still submitted a new story or article to a magazine every month was beyond him.

"So, will you?" Kat said, as she finished up her tasks for the afternoon and headed off to class.

"Will I—oh, the housewarming. I guess so. Can I bring anything?"

"Nope. Just come and check out the place and give your stamp of approval."

'What makes you think you need my approval?"

'We don't, really, but we know you'll worry yourself into gray hairs if you don't." She wrinkled up her nose at him and scooted out of the office when he burst out laughing.

Thursday, October 31

Moving day. Kat seemed as bubbly and carefree as ever, but Bekka confided in Daniel that Kat's stepfather had grumbled and whined and called Kat at least three times each week since she announced she was moving out of the dormitory to share the apartment. Mike Tyler seemed to think that if Kat wasn't living in the dormitory, it was a federal law that she had to live with her parents. Dr. Holwood had brought up the girls' move during the weekly prayer breakfast on Monday and mentioned that Amy was afraid Mike Tyler might try to interfere somehow.

The prayer group of teachers had larger concerns on their minds when a young woman living in Tabor Heights, Gretchen Sanders, vanished and then was found dead. Murdered by a young man who had been stalking her. Because of his demanding love letters and the white roses he left for Gretchen, and because the police, her family, and the dead girl herself had no clue who he was, the press had dubbed him the White Rose. That situation was bad enough, but when the news hit the media with all the details of the White Rose's weeks of letters and flowers and demands, another girl in Tabor Heights, Katrina Hooper, came forward with evidence that the White Rose had chosen her as his next "true love." What made the situation more disturbing, if that was possible, was that he had left his first rose and love letter, demanding her faithfulness and purity, the same day Gretchen had vanished.

Joel Randolph's daughter, Max, worked as a copy editor at the *Tabor Picayune*, and she passed on information to her father that the *Picayune* wasn't ready to publish, on the condition that it didn't go beyond the teachers' prayer group. Daniel thought of the three girls, so excited about getting their freedom, and wondered if maybe this once, Kat's stepfather might be right to be worried. Then again, according to Max, the police were putting together a pattern about the White Rose—if two targets could be called a pattern. His two "true loves" had long, black hair, lived at home, and didn't socialize much. Kat, Bekka, and Amy didn't have black hair, they weren't living at home as of that afternoon, and between all their classes and theater department activities, it was obvious they socialized. In theory, they were safe. That didn't mean their advisors wouldn't put them, and every other young woman in Tabor Heights, on their prayer list until the White Rose was identified and captured and stopped.

Daniel trailed Kat to the door after her last morning class, tempted to offer to drive over to her house where she had to pick up all her clothes and the dishes her mother was giving the girls, and run interference if Mike Tyler got nasty.

Marco Delaney, another sophomore, waited in the wide, double doorway of the Arts Building as Kat's class streamed out into the sunshine. Daniel knew him from his film appreciation class. Shoulders hunched, head tilted to one side, the boy watched the students chattering and groaning and laughing together as they exited. His dark head lifted and his dark eyes brightened as Kat emerged, books clasped to her chest, chattering in the middle of a knot of girls. He stepped out to follow and was immediately cut off by a flood of incoming students. It took all Daniel's self-control not to stomp out from the doorway where he watched and demand to know the boy's intentions toward Kat. His reaction surprised him and helped him relax and little. He wondered if Kat would laugh if he confessed how protective he felt about her.

By the time the stream of students passed, Kat had crossed the parking lot and headed for the cafeteria building. She was alone. Someone called her name. She turned, losing her grip on her stack of books.

She bent to retrieve the scattered load, and before her knee touched the ground, Marco was there, kneeling and gathering up all her scattered folders and books. Kat thanked him with a bright smile and hurried on, not seeing the young man frozen and grinning like a star-struck idiot.

Daniel grinned, seeing himself and Lynette playing out variations of the same dance twenty years earlier.

According to Bekka, Kat never dated anyone more than twice. Daniel wondered why that was, if maybe her dislike for her stepfather infringed on her relationships. He comforted himself that someday true love would appear and Kat would fall. Honestly, he was more concerned about Bekka's love life, or lack thereof, than Kat's. Bekka needed someone steady, who realized what a treasure she was. Maybe if she got rid of one of her jobs, she might have time for a social life.

Two hours later, he was gratefully distracted from those worries by a call from his contact in New York. Sam was a friend and collaborator and made his regular monthly call to complain with Daniel over their lack of progress in the industry. Daniel had his feet up on the only clear spot on his desk, his eyes half-closed and the receiver of the phone tucked between ear and shoulder when Kat came into his office at the end of her work period. She sighed, shifting her armload of copied and collated papers. Daniel looked up.

"Hmm? Finished already? Just put them —" He chuckled and swung his feet down to the floor, making a clear spot. "Right there. Thanks, Kat. I don't know what I would do without you."

"Learn how to order your own cappuccino, at least?" She put the papers on the corner of the desk and spun on one heel to leave. Quickly.

"Where are you going so fast? Aren't you dying to hear what I think of your script?"

"You're on the phone."

"On hold." Daniel hit the button on the phone, changing it to speaker. Elevator music spilled out and he grimaced. Sam loved his gadgets, especially his telephone system, which was more complicated than the space shuttles.

"I have to move." She stepped backward to the door.

"What's up?" He reached to stop her, then shrugged and raked his hair off his forehead to cover up the gesture. Kat never noticed.

"It's moving day, finally!"

"I know. Between you and Bekka, I'd have to have amnesia to forget." He laughed at her pretend scowl at his teasing. "What does your mother think of you getting your own place?" He again toyed with the idea of running interference by offering his car to help haul her belongings.

"I have no idea."

"You aren't talking to your mother?" He frowned. According to Bekka, Kat's mother supported the move.

"I have no idea! Nobody can get a word in edgewise with that jerk around. Why don't they write any nasty fairy tales about idiot stepfathers?" she said with a groan that turned into a giggle. "Bye!" Grinning in pure excitement, Kat spun and nearly danced out the door.

"Mr. Tyler?" Bekka said, when Daniel asked her about Kat's home situation, during her flying visit through his office less than twenty minutes later. "Unfortunately, I've run into him a few times. You wouldn't believe how he much he's butted into the whole process of getting the apartment. Like we were selling ourselves into slavery and the Tower is a roach hotel or something. To be honest..." She glanced at his door, which always hung open when a female student was in his office. Bekka looked out into the crowded work area between the three offices, currently empty of any listening ears. "I really don't know what Kat's mom ever saw in him. On the surface, he's fine. Kind of jolly. Always ready to cook up something incredible to eat, which is okay when it's his own kitchen, but not when he tries to take over someone else's kitchen. But he does know what he's talking about when it comes to food. Which is really evident from his waistline. A really good advertisement for his company."

Bekka didn't laugh as she said it, Daniel noted.

"But after about an hour, you notice how loud he is. Almost too friendly. Really pushy. The only expert on everything worth knowing—

and what he doesn't care about isn't worth knowing. Know what I mean?"

"Oh, yeah." Daniel had run into too many of those people in his lifetime. It was an occupational hazard in the arts and in big churches, unfortunately. "But? I get the feeling, from things you and Amy have said, or not said, he isn't exactly gunning for Father of the Year."

"Hardly. Maybe it's just girls who notice. When he looks at you too long—and he always seems to be staring—he makes the hairs stand up on the back of my neck, and on my arms. You know?" She shivered and rubbed her hands down her sleeves, as if just thinking about it made her arm hair stand up. "I don't know. Amy said it first, that he has a way of looking over every woman he sees, head to foot, like he has X-ray eyes. Amy's pretty, so she'd be more sensitive to things like that, but... Kat never says anything, except he's a jerk and no food is safe from him. I think it's more what she doesn't say about him that's so... condemning, I guess."

Daniel thought about that after Bekka hurried out. He couldn't detain her any longer to get more details or speculations. She had been living for a week already in the apartment the three girls would share, and had to rearrange a few things before her roommates moved in.

He had thought Kat's reaction to any mention of Mike Tyler was just the typical dislike of a girl for her stepfather. Especially if she never knew her father and had built him up into an ideal, and believed Mike was trying to steal her father's rightful place. Daniel supposed she considered her real father something of a hero, because he never had a chance to fail her or destroy her hopes and dreams.

Chapter Three

"Paradise, here I come," Kat murmured as she loaded the last bag into her trunk and slammed it.

Lynette stayed in the shadows of the open garage and watched her daughter finish loading her beater car almost past the safety limits. She smiled, with tears in her eyes, sharing Kat's excitement. There was something almost too wonderful to be believed about a girl's first apartment. She liked both Amy and Bekka and was glad they would be living with Kat.

The last year had been easier than she thought, when she first heard that Daniel Morgan was Kat's teacher, then had become her student advisor, and now their daughter now worked for him. She had been careful to attend performances, but never go anywhere near the places faculty might loiter. She had met Joel Randolph, the technical director, and had even encouraged Kat to audition for summer theater productions at Homespun Theater because the man impressed her so much. The General had overwhelmed her at the strike party after Kat's spring production last year. How could the man be so overblown and yet not come across as ridiculous? She liked the General, even though she came away with bruises from his energetic hug of greeting, and deaf from his enthusiastic compliments for Kat's talent.

She had yet to meet Daniel Morgan face-to-face. That suited her just fine.

Kat certainly adored him, and Lynette had to admit she had only heard good things about the man from Kat's friends. She thought about the few times Kat had endured a family dinner. Her daughter always brought theater friends along, and they always brought up the subject of their teachers. Mike was jealous whenever someone mentioned any of Kat's beloved teachers, and lately the more something irritated her overbearing husband, the happier it made her. Why had she ever married him? Why hadn't she paid attention to Kat's dislike of him? Her daughter was usually so good about sensing the person hidden under the polite social masks, so why had Lynette written off her negative reaction as jealousy?

Too late now, with that mistake behind her and a large portion of her life invested in the catering business. But it was never too late to make a life for herself in other areas. Lynette considered auditioning for some roles at Homespun Theater. After all, if Mike believed she was better off away from the theater, it would irritate him to no end if she spent evenings and weekends away from home. He didn't actually *want* her company or even to have her cook dinner for him. He just wanted her to be there, in the house and keeping the business running smoothly in the back office.

Lynette knew she would follow her inclinations in a minute if she could be sure she wouldn't run into Daniel at Homespun Theater. From what Bekka had said, the Randolphs and Daniel went to her church and were good friends. Daniel sometimes co-wrote scripts for Homespun with Max, the Randolphs' daughter. Bekka had invited Kat to her church several times, and Kat had admitted to her mother that she was tempted to go, just because both Bekka and Daniel attended Tabor Christian.

Lynette found it ironic and fascinating that Daniel had become religious. How had that choice and interest changed him? Every time Kat's face glowed and that happiness came into her voice when she spoke about her beloved Dr. Morgan, Lynette felt a flicker of guilt. What had she stolen from her daughter by denying her a father? Especially a father as talented, generous, and kind as the Daniel Morgan she had loved in college?

She sighed and watched Kat check over her car one last time. Her baby was moving out, officially and most likely permanently. At least when Kat lived in the dormitories, there was some chance of seeing her at holidays and breaks. She suspected Mike was glad for the current furor over the White Rose Killer skulking around Tabor Heights, just for another weapon to force Kat to come home. It took all her self-control not to snap at Mike and tell him that if he kept pushing, Kat would never come home again, even if the White Rose chose her as a target. Lynette kept her mouth shut and tried not to think about such things. She had thought she wouldn't get pregnant, had laughed at her friends who worried about such things — and look what had happened to her. It wasn't wise to tempt fate.

Kat was better off living with Bekka and Amy. There wasn't anyone Lynette would have chosen to be a big sister to her daughter, better than Bekka Sanderson. She should be happy for her, instead of feeling sorry for herself. Mike was a good provider, but Lynette had come to admit that money, comforts, and leisure time weren't all she had imagined them to be. Kat was certainly far happier with the car she had bought after working odd jobs for two years in high school, than she ever would have been with the Trans Am Mike wanted to buy her for a graduation present. Lynette had supported her daughter in refusing the gift, and she was grateful now. The less Kat owed her stepfather, the better.

Kat's beater car with its cracked and fading paint job and mismatched doors certainly didn't belong in front of this house with its manicured lawn and pristine flower beds, three-car garage and three-story, neo-

Tudor design. Lynette sometimes doubted she herself belonged there any longer.

'Don't kill yourself coming back for everything all in one afternoon, sweetheart," Lynette said, approaching the car. "Mike said he'd rent a truck to haul your bedroom furniture tonight."

"I have rehearsal tonight, Mom," Kat murmured. She leaned against the window and studied the pile of blue plastic grocery bags jammed full of clothes and groceries and linens, filling her back seat.

"Well then, tomorrow."

"We're having a housewarming party then. I can't move my furniture in during the party."

"If you'd just wait until your father got home—"

"Mike is *not* my father. I don't want to owe him for anything, either."

"He wants to help you." Lynette mentally slapped herself for that mistake. She didn't know why she kept trying to make peace between her husband and daughter. It simply felt like the right thing to do, even when she herself felt irritation every time Mike opened his mouth.

"Yeah, I'll bet." Kat turned away and reached for the door handle. "I'll be back tomorrow morning to get the rest of my stuff. You're invited to our party, you know."

"That might be fun. Do I know anybody besides your roommates?" Lynette managed a smile she was fairly confident looked genuine. She was still a great actress. Nowadays she had to be to survive.

"A few of the gang. Everybody you met at the last theater party. Oh, Morgan might come. You'll finally meet him."

"Morgan?" Her smile flickered.

"Dr. Morgan. My advisor. Remember? Sheesh, Mom, you're getting senile," Kat said with a grin. She yanked the door open and slid into the driver's seat.

"Better that than the alternative..." Lynette's heart hammered at the thought of running into Daniel at Kat's new apartment. What would she say to him? Besides ask why he had never contacted her, of course. And maybe burst into tears. Which was utterly ridiculous.

'Huh?" Kat frowned at her.

'Nothing. Well, this is it, then. You take care, and call me when you get settled in, all right?" She hugged Kat and pulled the seatbelt up for her. "You know, I have that neighborhood committee meeting tomorrow night," Lynette lied. She gladly named herself a coward. "How about if I borrow the Abernathy's SUV and bring your furniture over tomorrow afternoon?"

"Okay, I guess." Kat's eyes lost that happy sparkle. "I really want you to meet Morgan, Mom."

"I know. Some other time. Now, get going. Your roommates are probably wondering where you are." She hugged herself, shivering a little despite the warm October breeze, and stepped back from the car to let Kat close the door. Why in the world had the girls chosen to move on Halloween? Lynette wrapped her arms around herself and stayed standing in the driveway, watching as Kat pulled out into the street.

This was probably what Daniel had felt like when she slammed the door in his face and sent him away for the last time, just before she ran away from college.

"What goes around, comes around," Lynette murmured.

If he ever found out the truth, that his student assistant was his daughter, and Lynette had known where he was for the past year, could he forgive her? He went to Tabor Christian Church, and everybody Lynette had ever met from that church were warm, caring, fun people. Not a stick-in-the-mud among them. She liked them more because Mike grumbled that they always turned down his gourmet wine selection when he catered an occasion for the church. As if they did it on purpose, to irritate him.

Mike wouldn't admit it, but he was upset mostly because his largest profit came from the alcohol sales when he catered events. Lynette sometimes wondered if he would bite the bullet one of these days and give up his Sunday morning lounging time to attend the church, just to make connections and increase his business. From things Bekka had mentioned, a good number of the faculty at BWU attended her church. Mike still put some comforts ahead of grabbing more catering business connections, and Lynette was grateful. She couldn't stand the thought of the people at Tabor Christian meeting her husband. They might feel sorry for her.

Then again, why would they ever make the connection? She had no intention of attending that church, even if Mike begged her, for the sake of the business. What comfort could she get from a church? She had stopped attending church in college, when the pastor's wife and the head of the Ministry to College Students confronted her in the parking lot to encourage her to stop attending "for the time being." Translation: until she had her baby and gave it up for adoption and pretended the "unfortunate incident" had never happened. When Lynette cut through their euphemisms and cold-hearted sense of delicacy, and said she planned to keep her baby, they had been horrified and told her she had no right to pollute their hallways and flaunt the evidence of her sin. Lynette had tried to laugh at the mental image those words created. She had been five months pregnant with Kat and barely showed. There was practically nothing to flaunt, even if she had been stupid enough to be proud of her bad choices.

After that incident, she refused to ever go into another church again. She had only become more bitter when, after her mother withdrew her membership and her four-digit tithing checks from that church, a committee came out to the house to apologize and swallow their pride. Not only were they heartless and self-righteous, but they were hypocrites for the sake of money. What good was a church and religion if they didn't offer help when she needed it the most?

Maybe Daniel found comfort in religion, but Lynette knew she never could.

Tuesday, November 19

Kat invited Daniel to eat Thanksgiving dinner with the Musketeers.

"Why aren't you eating with your parents?" Daniel studied Kat's face, looking for signs of stress. He hadn't been able to get Bekka's words about Mike Tyler out of his head. What had Kat's stepfather done to punish her for moving out on her own?

"Chef Creepo is going to a convention in Denver, and Granny wants Mom to come visit in Chicago. She wanted me to come, but I have rehearsals and all these papers to write." Kat shrugged. No distress dimmed the excited sparkle in her eyes. "This is going to be our first big dinner party. You have to come. Swear, we won't have even a tenth of the people who came to our housewarming. You had fun there, didn't you?"

"Any time I can whip the General in Trivial Pursuit is a good time."

Daniel usually had Thanksgiving with his cousins, but a client of Abby's plane courier service had given her four passes for Disneyworld, and they were talking about going down for a short trip over the holiday. He suspected that their hesitation so far was guilt over leaving him in the lurch. This opportunity couldn't come at a better time. Just to be safe, he decided to consult with Dr. Holwood on the propriety of spending a holiday in the apartment of three female students. Kat did imply there would be other guests, didn't she?

Friday, November 22

"Hey, great, honey." Mike barely glanced at Lynette, busy with his TV program and the tray of cheese, beef stick, and crackers. "You won't be bored, and you can keep an eye on Kathryn. Sounds like a good idea."

"Glad you think so," she said, barely loud enough for him to hear. From past experience, Lynette knew Mike wouldn't have heard if she shouted. Now that the holidays were here, the big season for catering, he never let anything interfere with indulging in one of his rare evenings at home. Most definitely, listening to his wife counted as "interference."

Lynette turned from the TV room and wandered down the hall to her craft room. That vague feeling of discontent that had nibbled at her for years felt like a combination of shark teeth and indigestion now. What was wrong with her? Wasn't this what she wanted? She wouldn't have to endure Mike's yearly lecture on the food traditions of Thanksgiving and his "better ideas" for holiday eating. She wouldn't even see him from Tuesday night until Sunday afternoon, when he flew back from Denver.

Best of all, her mother had decided to go visit friends in France and had canceled her command performance for Thanksgiving, so Lynette didn't have to go to Chicago. Part of her suspected her mother really didn't want to see her because Kat wouldn't accompany her this year. Sometimes, Lynette thought her mother loved Kat more, and she was only tolerated.

"You're turning neurotic," she told herself, and nearly kicked the door closed.

A soft chuckle escaped her as she sank into her old-fashioned, overstuffed easy chair. She had saved it from being hauled out to the trash at least a dozen times since marrying Mike, and finally managed to put it in a room he never entered. The man cared more about style than comfort, and never understood why Lynette loved the scratchy old swaybacked chair with its permanently dented cushions and arms wide enough for people to sit comfortably on them.

Appearances were all that mattered to Mike. Being married and looking successful were all that he cared about. The surface was his priority. It never occurred to him that marriage required just as much work as his catering business. He knew nothing about putting work into the background details of a relationship. Of course, that was if she and Mike had a relationship at all, or ever had a relationship to begin with.

Lynette sighed and admitted what bothered her most about her conversation with Mike. She wished he had grown angry when she refused to go to Denver with him. He hadn't argued when she was going to her mother's house because Mike feared her mother. Or rather, he worshipped her mother's money and feared her stable of lawyers. Anything that kept Mother Teague happy was fine with him.

She wished Mike had grown angry. She wished he had erupted out of his recliner — if he could shift his increasing bulk that fast — or thrown something at her. She wished he had tried to hit her. Not that a man in his shape could ever hope to catch up with her.

Lynette wanted some excuse to leave Mike. Just one bruise, something tangible as evidence. His alcoholism wasn't much of an excuse, because he didn't fight her when she let nothing beyond two six-packs at a time into the house, and only permitted wine on special occasions. How could he get rip-roaring, sloppy drunk and give her an excuse to leave him when he wouldn't fight to have his scotch and whiskey? Complaining that he was a self-absorbed egomaniac and that he irritated her daughter so that Kat moved out would never stand up in court.

How had she ever gotten into this mess?

"Think of the positive," Lynette scolded herself.

Yes, she would think of the benefits of this. Mike, gone for five glorious days. Silence in the house and no one to clean up after. No one to argue with her about the menus she cooked. She would have Thanksgiving with Kat. Maybe they could revive a few of the holiday traditions they had abandoned when Mike barreled into their lives. Hadn't Kat said she and her roommates were going downtown the day after Thanksgiving, to watch the lighting of the tree on Public Square? Lynette liked Bekka and Amy and thought both girls liked her in return. They wouldn't mind if she tagged along, would they? She could volunteer to drive all of them, or they could take the Rapid and shop at Tower City. Would there still be window displays in the old May Company building, even though the May Company had moved out years ago?

"It'll be a great Thanksgiving," she told herself and the craft-filled room.

If she could stop talking to herself.

Lynette grinned at that thought. She knew the cure for that.

"Thanksgiving?" Kat said, her voice rising to a squeak when her mother called five minutes later. "Please tell me you're not kidding, Mom."

"Why, I actually think you sound pleased," Lynette said with a chuckle. "You don't mind my inviting myself at the last minute?"

"No! This is great. We are going to have a blast. You can finally —" Kat giggled, making her mother wonder what she had been about to say. "Amy's a really great cook, Mom. You'll finally have a Thanksgiving where you won't have to do a lick of work. Just sit back and be waited on."

"Sounds heavenly."

Whenever they stayed in Ohio for Thanksgiving, Mike insisted on commandeering the menu and doing the cooking, but he never could learn the secret of cleaning up as he went along. Then he ate himself into a coma, so it was always Lynette doing the final cleanup at nearly midnight. All by herself.

Yes, the thought of being someone else's guest at Thanksgiving would be wonderful. The day would be absolutely perfect. Just Kat and her roommates and their boyfriends.

Later, as she watched TV in bed and waited to get drowsy, she let herself explore her discontent, like exploring a slowly eroding tooth with her tongue. Mike used to be so charming, so eternally young and enthusiastic about everything. After only a few years of exposure, Lynette realized he was nothing but a spoiled brat, chasing after the newest thrill and dragging her along as a playmate. Had he really changed, or was it her? What could she do about her problems? She wanted someone to talk to about it, someone who could offer advice, maybe even help. If she went to her mother with a list of complaints, would she believe and help her?

Then again, the last time Lynette had a major problem, her mother had called in her lawyers and chased the man in question so far away, he never made any attempt in twenty years to get hold of her. Did he really take her so seriously when she said not to come after her and their baby until he had become a star?

Lynette watched the weather report, which predicted days of constantly falling snow. She snuggled down under the covers, reached for the remote and turned off the TV. Maybe Mike would get snowed into Denver and not come back for another week. Now, that would be heavenly indeed.

Thursday, November 28

The entire state of Ohio had been hit with the Storm of the Century. Thanks to Lake Erie's famed and much-maligned Lake Effect, the weather couldn't seem to decide if it wanted to be freezing rain or snow. Daniel gladly headed home Wednesday after his only class of the day and settled down by the gas fireplace to read. He listened to the wind howl all afternoon and into the evening and prayed several times the weather would let up enough so he could make it to the girls' apartment building.

When Daniel drove from his little bungalow on the northern edge of Tabor to the apartment building in the center of town the next morning, the sky looked like the snowy, gritty sludge along the main roads. He kept watching the sky, wondering if he should turn around. He didn't fear he wouldn't make it, but what if he got snowed in there? His mind went blank when he tried to remember if any friends or fellow teachers lived in that apartment building. He certainly couldn't bunk down with three female students, even if their boyfriends were stranded there, too.

"Please, Lord, let this be a good day for the girls," Daniel whispered, as he scurried the short distance from the parking lot to the front door. "And please don't let us get snowed in."

The crunch of the snow under his feet and the moaning threat of renewed storm winds were his only responses. The elevator was crowded with other guests coming into the building for the day, and he laughed at himself when he realized he didn't know anyone. Maybe Tabor Heights wasn't as small a town as he thought. There went his contingency plan to avoid scandal. He was in a slightly better mood when the door of the elevator opened onto the third floor.

The rich smell of pumpkin pie and fresh bread, and the sounds of Christmas music seeped under the door of the apartment to greet him. Daniel shifted the bag holding his contribution for the day to one arm and rang the doorbell. There was no response for just long enough that he wondered if he had come to the wrong apartment. He found it odd that he didn't smell turkey yet. The number looked the same since he had been at the housewarming party four weeks ago. Then he heard feet thudding on the floor and approaching the door. Kat flung the door open. She took a step back, clearly surprised to see him. Had he missed some message not to come? Had she forgotten that she invited him?

"Happy Thanksgiving, Kat." Daniel handed her two foil-topped bottles, glistening with condensation. "You said not to bring anything, but heck, my students don't listen to me half the time, so why should I listen now?" He shrugged, chuckling raggedly.

"Sparkling cider? Thanks." She glanced over her shoulder at something in the apartment.

"Is that relief I see? You wouldn't suspect your advisor of trying to get you drunk, would you?"

"Of course not. Let me put these into the refrigerator. Do you serve sparkling cider cold?" She stepped away from the door, finally gesturing for him to come inside.

"I hope so. I've been doing it that way for years." He started to unzip his jacket, then looked around the room.

It was empty, but for him and Kat. And the scads of decorations Bekka had warned him about. Kat insisted on decorating for every occasion. Pilgrims on the TV set and on the wall and as a centerpiece on the table. Turkeys everywhere. Even the napkins had been twisted to look like turkeys.

"You know, Meier's is a local company," he hurried to add. He had never felt so awkward, tongue-tied and out of place before in his life. "I figure, support Ohio business, right?"

"Are you nervous?" Kat laughed, and a moment later nearly dropped the slippery bottles.

"Who? Me?" Daniel raked his fingers through his hair, shedding a last few snowflakes onto the carpet. "Why should I be nervous? I'm an over-forty professor spending Thanksgiving with three female students and not a boyfriend in sight yet. What's to be nervous about?"

"Oh... so, that's why you were so iffy until you heard Marco say he was coming." Kat headed for the kitchen door. "You're just early, that's all. I'll put these away. If you hear a scream, that's Amy having a panic attack."

"How early?" He slid his jacket off and looked around for the closet.

"Well, I did say one. I know you wrote it down when I told you."

Daniel dug in his pocket and pulled out a much-folded scrap of paper. "This looks like eleven to me. Oh, that's a mark from the other side. I wrote another note to myself on the back... Sorry."

"That's okay." She bit her lip against what looked suspiciously like a smirk as she reached to push aside the curtain that stood in for the kitchen door. "My mother always shows up early, anyway, so she can help. You can keep her company and out of the kitchen."

"Your mother? You didn't say she was coming." Daniel wondered if he had made a mistake coming. The last thing he wanted to do was run into Kat's stepfather, after everything he had heard about Mike Tyler from Bekka and Amy, and other faculty members who had the displeasure. Then another thought occurred to him, and he laughed. "Does she know I'm coming?"

"No. Why?"

"Sometimes I think your mother is trying to avoid me."

"Well, don't you dare leave." Kat stepped back and yanked his coat out of his hands. "Chef Creepo is at a convention in Denver, so Mom is all alone. You two can keep each other company. I wish Mom had met you before she met him."

"Uh, thanks. I think." Daniel relaxed as Kat's infectious laughter rang through the room.

"You'll like Mom. She was a theater major at Northwestern, like you were." She vanished through the curtain into the kitchen, taking his coat with her.

"Yeah, you told me." He sank down onto the arm of the threadbare couch and looked around the room. What was he going to do for the next two hours? Talk to Kat about her latest script? Where was Bekka?

As if thinking of her was a signal, Bekka darted down the short hallway from the room at the end, through the door next to the living room. She wore a red flannel robe, three sizes too large, and moved faster than he had ever seen her go before. Daniel had a glimpse of towels hanging on the wall and the edge of the bathroom counter before the door slammed. It wasn't like Bekka to be in bed this late in the morning. Logic said she was sick.

Now Daniel knew he had to get out of here. Bekka would never forgive him if he saw her sick. She had always denied pain or illness, even when he thought she would start sweating blood, or suffocate from congestion.

The ringing doorbell startled him. He glanced at the kitchen, but Kat didn't hurry out to answer. A scream that sounded like Amy filtered through the curtain. Sighing, Daniel reached for the doorknob and prayed for a boyfriend to show up early.

Chapter Four

Daniel froze when the door swung open to reveal Lynette Teague standing in the hall. Her hair hung loose, as vibrant, silky and long as twenty years ago. Her cheeks were flushed with cold. Her silvery-blue suede jacket hung open and she held matching gloves in one hand. Vaguely, Daniel was aware of a bulky figure standing behind her in the hall, swaying from one foot to the other like a child in need of the toilet.

"Hey, is this the party?" The man shouldered Lynette aside and stomped through the door, oblivious to the fact that Daniel hadn't stepped aside yet.

The puzzle pieces in his mind snapped together with miniature explosions.

Lynette was Kat's mother.

The man with her had to be the infamous stepfather, Mike Tyler, aka Chef Creepo. He was just as Kat had described him: stylish dresser, overweight, and half a head shorter than his wife. He was loaded down with grocery bags. It looked like he carried enough food to feed the entire apartment building. He stomped three feet into the apartment and looked around like a conqueror, claiming new territory. Daniel bristled.

Wasn't he supposed to be in Denver? Daniel distinctly remembered Kat saying that.

Lynette was here. Lynette was Kat's mother.

Kat was his daughter.

"Is this the place? Doesn't look like much. You sure this is the right place?" Mike demanded, scowling at Lynette, who stayed in the doorway, staring at Daniel like she had seen a ghost.

Another puzzle piece slammed down in his mind, with the impact of Dorothy's house on the Wicked Witch of the East. Lynette had to know he was here in Tabor Heights because Kat would have mentioned her advisor.

No wonder it seemed Lynette had been avoiding meeting him — because she had.

That had to be absolute terror and guilt making her look like a deer caught in headlights.

Pity got Daniel's brain and tongue working and pushed aside the anger and hurt that wanted to rise up and choke him before busting out in a howl of anguish and fury. Followed quickly by glee.

Kat was his daughter!

"If you're looking for Kat, Bekka and Amy, this is the place," Daniel offered, deciding to show mercy and drag his gaze to focus on Mike.

"Who's Kat?"

"Kathryn," Lynette sighed. To Daniel, it sounded like she had given this answer dozens of times already. "She prefers her friends call her Kat."

"She never told me that," her husband said, with all the injured air of a spoiled brat.

Daniel caught a glimpse of Bekka as she stumbled from the bathroom back into her room, without giving a backward glance at the people in the living room.

"Great." Mike dropped his grocery bags. "The john's free. I've been ready to burst since we were halfway here. Why'd Kathryn have to move so far away?" He waddled across the room and slammed the bathroom door behind himself.

"Gee, I wonder why," Daniel muttered, consciously not looking at Lynette.

"What are you doing here?" Lynette said in a harsh whisper. She glanced at the kitchen, where a frantic, muted discussion took place behind the curtain.

"Kat invited me."

"Why? What did you tell her about us?"

"Nothing! How could I tell her anything when I didn't know — anything," he added on a growl.

Lynette backed up a step.

"You knew I was here, Lyn. You had to. Why didn't you tell me? Why didn't you tell her?"

He gestured at the kitchen doorway and lowered his voice even more. No matter how much he wanted to wrap his arms around Kat and tell her he was her father, he knew the value of timing and staging. This was not the time or the place for a family reunion. Especially when one look at Lynette's face would convince everyone in the room that she was terrified of him.

"I couldn't." She finally came into the apartment and pushed the door closed. "Why didn't you ever come back for us?"

"How? Your mother's lawyers made it really clear that if I ever came within ten miles of you, I'd end up in jail, and they'd have a dozen witnesses lined up to testify I was a danger to you. Kind of hard for a guy with no money and no connections to fight, you know?" He took a step toward her without meaning to and she immediately backed up against the closed door. Daniel fought the acid in his throat and the frantic, furious racing of his heart, and gentled his voice. "Why didn't you call me when Kat was born?" His voice cracked. "I missed so much..."

"I couldn't." She looked around the room, focusing on the bathroom door. Did she hope her husband would come out and rescue her? "You never guessed?"

"At the beginning, yes. She looks so much like..." He tried to offer an olive branch. "You did a great job with her, Lyn. She's a great kid. She has a great future as a writer. A whole lot more future than she does as an actress, if you want my honest opinion."

"You still haven't gotten to Hollywood."

"Neither have you."

"I had better things to do than chase a dream across the country. I had my daughter to raise!" Lynette winced and glanced at the kitchen curtain.

"I wanted to help you. With *our* daughter." Despite the clashing emotions fighting for dominance, Daniel felt his heart leap at finally being able to say that, make that claim.

Thank You, God. No matter how this day ends up, thank You! She's my little girl. My daughter. I have a daughter.

"You can't even help yourself! You could have made something of yourself, but you gave up."

"Teaching at Butler-Williams is nothing to be ashamed of."

"You know what they say—those who can, do. Those who can't, teach."

"And those who have given up—" Daniel looked away for a moment, took a deep breath and said a quick prayer. This wasn't how he imagined his first meeting with Lynette. He turned around and held out his hands, begging for peace. "Just like old times." He tried to smile. It hurt.

"I think we just proved it's good we didn't stay together." She took a deep breath and tried to smile. Despite the hot flush in her face, she looked frozen to the core. "I'm sorry, Daniel. Seeing you startled me."

"Can we try to get along today, for Kat's sake? Let's agree that she has a lot of talent and we both should help her all we can, all right?"

"I almost wish she'd give up on acting. She gets the strangest parts... when she gets any at all." Lynette took a few stumbling steps toward the couch. She stopped, blocked by the bags Mike had left on the floor.

"You never know. The General has friends in a few of the big studios. One thing could lead to another—"

"She could end up on the West Coast instead of us."

"Dramatic irony?"

"Kat didn't tell me about the studio connection." She sighed again. "You probably have more of her life than I do, now."

Kat and Amy emerged through the kitchen curtain, carrying trays of olives and pickles, cheese and crackers, and little sausages set around a smoking bowl of some red sauce for dipping.

"Mom, when did you get here?" Kat smiled as she put down her tray on the coffee table. Amy groaned behind her.

"Not too long ago. Dr. Morgan and I were getting acquainted."

"What did I tell you? Mom always shows up early." Kat went to hug her mother and stopped, blocked by the bags. "Gee, Mom, you brought the whole kitchen with you. All I asked for —"

"There's my little girl!" Mike bellowed, emerging from the bathroom. "Come on and give your old dad a hug."

Daniel bit his tongue against shouting, *My little girl!*

"I don't think I should." All animation fled Kat's face. "Bekka is sick and I don't want to pass it on to anyone."

"Hold onto your hats, girls. Chef Michael is here to save the day!" He snatched up the grocery bags and hurried into the kitchen.

"I thought he was going out of town," Kat moaned.

"Excuse me — bathroom?" Daniel knew a cue for a strategic exit when he saw it. Lynette wouldn't appreciate him witnessing this stress between her and Kat.

What a time for their family to be reunited.

And what was Mike Tyler doing there, anyway? He was supposed to be out of town. Daniel closed the bathroom door and sat on the edge of the tub, head bowed, hands pressed against his face, and prayed. Hard. He wasn't sure what he prayed, but he knew this was the only smart thing he could do.

~~~~~

"Ah... maybe I should see what he's doing in my kitchen." Amy gave Kat a sympathetic look and ran for the kitchen.

"Mom?" was all Kat could manage to wail.

"Believe me, sweetheart, I wanted to spend Thanksgiving alone with you and the girls." Lynette flinched and glanced at the bathroom door, where Daniel had vanished. She didn't know if she appreciated his tact or hated him for being a coward. "Mike was all packed and ready to hop that plane for his convention. You think the snow is bad here? Colorado has six feet."

"He could have landed somewhere and rented a car," she grumbled.

"Oh, come on, it won't be that bad."

"But Morgan is here! The last thing I need is him feeling sorry for me." Kat crossed her arms over her chest and turned away, hunching her shoulders.

"You think he will?" Lynette murmured. Would he feel sorry for her, too, or consign her to suffer for her mistakes?

"Mom, Mike is a *jerk*. Even *you* have to admit it."

"He's a lovable jerk. And he's a great cook."

"He's his own walking billboard." Kat moved her hands to outline a belly that would make Santa Claus jealous.
~~~~~

"What about your Dr. Morgan?" Simply saying his name, after seeing him face-to-face for the first time in twenty years, sent a shiver through her.

He had aged so little. Maybe a little thicker, more solid. No gray hair. The wrinkles around his eyes and mouth were all laugh lines. Lynette remembered how much they laughed together. She had loved to hear him laugh. The warm sound of it always made her feel everything was right with the world.

She had feared the laughter would stop once he gave up his future to take care of her and their baby. She had been afraid he would hate her, resent her, and leave her. Sending him away, she had admitted years ago, had not been smart. But it was the only thing she could think of to do to save them both from greater misery.

And what good had her sacrifice done? He taught theater history and writing at a private school in Northeast Ohio. Even further from Hollywood and Broadway than Northwestern University had ever been. Yes, he was happy and admired and students fought to be in his classes. Kat certainly loved him.

What would Kat say if she knew her beloved Dr. Morgan was her father? Lynette shivered, positive her daughter — *their* daughter — would hate them both. Kat must never know.

No matter what sort of a deal she had to strike with Daniel to ensure his cooperation, Kat must never know.

"What do you mean, what about him?" Kat finally turned back to face her mother.

"I know you're his assistant and he's your advisor, and he's helping you make connections for your writing. But do you think it was — well — wise, inviting him over today?" Again, Lynette glanced at the bathroom door, and this time Kat saw it.

"Morgan is a great guy, and he's all alone today, okay? I heard him tell the General that his cousins were taking their kids to Disneyworld this week. He's got nobody. Bekka and Amy both had him for classes, and they like him. I wish you'd met Morgan before you met Mike."

"Why doesn't that surprise me?" Lynette choked. If only her daughter knew the truth! She tried to laugh. "You've been trying to split me from your father since you were twelve."

"He's not my father!"

"He's a lunatic!" Amy yelped, racing from the kitchen. "He's rearranging my entire kitchen. He thinks he's going to empty out my turkey and start all over. I swear, the only carving anyone does here today is going to be on him!"

"Why am I not surprised?" Kat sighed.

"Mike!" Lynette rolled up her sleeves as she stomped toward the kitchen. This was a fight she was learning to handle, if not win all the time. "You promised you'd leave the girls' kitchen alone!"

"I thought you said he wasn't coming," Amy hissed as Lynette vanished behind the curtain.

"Mike Tyler, what did we agree on in the car?" She tried not to growl as she took up a stance in the middle of the kitchen that resembled a galley in a sailboat. Efficient, everything within arm's reach, but how in the world did Amy create her gourmet delights and baking experiments in such cramped surroundings?

"Honey doll, I just want to make sure this is the best Thanksgiving for Kathryn. My little girl—"

"She's not little, and she was never *your* little girl," Lynette said, with a sigh that was more a growl than she liked to admit. "Kat has never even liked you. Why don't you give up trying to buy her affection?"

"Buy?" Mike turned white. He gaped at her a few seconds, then a tidal wave of red came rushing back into his face. "What has she told you? You can't believe half the things she's said, Lynette. The kid was almost a teenager when we got married, and you know how much teenagers hate authority."

"Kat's told me nothing," she hurried to say. Lynette didn't like the shiver that ran through her. Gut instinct said there was more to Mike's words than his usual defensive, self-righteous babbling. It was typical of him to pass the buck as soon as someone caught him in a crime. "Kat doesn't talk about you, Mike. Do you want to at least be friends with her?"

"That's all I've ever wanted, honey. You know that. She's your daughter, and I want her to love me just like you love me." Mike picked up a grocery bag from the drop-leaf table tucked into the corner. "Now, help me get organized and we'll make this a fantastic day for the girls."

"Mike, take a deep breath."

"Huh?"

"Just take a deep breath." She jammed her fists into her hips and tried to tower over him—easy to do, when she was a good three inches taller than him even in her stocking feet. "What do you smell?"

"Turkey with sage and onion dressing. Needs some white wine in—"

"Stop right there. This is Kat, Amy and Bekka's house. They have rules here. The first one is, no alcohol. The second one is, *they* provide for their guests," Lynette hurried on, when Mike opened his mouth to protest.

She knew he was going to launch into his usual diatribe about Bekka. How someone so straight-laced and Mary Poppins-ish couldn't be good for Kat at all. Lynette knew Bekka was probably the best thing that had happened to her daughter in years.

"You smell turkey, right? That means they already have a meal prepared. You are not going to make friends with Kat by throwing out all the hard work her roommates did. Understand? This is *her* house, you do things *her* way. You ask before you do something, understand?" She glared until Mike deflated a little and gave her that endearing little nod and crooked grin and hunched his shoulders like a mischievous little boy who always got three hugs for every swat.

That was probably why he was such a jerk now, Lynette decided, staggered by the insight. She wished she had realized it years ago. He used cuteness like a shield to get his way and make people forget he was selfish, pushy, and self-righteous. She sighed and resolved to ignore Mike as much as she could today.

She had bigger problems to fill her mind. She, Kat, and Daniel Morgan were together in one room, for the first time since she told him she was pregnant.

When Mike and Lynette emerged from the kitchen several minutes later, she found the three roommates standing around the table set with mismatched plates and Kat's usual flair for seasonal decorations. Bekka looked like she fought a major bug, and still wore a heavy flannel robe with gray sweatpants underneath. Kat and Amy gave Lynette and Mike wary looks. Lynette wished she had taken Mike's chef hat and *Kiss the Cook* apron away. Even thrown them into the garbage. What was the line about choosing your battles?

"It's all right, girls," Lynette said with a sigh. "The kitchen is once more safe to enter. If you let Mike do dessert, he'll let you take care of the rest of the meal. And he won't offer any helpful criticism, will he?" She gave him a meaningful glare and wished she could win so many other battles in their marriage so easily.

"Sure, honey," Mike hurried to say. "Anything you say. Truce, girls?"

"Well, his desserts are pretty good," Kat admitted grudgingly.

Daniel stuck his head out the bathroom door and glanced around the room. He very carefully didn't look at Lynette, and something inside her cringed, remembering that last conversation, just about this time, twenty years ago. He had every right to hate her, didn't he? Any half-intelligent man would know now was the perfect time to reveal the truth. A man with one-quarter Daniel's acting talent could sway Kat to side with him in the resulting explosion of hurt and accusations.

"Is it safe to come out now?" he asked with a grin Lynette remembered quite well. Not the smile that made her melt. The one that could calm angry theater students who had tangled themselves into frustration during a rehearsal. The grin that meant he could be a troublemaker, but no one would ever get hurt.

Daniel Morgan had always been a gentleman. That was probably why he hadn't marched into the kitchen the moment he realized who she was, who Kat was, and made a loud, dramatic announcement sure to turn their daughter against her, in his favor. Lynette wondered how she had been so lucky.

How could she have been so stupid, to send him away?

"Hey, you like football?" Mike gestured at the TV set hidden under a scarf with a turkey painted on it.

"Are they still waiting for Godot?" Daniel asked.

"Huh?" Mike stumbled toward the TV as Lynette and Daniel shared a longsuffering look that turned into matched grins, from shared memories of theater in-jokes from college days. A moment later, they both blushed and looked away.

~~~~~

Mike Tyler was a jolly guy, but he was a self-absorbed jerk, hands down. He could be charming when he made an effort, and Daniel could see how Lynette had fallen for him. Especially since he offered everything that a drama student with outstanding loans and no agent or prospects for the future couldn't have given her and Kat back then. But the gloss had definitely worn off the marriage. That was obvious, just from the way the two of them had come out of the kitchen, looking more like scolding nanny and spoiled brat than husband and wife.

Why hadn't Lynette left Mike years ago? Or was that thought wrong? Divorce was wrong. Just because a guy was a social pain was no reason for divorce. Daniel didn't know whether to admire Lynette for sticking to her guns or shake her until she got some sense. Could she still love him?

No, Lynette didn't love Mike. She didn't even like him much. Daniel could tell just by the way Lynette avoided looking at her own husband, the way she leaned forward every time he put his arm across the back of her chair. Even if those things were unconscious, couldn't she see how uncomfortable Mike made Kat? It made Daniel bristle every time Mike tried to touch Kat as she scurried around with plates or guided the guests to their chairs. Each time, Kat made a visible detour and her smile dimmed. Daniel hadn't solved problems with his fists since long before college, but watching the interaction between Kat and her stepfather, he felt tempted now.

Bekka emerged from her room twenty minutes before dinner, showered and dressed and with some color on her face, and Daniel hoped she had gotten over whatever bug had hit her. He wondered how much of that drawn look on her face was the dregs of her illness and how much was dislike for Mike Tyler. Bekka watched the fat man almost as much as he did. Daniel said a few prayers of thanks during that long day, grateful Bekka was there to watch out for his daughter when he couldn't.

His daughter. Every time the realization hit him anew, he had to turn and stare at Kat and feast his mind and heart on the amazing, surprising
~~~~~

revelation. Kat was his daughter.

When Amy brought the turkey to the table, their guests cheered. Daniel speculated some of the cheers were in hopes that eating would get Mike to shut up and let someone else talk for a change.

Marco had finally won Kat's attention and had been invited for Thanksgiving. Joe and Amy were together for the holiday. Bekka didn't have a date. Daniel wasn't surprised, though he did think it a shame. Bekka had a lot to offer a good man, if she would just slow down enough for one to notice her. But then, who was Daniel to get critical? He hadn't dated anyone since Lynette shoved him out of her life. Summer theater flirtations and casual dinner dates in large groups didn't count. Not when he remembered what it was like to be with one person who seemed to be the other half of his soul.

Marco held the chair for Kat, and Joe followed his example before Amy could even give him an expectant look. Mike threw himself into his chair, rubbed his hands together, and reached for the bowl of dressing before Lynette had even crossed the room to the table. She sighed, softly, but loudly enough for Daniel to hear.

"Lyn?" he murmured, stepped up next to her, and reached for the back of the folding chair. Something warmed down deep inside when her lips twitched into a tiny smile, a flush brushed her cheeks, and she let him hold the chair for her and scoot her into the table.

Daniel glanced around the table and didn't know whether to laugh or cheer. The girls had pulled off a minor miracle and did it with style. Somehow, eight people were now jammed together around two card tables put end to end, with mismatched folding chairs, a hassock and the desk chair from Kat's computer center. Daniel finally understood what Bekka meant when she said their apartment was furnished in Salvation Army Classic. Patched furniture held mended cushions, covered with throws. Their bookshelves were built of plastic milk crates or the classic college student's trick of boards and bricks. Movie posters brightened the otherwise dull beige walls, and Kat's computer desk sat crammed into the corner next to the balcony door. Turkeys, pilgrims and cornucopias were everywhere as either figurines, candles or cardboard wall hangings.

They had gone all out to make the place a home. Daniel chuckled silently to realize he felt far more comfortable here than he had ever felt at far richer, more stylish homes. It reminded him of the Randolphs' house. Their living room served as the Green Room, make-up room and whatever else they needed for Homespun Theater. Daniel had always felt comfortable and part of the family there. Just like he felt here. Despite it all. For a moment, he stood still and savored the sensation, right behind Lynette's chair. He was loath to move away from her to sit at the head of the table, where a turkey card with his name on it waited.

"Dr. Morgan, could you say the blessing?" Bekka asked. Her innocent look took on a nasty twinkle when Mike nearly dropped the bowl of dressing and his mouth dropped into a stunned 'O' of surprise.

"Ah... sure, Bekka. I'd be honored."

Daniel glanced at Lynette and his face warmed. She didn't look at him, didn't seem surprised by the request. Had Kat told her mother about his faith? He had never made a secret of his beliefs, but Daniel always kept two steps back from the line that couldn't be crossed while teaching in a secular university. He stayed standing, bowed his head, and folded his hands while he waited for everybody to take their seats. Bekka watched her two roommates as they fidgeted and glanced around and finally folded their hands and closed their eyes. She glanced at him, offering a tiny smile. Daniel had to smile. He hoped she knew how much he appreciated, and yet dreaded, this opportunity.

"Father God, thank You for this day. For these friends. For the warmth and bounty spread out before us while so many in this world have no home, no friends, no family, no food. Please help us to carry our gratitude away from this table and spread it in the world. Thank You for the miracle of just being together today, of being a family for just a moment in time."

Lynette's head jerked up, her eyes opened, and their gazes locked. Daniel felt as if ice filled his belly. That had been a stupid thing to say, hadn't it?

Instead of the fury he expected, Daniel saw tears glimmer and fill her eyes. She offered a smile.

It was more than he expected. He smiled back.

What he said in the rest of the prayer, he could never recall. It had made some kind of sense, because no one looked strangely at him when he finished and they raised their heads. Lynette looked away and tried to wipe her eyes without looking like she wiped her eyes.

Daniel stayed standing, not sure what he was going to do. He only knew he had to divert attention away from her. He owed it to her.

"A toast." He spied the chilled bottles of cider on the serving table set a few feet away. He bowed, earning grins and chuckles from his students. "To our hostesses." He stripped the foil from the bottles and twisted the metal caps open as he spoke and filled the mismatched glasses Kat had pulled out for the cider. "To friendship. To all the dreams filling this apartment. I hope all of you go wherever your dreams lead you." Joe passed the glasses around the table as Daniel continued. "May we always stay friends, and always have fond memories of this day." He raised his glass and met Lynette's now-dry, composed gaze. She nodded and raised her glass a little before she sipped.

Chapter Five

The glow of that day stayed with Daniel as school resumed after the Thanksgiving weekend, even when the General's legendary pre-production hysteria tripled in force and volume. He kept busy as the best antidote against brooding and spent his non-class evenings helping with the rehearsals for the Christmas program, mostly as liaison between frazzled students and their director. Daniel enjoyed those times, his hands-on exposure to the theater and the validation that he had chosen the right path. Maybe he only made a fraction of the income he could as an actor, but he loved working backstage and helping guide talented students toward their dreams.

It was a bonus to be able to work with Kat, knowing what he knew about her now. Marco returned to being a shadow in her life, relegated to her past after the ritual two dates had gone by. Daniel felt sorry for the young man, but what could he tell him? He suspected Kat's inability or refusal to go beyond two dates with anyone was mixed up with the absence of her father in her life, and Mike Tyler's influence. Daniel didn't see Marco as a stalker anymore. He knew exactly what the young man was going through. Lynette hadn't said anything to him about not telling Kat that he was her father, but he could see her fear, the pleading in her eyes. Daniel kept silent because of the memories of what they had once meant to each other, and because he suspected the only way Kat could learn he was her father was for her mother to make the confession.

So he waited and prayed. He called his aunt and uncle the day after Thanksgiving to tell them that their long-standing prayers had been answered, and he told Al and Abby when they returned from Disneyworld. Abby flung her arms around him and cried. He went to Pastor Glen for counseling, to sound out his reaction to the revelation, and to ask for prayer to endure the waiting.

And sometimes, late at night, as a reward for controlling himself and for being patient one more day, he daydreamed multiple scenarios of Kat calling him *Dad*, with joy and love.

Friday, December 13

"Mike, please tell me you didn't force yourself on Kat's strike party," Lynette moaned as she stomped into her husband's TV room.

"Force myself? Honey, all I did was offer to cater closing night." Mike barely turned his head away from the hockey game. "Come on, we gotta celebrate. Kat's finally got a decent part. How am I gonna show my little girl how proud she makes me?"

"What have I told you about sneaking around behind Kat's back?"

"I didn't sneak around!" He nearly rose out of his chair, but a moment later a fight broke out and he sank back into the cushions with his gaze glued to the screen.

"Did you ask her if she minded if you got involved?"

"Geeze, Lynette, sometimes I think she wants to cut me out of her life completely. I wouldn't even have known about closing night if I hadn't seen those tickets she sent."

"Hmm. Yes."

"Come on, who's going to give those kids a really great party for free?" He turned on that smile that was part charm/part mischief that had originally won her heart. Was it only eight years ago? It felt like forever.

And in some ways, it felt like a dream. Something that never really happened. Lynette wondered if she had been so desperately lonely she had created an illusion for herself. And Kat suffered for it.

The truth was, Kat had sent the tickets for closing night for Lynette to take a friend. Nothing was said at all about her stepfather. Lynette knew that was deliberate.

She also knew she didn't want to show up at closing night and have to endure the strike party without someone at her side to shield her from Daniel. He would be there. Kat had reported a dozen incidents where Daniel had come to the rescue, saving the General from irate performers or stage crew, or saving the crew from crazy ideas the General came up with at the last moment. Everyone adored him.

Lynette wondered if Kat would be so enamored of Daniel if she knew he was her father. Would she whine to her mother about his interference, exactly as she had just done by phone, when she found out Mike was catering the strike party?

"Just behave yourself, Mike. Don't go running around telling everyone you're her stepfather. Let Kat enjoy her night with her friends her way, okay?"

"Geeze, you make it sound like I deliberately set out to embarrass Kathryn." Mike pouted, and the next moment his eyes glazed over as an instant replay filled the TV screen.

"No, you would never do that," she whispered, and backed out of the room. Mike had become so desperate to win business from Butler-Williams, he was willing to provide a party for free. There was no talking to him now. The damage had been done. She definitely had to go to closing night, just to stand as shield between her daughter and her husband.

Especially when Mike found out that her stage name was Kat Teague, rather than her legal name.

Would Mike be any good as a shield against Daniel?

Did she really want a shield?

"Oh, don't be a ninny," Lynette snapped, her voice echoing in the living room as she picked up a dusting rag and continued her housecleaning.

She was being silly, fearing her next encounter with Daniel. It would be out in public, with lots of witnesses. If he hadn't sat Kat down to reveal he was her father, then he was waiting for Lynette to do it. He didn't hate her. Didn't want to punish her. He hadn't been the kind of man to plot revenge when they had been in college. Kat and Bekka had talked about their beloved Dr. Morgan enough, Lynette thought he was even more honorable now.

The only thing she had to fear... wasn't a fear, she realized, now that she made herself face the nebulous ideas that had haunted her since Thanksgiving.

Lynette remembered enough about church to know that the people who practiced what they preached believed in the sanctity of marriage. Daniel would never try to resume their college relationship simply because she was married to someone else. Lynette knew there were many so-called Christians who didn't care about such barriers, and then made excuses so it seemed God even approved adultery.

Adultery. That was the word. But it was more than just having an affair, wasn't it? Wasn't adultery wishing herself free of her husband? Wishing for the carefree, dream-filled days of her youth? Wanting the handsome man who had once begged to share her life?

"I don't know why I'm worried. Mike abandoned *me* a long time ago. I don't even believe in church anymore," Lynette muttered as she cleaned.

But she knew Daniel believed. He was the kind of man who would throw himself wholeheartedly into what he believed. He had been almost straightlaced in their university days. Not straightlaced enough to keep them from sleeping together, but he had been nicknamed "Father Daniel" because of his clean lifestyle among their fellow theater students. Daniel would never approach her. Even if she asked him.

Would she ask him? Could they be friends and work together to look after Kat and her dreams, just like he had proposed at Thanksgiving? They hadn't talked since then, hadn't had much chance for a private word all during the dinner and long, lazy afternoon. Still, Lynette sensed Daniel had forgiven her. She saw the love and pride shining in his eyes when he looked at their daughter and knew he would willingly do anything for Kat's sake.

Could they work together for Kat's sake? Could she survive the flood of longing and bitterness over dreams abandoned? Could she live with the renewed guilt and self-anger? She had made her choices and sent Daniel away. She had lived with it for twenty years, but now she truly wondered if she had made the right choice.

Saturday, December 14

Daniel stood in the doorway of the back parlor at Haven Funeral Home, watching Andrew and Helen Gray droop, little by little, as the line of mourners greeted them in front of their daughter's coffin. He knew Andrew from two men's retreats at Tabor Christian. They had run into each other maybe a dozen times at Heinke's Grocery. They had worked together at the ice cream table at the Sunday School picnic last summer. That was enough of a friendship to prompt Andrew to ask him to be pallbearer at Annalee's funeral. The Grays hadn't been living in Tabor Heights more than a year. Long enough for evil to target their daughter and take her from them.

Annalee Gray had been the White Rose's third victim. Daniel shivered, wondering who the next target was. His gut churned with relief and guilt. Relief that Kat wouldn't be the man's target, because she didn't fit the physical and social pattern established with the first three victims. Guilt that he could feel such relief while looking at the grief that aged Annalee's parents. The only comfort Daniel could find was that Annalee's parents knew her eternity had been assured.

Please, Lord, protect Kat. I don't know if she knows You. Don't let anything happen to my daughter.

Friday, December 20

Lynette knew Kat was a tree in the Christmas production. Her daughter had described her costume and even recited her lines several times, asking her opinion on different inflections and hand gestures. The reality of it didn't sink in until the curtain opened on the second act and she saw Kat on the stage. Mike, sitting next to her, jerked, snorted, and mumbled about "lunatic artists" until she jabbed him in the ribs. Harder than she had ever jabbed him before.

She had no trouble losing herself in the world of make-believe. For those two hours of the performance, she knew she and Daniel were united, agreeing in at least one area. Their daughter had talent, she was beautiful, and she could handle even the strangest roles with style and poise. Even if she did have to act through green glitter all over her face and a clunky costume that inhibited her stride.

The audience applauded wildly as Kat delivered her final line, surrounded by the weaving dance of surrealistic fairies and stars and half-human animals. Lynette clapped with all her strength, laughing with delight and pride, tears glimmering bright in her eyes. Mike just slouched a little further in his seat, clapping awkwardly. His disgruntled frown clearly showed he was confused about what had happened. She fought to ignore him and to hold onto her delight with the performance.

She prayed Kat couldn't see her stepfather for the lights in her eyes. Why, oh why, had Mike forced himself on her director and intruded on this one special night of her life? After all Kat's obvious avoidance and distaste for him, couldn't Mike see he was only pushing her away, not winning her affection?

Of course, Mike couldn't see that his own wife was disgusted with him. He thought everything was wonderful, everybody loved him, and he pouted whenever something didn't go the way he thought it should. He had been too busy conferring with the serving crew via cell phone before the house lights went down to read the program and realize *Kathryn Tyler* wasn't listed anywhere in the cast. Kat didn't want him to profit from the reflected glow of her success. If Mike realized what she had done, would it finally sink in that she wasn't "his little girl" and she wanted nothing to do with him?

Some things were going to have to change, Lynette knew. Maybe when they were in Chicago, visiting her mother for Christmas, she could get Mike to sit down and actually listen to her for a change. For Kat's sake, if no one else's.

~~~~~

Mike Tyler did understand food. Daniel had to give the man that much credit. Even Kat had to admit her stepfather could do one thing very, very well. Even though the man was a complete dud with almost everything else, his catering company was top rank. Everyone seemed to enjoy the food, and the catering crew was made up of fellow students, in black slacks and matching red sweatshirts, who laughed and chattered as they served. Everything was fantastic. More than worthy of the stellar performance of the cast and crew that night. Still, Kat cringed every time her stepfather passed her as he scurried around the theater backstage, overseeing his workers. Daniel could only be glad the man didn't grab her every time he passed her and shout to the whole world that his little girl was the star.

Daniel understood the impulse, though. He wished he could do it tonight. Wrap an arm around his daughter's shoulders and hug her, tell her how wonderful she was, give her roses, and proudly lead her to the theater critics who even now trailed in the General's wake, meeting the various cast members.
~~~~~

The strike party passed almost as quickly as the closing performance. Everyone moved with turbo speed to remove costumes and makeup and get everything cleaned up and put away so they could relax and talk and enjoy the food. The General had requested a relatively simple set when he wrote his script, all black curtains and flies, and most of the decorations were incorporated into the costumes. In what seemed like moments, the stage had been reduced to scuffed hardwood. Curtains were folded and hauled up into the storage area next to the grid. Costumes were hung up, waiting to be cleaned. Chairs and tables appeared and actors wearing street clothes and glitter makeup descended like the proverbial locusts on the long rows of steam tables where Mike's crew waited to serve them.

As the party settled in and people found places to sit and congregate in little knots, there was even room for dancing once someone found a CD player.

Daniel found the three roommates sitting in a shadowy corner of the stage near the proscenium, with Lynette. They were all visibly exhausted, the afterglow fading, leaving them mostly smiling at each other and not saying much. Daniel was glad to stand in a quiet corner and watch them. Amy and Bekka had worked backstage during this production and seemed to enjoy their part far more than the actors on stage had. Considering the histrionics the General could display, Daniel didn't blame them. They also didn't show any jealousy of Kat's temporary stardom, and he was glad. Of course, it was Bekka's nature to be glad for others' triumphs and not be jealous, but not Amy's. Maybe Bekka was having more of an influence on her poet roommate than she thought.

The General bombed through the dancing, around the knots of chairs, dragging the two theater critics in his wake. One was from the state arts board, the other from the college association that judged new productions and published a magazine devoted to collegiate theater. Not bad, Daniel knew. Next year, if the reviews this year were good enough, someone might come from Broadway. The General had no ambitions to work in New York or Hollywood, but he did love the exposure that gave his beloved students a chance to follow their dreams.

"There is my pretty little tree!" the General boomed as he zeroed in on Kat and her roommates. He spread his arms wide in profligate blessing on the entire cast and crew. "Darling girl, you must catch up on your sleep. Such a hard worker. You spelled her name right, didn't you? Kathryn Teague."

Daniel groaned when he saw Mike drop the fresh plate of pastries he inspected, frown, and waddle over to join Lynette and the girls. He just knew the clod would do or say something to spoil Kat's moment in the spotlight. He had to do something.

"That is spelled T E A — yes, I see you have a program," the General continued. "Very good. And over there is my star — my star of all my stars, yes?"

He laughed richly and led the two reviewers across to the other corner of the stage, where the girl who played the Christmas star huddled with her friends. Daniel had heard her laughing and complaining about her accumulated bruises from the harness to make her fly.

"He's rather tiring, isn't he?" Lynette said with a chuckle as Daniel stepped within hearing distance. She wiped her forehead.

"The guy's crazy, if you ask me," Mike said, joining them.

Kat rolled her eyes. Amy and Bekka traded glances, and Daniel saw them press their lips together to fight grins. Maybe even laughter.

"He's right, though," Mike continued, reaching out to squeeze Kat's shoulder. "You really do need your sleep, baby doll."

Kat leaned out of his reach, her smile dying instantly. Something twisted in Daniel's stomach. Whatever was wrong between Kat and her stepfather, it had depths and implications he couldn't understand. Lynette wouldn't allow the man to actually hurt her daughter. Nothing beyond irritating and embarrassing her, at least. Right?

Daniel prayed he was right. But then, seeing the frown Lynette lowered on her husband, he wondered. Maybe this was a recent development and she was just starting to notice?

"He can't even spell right," the man said with a snort.

Alarm sparked in Lynette's eyes. Daniel flashed back to a discussion in his first level playwriting class only two weeks ago, on the value of stage names and why some writers used pen names because of the lack of support from their families, or to protect them from mockery in the days when writers weren't respected. Kat had made the point that some people used stage names because they didn't want their families to take credit for their successes. In a heartbeat, he knew that was what Kat had done — she had used her mother's maiden name as her stage name because she didn't want Mike Tyler to get any credit, any benefit from her stardom.

"I think someone who performed as well as Kat did tonight, and through all the rehearsals, has the sense to take care of herself," Daniel hurried to say, using what he considered his *professor voice*. "Don't you?" He tilted his head just slightly toward Mike, challenging him with his unsmiling face.

From the corner of his eye, he saw Kat glow.

Daniel hadn't set out to be his daughter's hero, but that was what he felt like right that moment.

He liked it.

Lynette even smiled. A little bit. Daniel wondered if they would be able to have that talk about Kat soon, if she welcomed his presence and his intervention with Mike.

"Yeah, maybe," Mike muttered. "What's the world coming to, when lunatics are allowed to work with little kids like Kathryn and Becky and..." He gestured at Amy, clearly unable to remember her name.

"He's an award winning director, he's part owner in an off-Broadway theater, and knows half the studio people in L.A. That's why," Daniel retorted. He had a dozen other accomplishments to list, if that wasn't enough for Mike.

"You're kidding me?" He released that hearty laugh that seemed to condemn to the dustbin anything besides football and catering. "Theater won't pay the bills. Lynette here was a theater student. She wanted to be in movies, but she got smart and gave up on it before she wasted too much time." He slid an arm around his wife, who stiffened visibly.

Kat jumped to her feet and scurried away, with Amy and Bekka right on her heels. Daniel silently cheered them.

"You should be very proud of Kat tonight, Lynette," Daniel offered. "She did a wonderful job. She's a credit to you. I really believe she inherited all your talent."

Lynette's eyes glowed, then the glitter turned into tears she could barely restrain. She smiled and nodded her thanks. Mike snorted and muttered something about incompetents at the punch bowl and waddled away.

"I wonder sometimes how she would have turned out if you had — if I had let you be her father," she said on a sigh.

"I hope not much different." He nodded and knew it was the truth. "There are times I wish I could tell her who I am, just so I could help her more than I do now, but..."

"You think she'll hate both of us." Lynette turned to stare across the stage that slowly lost its crowd as the night wore on. "I've been thinking lately — a lot — about what would have happened if I hadn't called in my mother and her lawyers and sent you away."

"I should have fought harder."

"You wouldn't be where you are, who you are, if you had. Maybe we're both better off. I just wish... are you really happy, Danny? The kids all love you, and I know you're doing what you love and you're part of the community and..." She shrugged. "I don't know what I mean, but are you happy?"

"My life is great. I wouldn't have it any other way." Daniel dropped down to one knee in front of her and dared to take hold of her hand. She didn't pull away. He shivered, hot and cold at the same time, at this first touch of her hand in twenty years. "Lyn, I put my life in God's hands when I lost you and Kat. I learned to trust Him, and He's taken care of me. And now you two are back in my life. You know I'll do whatever I can to help both of you, whenever you need me. Kat is my assistant, my best student, and I think maybe she likes me more as her teacher than she would if she knew the truth. You know, the difficult teen years."

"Too well." She tried to laugh, but the sound caught in her throat.

"Morgan!" the General bellowed from the back of the auditorium. His bullhorn voice could be heard through a riot, let alone in the acoustically enhanced theater. "We need you!"

"Gotta run," Daniel said, standing slowly. He rolled his eyes, just imagining what petty problem the General had blown out of proportion. Lynette chuckled, sounding more natural this time. He gave her hand one last squeeze. "Maybe we can get together when you get back from Chicago, and talk about... I don't know. Kat's future?"

"I'd like that." She nodded, managing a smile.

Daniel felt her watching him as he crossed the stage and went down the wing stairs and hurried up the side aisle to where his fellow teacher waited with the two reviewers and Joel Randolph. Of course. Daniel almost groaned. The requisite theater faculty Christmas picture. He glanced back over his shoulder, and Lynette was no longer seated where he had left her. He sighed and held onto the promise of that talk when she got back from Christmas break.

Tuesday, December 24

"Please, Lord, bless Lyn and Kat," Daniel whispered as the strains of *Silent Night* filtered through the sanctuary and the golden glow from dozens of tiny white candles grew to hundreds as the flames passed from one worshipper to another.

He loved the candlelight service on Christmas Eve almost more than any other celebration of the church year. This year, however, he had a near-tears ache of wistful longing. How wonderful it would be if he could share the service with Lynette and their daughter. His regret had a jagged edge as he thought of all the missed years of filling stockings for Kat and telling her stories and tucking her into bed. Playing favorite uncle for Candy and Chad had been soothing, but never filled the empty ache.

He glanced down the row at his cousins. Abby sat next to him, dark hair cut short and swept back in that severe style that just made her look more pixie-ish. Ten-year-old Candy sat next to her, sitting still for the first time since the service started, looking so dressed up in her burgundy velvet, lace-trimmed dress. Nine-year-old Chad next to Candy, tugging on his tie to loosen it for the thousandth time that evening. And Al at the end of the row, his linebacker body slumped in the pew. He looked weary and cold from a long day towing stranded cars out of ditches and coaxing recalcitrant engines to start in this cold weather.

Al was a good man. He and Abby and their parents had helped

Daniel through the pain of losing Lynette. Daniel wished Al's wife, Bethany, were still alive to fuss over his daughter when the day finally came to introduce her to his family. He wished Kat could meet her cousins tonight. There was so much they had all missed.

Not that he missed the trauma of Kat taking driving lessons or going on her first date. But he hadn't seen her prom dress or held her while she cried over her first broken heart.

Please, he repeated silently. *Please, Lord, I believe You've given us a second chance to be a family. You've given me my daughter, finally, after all these years not even knowing if she existed. I have to believe...* A wry chuckle escaped him. *Lord, we need a miracle. We don't have a chance with Mike Tyler around. And I don't really wish the man harm, Lord, but he needs to be dropped off the Terminal Tower a couple dozen times. You're going to have to do something about him. But if You don't, Lord, I'm going to trust You. It's all I can do. Even if it's killing me.*

At the front of the sanctuary, Pastor Glenn raised the four-inch-wide gold candle high, and the congregation raised their tiny candles. The arched ceiling blazed golden with light.

"So let your light shine, the light of Jesus' birth and life and death and resurrection," the gray-haired, stocky minister called out, his voice joyful and ringing.

The congregation responded with an "amen" like a roar.

In unison, with the practice of dozens of years of the ritual, the people lowered their candles and blew out the flames. As tiny spirals of candle smoke twisted up toward the ceiling, the golden lights of the sanctuary came back on. *Joy to the World* blasted from the organ as the congregation slowly dispersed. Daniel grinned, imagining the unseen organist jamming on the staid old instrument, dancing in her seat as much as a proper, dignified church organist could ever do.

"See you at the house?" Joel Randolph said, leaning forward from the pew behind him to tap Daniel's shoulder.

"Wouldn't miss it." Daniel grinned and turned to exchange smiles, nods, and greetings with the Randolph family: Joel, his wife Emily, their daughter Max—as dark in hair and eyes as Joel, and their sons, Joe and Jeremy—as golden blond and gray-eyed as their mother. For the past ten years, he had spent Christmas Eve with the Randolphs and Christmas Day with his cousins. It wouldn't be Christmas anywhere else or any other way.

Maybe next year, Lord, I'll bring Lyn and Kat... or we can invite the Randolphs to be with us?

Chapter Six

Lynette and her mother came back from the traditional Christmas Eve gift baskets delivery more than an hour early. The aroma of wassail warming in the parlor and the spicy pine scent of the live trees in five downstairs rooms met Lynette like a gentle embrace. She sighed and inhaled deeply, relishing the quiet, and then sighed again, tensing. The lovely, quiet, relaxed preparations for Christmas were about to end.

Mike hadn't come with them to Chicago, because of several last-minute Christmas parties he had to supervise personally. He was due to fly in this evening but had been vague about the flight details. She expected him to call in another hour to demand someone come pick him up. Considering how he had grumbled so much after the Christmas production that Kat didn't even want to acknowledge that she knew him, much less that he was her father, Lynette suspected he would demand Kat drive to the airport to pick him up. Ever since she moved into the dormitories for college, Mike kept demanding "daddy and daughter time," and pouted when Kat consistently refused.

Lynette planned to send the driver, no matter how much Mike whined and begged and tried to charm her into giving him what he wanted. If that meant he sulked all Christmas Eve, that suited her fine. He wouldn't spend the entire evening making himself the center of attention. Even her mother had finally grown tired of his charming little boy façade.

She listened to her mother's voice coming from the kitchen, checking with Patricia, the housekeeper, to make sure everything was in place for their traditional dinner. Lynette smiled, knowing the same old routine would play out—her mother would insist on sending the staff away to spend Christmas Eve with their friends and relatives, and the staff would refuse. They were family. Most of them had been with Mrs. Teague since before Lynette was born. It wouldn't be Christmas without them. She remembered creeping into the staff living room, to visit the tree and see what treats had been hidden for her around the room. It had been even more fun repeating the tradition with Kat when she was little.

Where was Kat? She hadn't gone out with her mother and grandmother, preferring to visit her friends by catching a movie and doing last-minute shopping. Lynette wondered if she should encourage Kat yet again to consider staying in Chicago with her grandmother. Andrew Fontaine had adored Kat since kindergarten, and he hadn't settled on a girlfriend yet—maybe Kat hadn't chosen a steady boyfriend because she subconsciously wanted Andrew?

"Like father, like daughter?" she murmured, and flinched as an image of Daniel's face filled her mind.

Last summer at the Stoughton Mall, she had seen Abby Morgan and the children she had seen at the theater with her more than a year ago. They called her Aunt Abby. A little questioning had revealed she was Daniel's cousin, and the children belonged to her brother. Lynette had been shocked at the giddy relief that swept through her when she realized Daniel wasn't married.

Now, it struck her anew that Daniel hadn't settled on anyone in all the years since she had turned her back on him. She had even asked Bekka once if Daniel dated, and the girl had given her a stunned, yet amused look, as if she thought it the most ridiculous thing in the world for Dr. Daniel Morgan to date anyone.

What were the chances Daniel had been waiting for her to come back into his life?

"You're too old for romance and for Prince Charming to come back—"

"Leave me alone!" Kat shrieked, her voice echoing down the stairwell from the bedroom suites on the third floor.

A thud, like a falling body, and a door slamming jolted Lynette into action. She bolted for the stairs, dropping her purse on the landing between the first and second floors. Her boot heel threatened to catch in the thick carpeting. Her racing heart muffled her footsteps. Mother instincts pictured Kat lying bloody and still in her room. Who would threaten the girl in her grandmother's house?

In the few seconds it took to get from the second to third floor, Lynette wondered if Kat was on the phone and had thrown something at the door in her fury. But who would call her in Chicago? Who knew her grandmother's phone number? For Kat to be on the phone, she would have had to call someone. Hadn't she broken up with her latest two-date-limit boyfriend?

"Why won't you leave me alone?" Kat screamed, her voice breaking with sobs as Lynette reached the landing and ran down the third-floor hall.

"There's nobody in the house," Mike said, his voice strained, a low growl Lynette only heard twice. Both times, he had drunk himself from the jolly, silly stage to vicious and bitter. Her steps fumbled as she tried to accept it was his voice she heard. "You owe me."

"I don't owe you anything!"

"Time to pay up!"

"No!" The door banged hard in the frame from something hitting it and bounced open just two seconds before Lynette reached the door.

She pushed it open to see Kat staggering across the room with Mike following her. Her daughter hit the wall, scrabbling at the intercom panel. Mike grabbed her one-handed by the waistband of the pretty jade green lounging outfit her grandmother had just given her and flung her across the front room of her suite. She tripped over the ottoman and tumbled, landing on her back.

The piercing aroma of whiskey filled the room. Only Lynette's father had ever drunk whiskey in this house, and the liquor cabinet had been locked since the day he died twenty-six years before. She could only stare, trying to process what didn't make sense, and saw the bottle Mike held in his hand as he stomped across the room and stood over Kat. He tipped up the bottle and poured it over her face, making her sputter and choke.

'Drink up, baby doll, and we'll have some fun." He chuckled, and it was a vicious, triumphant sound Lynette had never heard before. "Just relax, and it won't hurt at all."

"No." Kat rolled, and he stepped on her arm, stopping her.

"Michael!" Lynette shrieked, finally getting her voice.

"Get out of here, Lynette," he growled, turning to glare at her. His face was brilliant red. His shirtfront was wet and dark. Probably more whiskey he had spilled on himself.

Kat shrieked and kicked up, hitting Mike low in the groin, but missing her obvious target. He swore and dropped down on her, spilling the rest of the whiskey, punching and clawing. Lynette leaped the fifteen feet between them in what felt like one step, but not before she heard the shriek of tearing cloth and Kat's scream.

Then she was on top of Mike, scratching and kicking and punching and shrieking at the top of her voice, wordless ranting, while ice filled her mind and fury burned through her belly.

Vaguely, she saw Kat roll out of the way and scramble backward until she hit a wall. Lynette pounded Mike, felt the tears streaming down her face, but it was as if she watched through a curtain.

What would have happened if she hadn't come home early?

Mike had lied about his flight arrangements — he had planned to get here early.

He had stolen her father's whiskey.

He had attacked her daughter.

Mike's flailing fist hit her in the gut, knocking the breath out of her, and she went down, gasping. Lynette's eyes watered, but she saw him grab onto Kat's easy chair and haul himself to his feet.

'Mom!" Kat shrieked. "Look out!"

'You shut up, you little tramp!" Mike snarled.

He bent over Lynette, slapping her hands out of the way when she tried to ward him off. He grabbed her by her hair and yanked her halfway to her feet, then pushed her hard, so she hit the wall. The framed photos from Kat's Girl Scouts photography badge rattled, threatening to come down on her.

"You get out of here right now, Lynette. Or do you want to watch? How about a threesome?" He wiped his mouth and staggered back, leering. "Kat hasn't played her little game with her step-daddy in too long, and she owes me."

"Mom, I never—"

"Shut up!" Mike roared.

The sound broke off with a yelp as a black, gold-tipped cane whipped down from the edge of Lynette's vision and cracked across Mike's face. It broke in half. Mike howled and went down, his hands coming up to cover his face as blood gushed from his broken nose.

"My granddaughter," Lynette's mother snapped in icy, regal fury. "My daughter. In my house!"

Then Ramsey, the driver, dove in and hauled Mike to his feet and dragged him, bleeding and whimpering and struggling, out of the room. Lynette turned to watch, stunned at how rescue had showed up so quickly. Patricia, the housekeeper, and Gloria, the cook, stood in the doorway, their faces white with shock. Gloria kicked at Mike as Ramsey dragged him out of the doorway and headed for the stairs.

"Mom?" Kat whispered.

"Baby." Lynette never quite got to her feet as she scrambled across the room to wrap her arms hard around Kat to hold on as tight as possible. Then the trembling took over. "How did you—" she managed to blurt before her throat closed with sobs.

"We heard everything," her mother said, tottering across the room to join them. She went to her knees and wrapped her arms around her daughter and granddaughter. "The intercom."

Kat giggled, the sound breaking into sobs, and the three huddled together. Vaguely, Lynette heard Patricia assuring them the police were on their way, and Gloria muttering about needing to clean up the spilled whiskey and the blood spatters on the carpet before the stains set.

"Don't you dare change anything," Patricia said. "After all those CSI shows we watch, you ought to know better than to destroy any evidence. The police are going to need it."

Gloria was properly contrite, and any other time Lynette might have giggled over the incongruity of the two elderly women talking police procedural.

When Kat's tears slowed and Lynette thought she could stand up without collapsing in a boneless heap, her mother insisted they leave the room and get cleaned up.

"The nerve of the man, helping himself to your father's eighty-year-old whiskey," she muttered.

"He's always had a lot of nerve," Lynette rasped, as she got to her feet, and helped her daughter stand. "Kat, I'm so sorry—"

"I never did, Mom," Kat blurted, wrapping her arms around her mother's waist like she hadn't done in years. She trembled and hid her face against Lynette's shoulder. "He said he had to teach me how to please a man. But I never let him and I would never like it. I swear."

"You don't have to tell us anything, Kathryn," her grandmother said. She came up on her other side and rested a hand on the girl's head, stroking her hair.

"I think she does, Mother," Lynette whispered. "Kat hasn't been able to tell anyone—he threatened you to keep you quiet, didn't he?" A sob choked her when her daughter nodded and then pressed her face even harder into her shoulder.

"He told me I had to take my clothes off for him when you got married. He kept trying to come in the bathroom when I took showers. He said I was his property, he had put his name on me."

"You're changing your name back. My Christmas present," she hurried to say.

~~~~~

Daniel and Joel sat on one of the three old, saggy, much-loved sofas in the living room and Green Room for the Randolphs' Homespun Theater. They worked a crossword puzzle, discussed the upcoming theater season at BWU, and listened as Joe, Jeremy and Emily wrangled and laughed over a board game. Max sat on another sofa with her best friend and writing partner, Tony Martin, a fixture in the Randolph household since Daniel had known the family. Max—named Maxine for her great-aunt—was twenty-four, and Tony was thirty-two. Best buddies, they acted like kids one-third their actual ages when they got involved in a project together.

Daniel and Joel grinned and sometimes exchanged glances and shook their heads as they listened to the pair talk. Tony had arrived at the house just after the Christmas Eve service with an idea for a plot twist in the latest book they were writing. He and Max had paid almost no attention to the others in the house for the last two hours, except for helping dispense eggnog and cranberry juice, or get themselves bowls of Emily's traditional Midnight Soup or homemade pizza. Max and Tony lost in another story idea were as much a Christmas tradition as Midnight Soup and pizza.

"I don't know how they do it, sometimes," Joel said. He slouched and raised his arms above his head, stretching. "Must be getting old. All these gray hairs just drain the brain cells."
~~~~~

"You've been gray since I've known you, and you're still going full tilt," Daniel said.

"So are you. Watching these kids of ours grow up makes me so aware of time just flying by. Easier for you, though, right? You only get the kids for four years, then they're gone and you have a new batch to train and try to pound something worthwhile into their heads."

"Hmm. I suppose."

"You suppose?" Joel turned to really look at him. "What's got you thinking such somber thoughts?"

"Did I ever tell you about Lynette?" Why that slipped out, Daniel had no idea. Was he just tired, or did he need that badly to talk with someone about the mess he had made of their lives? Maybe it was God's prompting? He certainly did believe in miracles—at least, on Christmas Eve.

"No. Unless she's that pretty girl in all those pictures from college."

"That's the one. We had big plans. We were going to be stars. We were going to have our pick of Hollywood and Broadway and nobody was going to stop us."

"You got into writing and teaching. What happened to her?" Joel asked after a few moments, when Daniel said nothing.

"She left school, sent me away, had her mother file a restraining order, and raised our daughter without me." He forced a thin, crooked smile, and met his friend's gaze.

"Whoa. That's a lot to keep buried." He glanced over at Emily, who looked up at the same moment in that strange kind of communication Daniel had witnessed many times over the years.

"It gets better. You had Kat Tyler in your set crew last spring, right?"

"Kat Tyler... oh, yeah. Single-handedly built the rigging for *Pinafore* last spring. Good kid." His friend's smile faded a little and he studied Daniel for several long moments. The air seemed to crackle; Daniel could almost hear the thoughts buzzing in his fellow-teacher's head. "Yours?"

Daniel could only nod.

"She doesn't know, I'm guessing. Girl like that wouldn't keep news like that secret." He offered a grin, and Daniel managed to mirror it. "Does her mother know—"

"That I'm her advisor? Oh, yeah. Lynette and I ran into each other at Thanksgiving. We were both invited to dinner with Kat and Amy and Bekka. That was how I found out who Kat was."

"Ouch. I bet that was awkward." Joel winced in sympathy, but his eyes twinkled with mischief. Daniel could just imagine the comments, the questions, and the humorous side his friend would find in all this, at some later date.

"God's mercy at work—there were lots of witnesses to our first meeting in twenty years, so we had to be civil. It helped ease a lot of the tension. I keep meaning to call her, work out some arrangements. We have a truce, but I've been too busy..." He shrugged. It sounded lame, now that he thought of it, to admit that he wanted Lynette to make the first move.

"How does she keep it secret from Kat?"

"Lyn doesn't see her much since Kat moved out. I don't really think she's angry with me anymore, and we both agree we're going to be civil and work together for Kat's future."

"Do you think you two have a chance of getting together?" Joel glanced over at Max. "A kid needs a father, no matter how old she gets."

"Lyn's married... and Kat can't stand him."

"Ouch. Again."

The two friends sat together in silence. Daniel decided that despite the rather deflated feeling that followed the confession, he did feel better. He knew Joel would keep his confidences and pray for him. More important, he knew Joel understood and wouldn't condemn him. Maybe he could even give him some advice.

"Do you mind if I tell Em?" Joel asked, after a particularly rowdy finish to the board game sent the three participants away from the table, laughing and threatening rematches.

"Why not?" He tried to grin. "Her opinion of me can't get any lower."

"That's what you think." Joel winked, heaved himself up out of the sagging couch and followed his wife into the kitchen.

Now it was Daniel's turn to slouch boneless in the couch. Max and Tony continued to talk and scribble notes and laugh when their ideas came so fast and furious they talked over each other. He watched them, remembering how it had been for him and Lynette, playing with ideas and dreams, plotting how to handle scenes for acting or directing classes. The big difference was that they couldn't keep their hands off each other twenty years ago. Today, Max and Tony were barely aware she was a girl and he was a boy. Daniel wondered if everybody in the world wouldn't get along better if they could ignore gender and sex and romance.

~~~~~

"Mr. Tyler surprised everyone when he arrived. We weren't expecting him until just before dinner. He took a taxi instead of calling from the airport, like we expected," Patricia said, calm and somber and dignified at the end of the table where two of the responding police officers sat, gathering information against Mike.

Lynette and her mother sat together, holding hands, on a couch at the far end of the room. Lynette was more grateful than ever for the influence of her mother's money. Besides the police station being only a mile from the Old Money neighborhood, her mother's close association with the annual police fundraisers made her well-known and admired. They
~~~~~

responded a little faster because the police knew the situation. When Mrs. Teague said, "Come immediately, my granddaughter is in danger," they came as fast as ordinary physical laws allowed.

And that also explained why one officer sat in the small auxiliary kitchen with Mike, while two officers, one of them a woman, talked with Kat and the staff. Brenda, the female officer, was a childhood friend of Lynette's. She had given Kat an enormous, floppy dog when she was born. She oversaw taking pictures of Kat's bruises and torn clothes. The gentle, somber concern was the right tactic, and Lynette was ready to believe in God looking out for her again.

She had come downstairs with Brenda, to let Kat get washed up in private, and listen to the testimony of the staff. Lynette felt ready to cry from pride that Kat had been clear-headed enough to hit the intercom and feed the sound of her battle with Mike to the entire house. She hadn't believed him when he claimed there was no one there to hear her and come to her rescue.

"He didn't ask when Mrs. Teague and Miss Lynette were coming back, all he cared about was whether Miss Katie was with them." Patricia shook her head, lips pressing flat in disapproval for a moment. "He said not to tell anyone he was here, that he had a nice big surprise for everybody, and that as soon as Gloria and I had everything ready for dinner, we should go."

"Go where?" Tom Peters, Brenda's partner asked, his voice a gravelly, tired sound that belied the sharp mind Lynette had admired in high school.

"I'm sure I have no idea. He still doesn't seem to understand that we live here. He thinks we come in every day." She shook her head again. "I heard a banging sound, and then he went upstairs before I could figure out where he had been and what he had done." Patricia turned to the couch at the end of the room. "I'm sorry, Ma'am, if I had known he got into the liquor cabinet—"

"It's not your responsibility, Patricia. I should have emptied the cabinet years ago. Nobody here drinks anything stronger than wine. It's nothing more than a dusty memorial..." Mrs. Teague gestured at the officers. "Please, go on. The sooner this unpleasantness is over, and that foul man is out of my house permanently, the better."

"Miss Katie came home just after he went upstairs. I heard Gloria talking to her in the kitchen. Miss Katie called on her way, asking if we needed anything from the store. She's always been like that. We're her family. We didn't say anything about him being here when she arrived, because Mr. Tyler told us not to." Her voice cracked.

"Did he know Kat was on her way home?" Brenda asked. When Patricia nodded, she asked, "Did he tell you to keep quiet about him being there before or after he knew Kat was coming?"

The housekeeper thought a moment, then her eyes widened in dismay. "After."

Lynette shuddered. If she knew Mike, he had been drinking on the plane and had slid into his jolly, I-can-do-whatever-I-want-because-everybody-likes-me mode by the time he landed. He was probably already shifting into his mean, selfish side by the time he walked in the door. Remembering how he had said Kat owed him, Lynette wondered how long he had been waiting for this opportunity.

Gloria had a slightly different viewpoint on the events, because she had been in a different room, had overheard some things and talked to Kat when Patricia didn't. Lynette didn't wait to hear what Ramsey said. She had already given her statement to Brenda when the woman examined and photographed and questioned Kat, so she wasn't needed anymore. Her daughter needed her more.

"By all means," her mother whispered when Lynette said she was going upstairs. "I'm being selfish."

"Never, Mother." She bent and kissed her mother and hurried out of the room.

On the way, she detoured to the auxiliary kitchen. Morbid curiosity or the knowledge that she wouldn't have to look at Mike Tyler again until they faced each other in court gave her the strength to knock on the door and walk in.

Mike slouched at the small table where Kat had learned to roll cookie dough and drink tea that was mostly milk and honey. He was still drunk, but as the alcohol faded from his system, he slid back into the jolly, little boy phase. His cuffed hands rested on the table, his head tipped to one side, his nose was swollen, and his eyes were just turning black. He obviously felt no pain, and that infuriated her again. He offered her a sloppy grin when she halted in the doorway and just stared at him. Maybe it was the blood on his face and the bruises she had given him, and the corresponding aches in her hands and the ache in her ribs where he had hit her, but his smile, his charm had no effect on her. How could she have been blinded, taken in by him for so long?

"How could you, Mike?" she finally asked.

"Come on, Lynette, I just wanted a little fun, like we used to have when Kathryn was little. What's the harm?" Mike said with a lopsided grin. He raked his pudgy fingers through his hair, wincing a little when he had to raise both hands to do it because his wrists were cuffed together.

"The harm is you've been molesting my daughter all these years. I can't believe she wouldn't tell me. You frightened her into not telling me!"

"Kathryn never told you because she liked me touching her. She knows I've got rights. She knows I'm not doing anything wrong. She's only fighting now because that self-righteous little religious witch got hold of her and started twisting her head around."

"Bekka is the best thing that ever happened to Kat!"

"Yeah, that's what you think. She thought differently when she was little. Why'd she have to grow up, huh?" He chuckled and slouched a little more.

Lynette glanced over at the police officer, someone she didn't know, but she trusted him because he came with Brenda and Tom. He met her gaze and tipped his head to the pile of equipment sitting on the counter lining the wall. Lynette's eyes widened as she caught her breath and realized that small glossy black box was a tape recorder. She guessed the officer had been getting Mike's statement, and simply left the recorder going when she knocked on the door.

"Kat says she never liked it, never wanted you to touch her, and she always told you to leave her alone."

"Yeah, that's what she says now. I know differently. She's got nothing to be ashamed of. Why don't you send her on down to talk with me again, hmm?" He winked. "We'll get this all straightened out and have a really happy Christmas. For a change."

"For a change?" Lynette fought the urge to lunge across the table and strangle him. She couldn't believe what he implied.

"It's all Kathryn's fault. Really." Mike belched and offered a mischievous grin. Lynette wanted to kick that grin off his face. "She's long overdue for a serious little talk about how girls should get along with their step-daddies. Maybe I should just go on up to her room and have it out with her."

Lynette all too clearly imagined Mike jumping on her daughter and raping her. Laughing while Kat screamed. And all the while claiming she liked it.

How could she have married this monster and not known it? The same way, she knew, Mike had harassed her daughter under her nose, and she never knew it.

Chapter Seven

"I cannot imagine for one minute that Kat willingly let you touch her." Lynette's voice cracked, and for several long minutes, she couldn't breathe.

"What's wrong with a guy kissing his daughter under the mistletoe?" Mike said. His voice was just a little too loud. "That's all I wanted. The little slut came on to me, dressed up all slinky like that, and —"

"There is no mistletoe in this house, and Kat says you walked into her room while she was changing her clothes."

"Hey, it was an honest mistake. I knocked. I just thought she didn't hear me."

"Just like you made an honest mistake, trying to walk in on her when she was taking showers? If you were sober, if you weren't such a selfish monster, you'd know that three closed doors and no one answering means you stay out!" She stomped up to the table and slammed her clenched fists down on the surface. To her delight, Mike jumped and his ruddy face paled for a few seconds.

Lynette shuddered as her imagination filled in, again, all the things a big, strong man could do to a slender girl, who for some reason believed her mother would never listen if she told her what happened. Why hadn't Kat told her? Had Mike intimidated her that badly, from the very beginning?

Daniel would never... Lynette swallowed a sob. A dizzy, nauseating wave overwhelmed her, as she thought of what Daniel would do if he ever found out what she had allowed to happen to their daughter, right under her nose.

That talk with Daniel after the holidays, to discuss how they would tell Kat the truth, how he would become part of their lives, would simply never happen. She couldn't bear to see the scorn, the condemnation, the fury in his face.

But Kat would tell him, wouldn't she? Lynette suspected that even if Kat didn't know Daniel Morgan was her father, he had become the father figure she had never had, the one she wanted. It was ironic, she supposed, that Kat would turn to her real father. Fate? Instinct? Maybe her punishment for throwing Kat's father out of their lives before she had a chance to know him?

"Come on, Lynette, you really believe what she said?" Mike shook his head. "Sheesh, what's wrong with you, in this day and age? We didn't do anything wrong!"

The police officer snorted and sat up a little straighter. Lynette saw his hand close around something at his waist — she hoped it was his billy club, rather than a can of pepper spray. Maybe she would ask to borrow it, and ask him to leave the room for a few minutes? It wouldn't take long to batter Mike Tyler's face until he could never give anyone that nauseating, charming smile ever again.

"We would have had a little fun, like we did when she was a kid, that's all," Mike continued, shrugging. "No one would have been hurt."

"You were hurting *her*!" Lynette choked, fighting for control. "How long have you been hurting her?"

"I swear, Lynette, whatever the little tramp told you, it's a lie! She wanted it. I was just giving her what she wanted, like any good daddy would. How's a girl gonna learn how to treat a man if her daddy doesn't teach her?"

"Kat's father would never do that to her!" An image of Daniel beating Mike to within an inch of his worthless life filled Lynette's mind and she wished it could be true.

"Yeah, and if he's so perfect, how come you didn't stay with him?" he shot back.

"I wonder, sometimes."

Lynette nodded to the police officer and turned to leave. It gave her great pleasure to walk out of the room, free to go anywhere she wanted, while Mike was headed for Christmas in jail. She doubted he would be able to get anyone from Ohio to come help him out until after Christmas. If anyone came at all. All Mike's friends in the legal community were business lawyers. They wouldn't have the slightest idea what to do for a man in jail for assaulting his stepdaughter. She thought about her mother's vow, that by the time Mike got back to Ohio, he wouldn't have a dime to his name. The business they had built together would belong entirely to Lynette, and Mike wouldn't be able to start a business anywhere in the surrounding states without the community knowing what a predator he was. Most of Mike's employees were college and high school students, willing to work odd hours and weekends. How many of them would be willing to risk working for a man who had been revealed as a molester?

Lynette paused halfway up the stairs and shuddered as she imagined the torment Kat would go through when everything was revealed. She had to find a way to do this as quietly as possible — punish Mike as much as she could without Kat being shamed and forced to relive the abuse and harassment.

She found her daughter huddled in the window seat in her grandmother's suite. Lynette could understand Kat not wanting to go back to her room, with blood on the carpeting, the stink of spilled whiskey heavy in the air, and other signs of Mike's attack. A sob choked her, when she realized that Kat hadn't come to her room for comfort in years—because Mike had always been sure to walk in on them. Come to think of it, Lynette didn't want to stay in her suite, simply because she had shared it with Mike for so long. Maybe the three of them could all camp in Grandma Teague's room tonight. Or sleep in the parlor, in front of the Christmas tree, like Kat had loved doing when she was little.

Kat's hair was wet from a shower. She wore her favorite blue flannel robe, and Lynette thought of her pretty new green lounging outfit that she had loved, torn and ruined now. Even if it could be repaired or replaced, Kat would never wear it again because of the memories attached. Her daughter sat with her legs folded up and her arms around them, her chin on her knees, staring at the falling snow.

"Baby," she whispered, and clutched for support at the doorframe.

"I didn't, Mom. I never did."

"I'm sorry." A strangled, half-hysterical chuckle escaped her. "Fat lot of good that does."

"You loved him," Kat whispered. She turned from the window, leaving a glistening spot on the glass where her tears had run and her warmth had melted away the frost.

"Honey, I haven't loved that... slob in years." She took a deep breath, trying to hold back tears. Kat was the only one who had any right to cry. "How come you never said anything? Didn't you trust me to stop him?"

"I figured... Mom, you knew I didn't like him, right from the beginning. You'd think I said it just to keep you from marrying him."

"Did Mike give you that idea?"

Kat opened her mouth to deny it. Lynette could see it in her eyes. Then she closed her mouth and looked rather nauseated and nodded.

"Honey, that's the best trick in an abuser's arsenal. Make the victim think she's alone and nobody will help her or believe her. And make her think it's all her fault, that she deserves what he's doing to her. Oh, Kat, if I had known. If your father ever... " Lynette felt as if the rug had been pulled out from under her feet.

What would Daniel do when he heard? The question kept slapping her hard enough to steal her breath. He *would* hear, eventually, either from Kat or her protective roommates, who despised Mike.

"Do your roommates know about—"

"Gee, Mom, if I couldn't tell you, how could I tell anyone else?" Kat sniffed and rubbed more tears from her eyes. "I could really use a hug."

"So could I." Lynette let herself enter the room, finally. She wrapped her arms around her daughter and held on tight.

I've done it again. The idea throbbed through her heart and soul as she and Kat cried together and rocked on the window seat, as they had done when she could hold her daughter on her lap. *I've messed up our lives again. First, I send her father away, then I choose a prince charming who turns out to be a toad that likes to pick on little girls. When am I going to learn? Please, God, I know I haven't prayed in years, but help me out in this. When am I going to get it right?* She could only sigh at the irony that she was praying now, after all these years of refusing to admit she needed or wanted God's help. This was definitely a time where she had hit the bottom. For Kat, she would swallow her pride and reach out for help. If she could figure out how.

~~~~~

"You've got great kids," Daniel said, listening to the sounds of the Randolph boys thudding around in their room upstairs as they prepared for bed.

It was late. Nearly midnight. Christmas tradition at the Randolph home was to put lights on the tree, but not the star or other decorations until Christmas Eve, after the children had gone to bed. Even though the children were twenty-four, sixteen and thirteen now. Max hadn't grumbled and pretended to be insulted when her parents sent her upstairs with her brothers. Her head was too full of the story she and Tony had laughed and argued over all evening.

Christmas tradition also meant Daniel helped with last-minute wrapping and decorating. He had always enjoyed it with a bittersweet aftertaste, letting himself imagine only this one time a year what it would be like if Lynette had married him and let him raise their child. Their daughter. Kat.

"Yeah, we do," Joel said with a satisfied sigh. He unfolded the ladder and shifted it around to get the best angle for putting the star on top of the tree. "You knew Max wasn't mine, didn't you?"

"Considering you and Em have only been married eighteen years and Max is older than that, yeah. Just because I'm not a techie doesn't mean I can't count." Daniel winked at Emily, who sighed a laugh and finished closing up the ornament boxes. "What does that have to do with the price of tea in China?"

"Max's father doesn't know she exists," Emily said. "We'd been fighting for weeks before he left me and left the country for a long-term film job. It was bad enough, bitter enough between us, he didn't want to take me with him. I was sick, I suspected I was pregnant, and I was scared to death because we weren't married. Even back then, in Hollywood, it was hard for a single mother. But I was so furious with him, I refused to say a word. And then too busy raising my child without any help but my Aunt Maxine. And then too ashamed to contact him."

"Okay, that's why you asked if Em could know about Kat." Daniel sighed and reached out to steady the ladder as Joel climbed. "What are
~~~~~

you trying to tell me?"

"Max knows who her father is. I want her to tell him, but the choice is hers. Someday, if her career in screenwriting takes off—"

"It will. Chuck Winters is the best in the business, and with him as her agent, she's bound to succeed," he hurried to assure her.

Daniel knew Chuck Winters was good, because the man represented him on both coasts as he tried to sell his screenplays and stage scripts. He always managed to get top dollar for options on every script Daniel wrote. It wasn't his fault that the production companies interested in the scripts could never raise the money to actually go into production.

"And when that happens, when her name is listed in the credits, what will her father's reaction be? He has a right to know," Emily said, a suspicious brightness in her eyes. "She's using my maiden name for screenwriting. Somebody is bound to ask if Max Keeler is Emily Keeler's daughter."

Daniel grinned for a moment, remembering what a jolt he had when Kat chose Teague for her stage name in the Christmas production. If he hadn't found out at Thanksgiving that she was his daughter, that would have been a dead giveaway, reawakening all his suspicions from the year before. He could imagine how Max's unnamed father would react when he found out Max was the daughter of Emily Keeler-Randolph. Since Max didn't look like her mother, then naturally she had to look like her father.

"It's not the same thing—I knew Lyn was having my baby, and I wanted to be that baby's father. Will Max's father be glad to know he has a daughter? It sounds like Max doesn't want him to know. Lyn doesn't want Kat to know I'm her father. Heck, she even told Kat I died before we could get married, so Kat wouldn't ask what happened to me. I think sometimes how much I'd like to hug Kat, just once, and tell her how proud I am of her. How much I love her." Daniel blinked hard against the sudden, hard, hot wet pressure in his eyes. "But what would that do to her?"

"She'd be the proudest kid at BWU," Joel said as he climbed down from settling the star. "Every one of your students thinks you're the greatest thing since the wheel. Give Kat some credit. Sure, she'll be shocked, but she's smart enough to know she'll be better off."

"Will she? Besides helping her career, what good can I do her?"

"That's Max's biggest excuse for not contacting her father," Emily said. "She knows he could help her career enormously, and she won't capitalize on that."

"Takes after me too much," Joel offered.

Daniel snorted. A grin broke through the mask of mock disgust he tried to hold onto. Emily sighed and went to her husband and put her arms around him.

Merry Christmas, Kat. Lyn. Wherever you are. Daniel watched the Randolphs kiss and hold each other and laugh, and tried to imagine Lynette and their daughter, right that moment.

They were probably tucked up in bed, smiling in their dreams, waiting for morning. Was Kat still young enough to get up incredibly early and dash to the tree to tear into her loot, like her cousins, Candy and Chad did? He hoped so.

~~~~~

"Merry Christmas," Lynette whispered. She took a sip of the chamomile tea her mother insisted she drink and winced. "Oh, this is awful."

"It is not. It's soothing," Mrs. Teague said, and delicately sipped at her own cup.

"I don't want to be soothed, Mother. I want a gun and ten minutes alone with that slimy Mike Tyler so I can..." She sighed, closed her eyes, and sagged back into the thick, puffy cushions of the couch in her mother's sitting room. Kat was asleep, finally, in her grandmother's king-size bed. Neither of them wanted to be out of earshot of her. "It's all my fault."

"It is not. Mike fooled you. He fooled me."

"He didn't fool Kat. Why didn't she tell me?" she nearly wailed.

"Because, my dear, your daughter loves you very much. She knew you were happy with Mike. Happy for the first time in years. And she didn't want to ruin it for you. Mike was the man you chose, so she obviously decided she could live with it if that would make you happy."

"I chose Mike, all right. I have a wretched history of bad choices." She set the cup down before she either clenched it tight enough to snap the antique, eggshell-fragile china, or flung it across the room. "Why did I send Danny Morgan away?"

"Besides the fact that he couldn't support himself, much less a wife and child?"

"He loved me."

"Yes, but he obviously didn't have the potential you saw in him. Where is he today, Lynette? You were determined he would be a star. That's why you sent him away, so he would have the opportunity to fulfill his potential. Why haven't we heard from him?"

"Because he became a teacher, and a writer. A very good teacher and a good writer. And all his students adore him." She took a deep breath. "Especially Kat."

"What?"

"Mother, haven't you heard a word Kat said, all the times she gushed on and on about her advisor, Dr. Morgan?"

"Yes, but I thought it was merely a... It's not a coincidence with the names, is it?" Mrs. Teague sat up. "Has he told her? Does he know?"
~~~~~

"Oh, he knows. He suspected, and then we ran into each other at Thanksgiving at Kat's apartment."

"Well, a university professor is a good, solid, respectable profession. Good for him. I did like him. Until he made himself a nuisance, coming here week after week, trying to find you." She sniffed and darted a sideways glance at her daughter.

"Mother, do something for me?" Lynette didn't wait for her mother's response. "You drove away the only man I ever really loved. Kat's father, who never would have done a thing to harm her. He'd spoil her rotten, if I'd let him." A tiny choked laugh escaped her. "You drove him away with those lawyers of yours. Now I want you to—to crucify that puddle of slime that fooled us and hurt Kat. I want him to suffer, for all the years he made Kat hate living in her own home!"

"It's already done, arranged while you were upstairs with Kat. I didn't have to ask Jacob. He was nearly foaming at the mouth to start the legal work by the time I gave him the details." Her mother nodded for punctuation. "But Lynette, if Daniel Morgan really loved you, he would have fought for you."

"Fought for me? You had an entire stable of lawyers and he was twenty years old, with a mountain of college loans to pay back. How could he have fought you?" She would have laughed if she hadn't felt a lifetime of tears choking her.

"I never did get those court orders as I threatened."

"What?"

"I knew he was the best thing in the world for you, but you kept insisting you had to drive him away to save him. I knew if he kept coming, kept trying, you'd eventually give in and let him love you, and live happily ever after. But he went away."

"Mother, he had no hope. We both took it away from him."

"Yes... I suppose we did." Her mother thumped the arm of her chair with her fist. "But you're free of Mike, now. It's destiny, Lynette. You're living practically in the same town. Kat loves him. Does he like Kat?"

"He adores her. The few times I've run into him, Kat is always there. He tries to act like he's just her teacher and she's his favorite student, but I can see it in his eyes. He's so proud of her."

"Well, then, go to him. Fix up things between the two of you. Then tell Kat. It'll all work out."

"No, Mother. It won't."

"You're free now."

"Mother, Daniel's religious."

"So are we. I raised you to go to church every Sunday."

"Until those hypocrites drove me away, before Kat was born."

"Yes, well..." She sniffed and waved her hand, as if dismissing those people and that church. Lynette recalled her mother had found a new church soon after she had stopped attending any church whatsoever. She wished that she had at least given the people in her mother's new church a chance. Would things have been different now, if she had?

"I've heard about the church he goes to. The people there are so active, so... they really believe their Bibles. They believe divorce is wrong. Even though I'm free, almost free of Mike, I'm still off-limits to Daniel."

"We'll see."

"Mother—"

"You have to learn to forgive yourself, Lynette. And forgive all those religious hypocrites who hurt you. And forgive Daniel Morgan for not being your prince charming and going off on a quest for fame and fortune when you told him to. Just because you gave up on happily ever after twenty years ago doesn't mean you have to give up on it now."

"I can't," she whispered.

"You can't forgive, or you won't?"

"How can I tell him what I let happen to our daughter? He'll never forgive me."

"If he has a shred of love left for you, Lynette, he will."

Yes, that was probably true. But Lynette knew she could never face him. She couldn't stand to see the anger on his face, the sorrow for Kat's sake. She couldn't stand to hear his condemnation, or worse, hear him forgive her. She didn't deserve it. She had ruined all their lives.

Eventually, Daniel would hear about Mike and Kat. When that happened was time enough to face him. She wouldn't seek him out. She couldn't.

Sunday, December 29

The Sunday after Christmas, Daniel wanted to stay in bed. It had been a long, strange week, and he had only been grateful that he hadn't had to deal with classes while insanity seemed to reign in Tabor Heights.

The day after Christmas, the *Tabor Picayune* ran a story following up on the hunt for the White Rose and revealed that Hannah Blake was the latest target. It didn't make sense—Hannah was a strawberry blonde and she lived on the top floor of a converted house on Main Street, not with her parents. She didn't fit the pattern of the White Rose's victims. What made the story even more twisted was that Hannah had found Annalee Gray's body, when she and her boss, Xander Finley, went to check out their new office space, another converted house two doors down from Hannah's apartment. The fire at their new office last Sunday, which Hannah had been in the middle of decorating and organizing, was somehow related to the whole investigation.

According to Max Randolph, passing on information to the prayer team at BWU, on the condition they kept it quiet, the police believed Hannah was the target of a copycat. A BWU student had also received white roses and love notes. The girl, Tracy Brickman, had fled the university when Christmas break came, and she wasn't planning on coming back to Tabor. Daniel didn't blame her.

He forced himself to get up and get moving. He had a quiet service at church to look forward to, and more room in the sanctuary while the students were home on break. Add to that the promise of lunch with the Holwoods after the service, he had enough incentive to face the day. On the bright side, Kat and Bekka were out of town and wouldn't hear about any of this until they came back to school after the holidays were over. The thought that this grim episode in Tabor's history might be wrapped up before they came home cheered Daniel immensely.

He arrived late to church and didn't see Kat and Bekka sitting in the back pew on the left side of the sanctuary until he was already on his way to his seat on the right side. Kat's hunched shoulders and the way she kept looking everywhere proclaimed she was nervous. She still had her coat on, ten minutes into the service, as if she considered fleeing the moment she got too uncomfortable. Daniel wondered how often she had been to church growing up. He had visited Mrs. Teague's church several times, trying to get the woman's approval. The sanctimonious, Old Money crowd had looked down on his sweatshirts and jeans and lack of pedigree. They had probably tormented Lynette for being an unwed mother. The Lynette he knew back then wouldn't have stood for that treatment for very long. It wouldn't surprise him if Kat had never gone to church her whole life.

But what was she doing here? Why wasn't she in Chicago with her mother and grandmother, enjoying Christmas in the lap of luxury?

He gnawed on the questions all through the service, hardly hearing any of it. Then when the congregation was dismissed, he lost sight of Kat and Bekka in the tidal wave surge toward the doors. Sighing, he prayed another verse of the same prayer he had begun the day he realized Kat was his daughter. Something was wrong, and he couldn't do anything to help her unless she came to him for help. As her advisor, not as her father. That knowledge made him ache. It made him seriously consider breaking that unspoken promise he had made to Lynette, in answer to the silent plea in her eyes, not to tell Kat, to let her break the news to their daughter.

His daughter was in good hands with Bekka Sanderson as her roommate. Daniel knew he had to trust Bekka, and God, and hoped Kat would open up to him when classes resumed in another two weeks.

Dr. Rance Holwood was head of the Humanities Department, which had umbrella authority over the Theater Department. He and his wife,

Doria, fostered children. Their enormous Century home, just a few blocks down the street from their church, was made for a large, active family. Daniel always looked forward to time spent with them, but he nearly turned his car around when he spotted two figures walking the slate sidewalk, heading straight for the house. Bekka had an oversized pea coat she had found at the Penny Pincher that she dearly loved. Daniel would have recognized it from halfway across town. And Kat's hair stood out like banked coals against all the snow piled up along the streets and sidewalks.

Bekka waved and hefted a white bakery box and smiled when he pulled into the Holwoods' driveway a few seconds before they reached it. Kat ducked her head, just like she had done in church, and Daniel wondered suddenly if she was afraid to face him. What had happened at Christmas?

"What a surprise, seeing you two. Weren't you supposed to be out of town for Christmas?" he said as he climbed out of his car. Daniel prayed his acting skills hadn't atrophied and his smile and casual tone were convincing.

"We were," Bekka said. "Both of us just had a little too much family togetherness, or whatever you want to call it, and headed back to the apartment. It's been a taste of Heaven, sitting around, sleeping late, pigging out, writing from sunrise to sunset."

"Don't get used to it," he said as they trudged up the salted sidewalk to the front steps. "Classes start soon enough, and both of you have first period classes."

"Don't remind me," Kat grumbled. But she managed a smile for him.

Doria Holwood opened the door before they reached the porch, accompanied by her current crop of foster children. Daniel had been to the house often enough for the children to know and like him. Judging by their welcome for Kat and Bekka, they knew the girls as well, because they instantly surrounded both of them and demanded to show off their Christmas presents. The near-twin boy cousins and dainty little girl were quite a contrast, all three blonde compared to their Black foster parents.

Bekka's reason for coming back to Tabor came out eventually. She was supposed to be visiting her grandparents in Florida. Knowing the elderly, narrow-minded Sandersons, it was no surprise to Daniel that she had grown tired of their company early and fled back to snowy Ohio and the relaxing quiet of BWU during holiday break.

Daniel had endured several unpleasant run-ins with the Sandersons, starting the day Bekka's grandfather came to his office to demand he talk her out of her "idiotic dreams" of being a writer. Bekka wore jeans every day but Sunday, rode a bike even in the snow, and pursued her career instead of a potential husband. It was a miracle, in Daniel's opinion, that her grandparents hadn't thrown her out of the house when she turned eighteen.

Even though he focused most of his attention on Kat, who was unusually quiet, he gathered all the friction between Bekka and her grandparents had finally reached the explosion point. One of their guests at their Christmas Eve party had monopolized Bekka, interrogating her about her writing until she agreed to send him one of her books to look at. He worked in publishing and specialized in giving up-and-coming writers their big break. Daniel thought such an opportunity was an answer to prayer; especially since Bekka hadn't gone looking for it. Her grandparents, however, insisted Bekka had pestered their guest and forced him to agree to look at her book. They had argued on Christmas morning. All their distaste for her chosen career, her quietly rebellious and independent lifestyle, her non-Christian friends came out in the explosion. Bekka had come home, and doubted she would ever hear from her grandparents again.

As she downplayed what had happened, Bekka's gaze kept drifting to Kat. Daniel paid more attention to the byplay between the roommates. It didn't take long to realize that every time the conversation drifted toward Kat, Bekka redirected it. Even at the expense of revealing her own wounds.

What had happened to Kat over Christmas?

The next day, Daniel drove out to Lynette's house in Stoughton. There was no sign of life in the big, elegant house. Someone shoveled the driveway and sidewalks, but according to Kat a service did that. He couldn't imagine Mike Tyler taking the time and effort to sweat over snow shoveling. There was no one home, no tire tracks in the light dusting of snow on the driveway. Why had Kat come home early, instead of spending two weeks in Chicago with her grandmother? She had been looking forward to it with such anticipation, bordering on giddiness.

What had happened to his daughter over Christmas?

"Please, Lord... show me what to do, what to say. I can't tell her. Not without Lynette's support and help. I don't want to hurt Kat. I don't want her to turn against either of us. But how can I help her if she doesn't know I'm her father?" Daniel rested his head on his steering wheel a moment. He had been asking that question far too often lately. He had asked Pastor Glenn two weeks ago, during another informal counseling session at the Perk and Perch.

"God probably feels the same way sometimes," the senior minister had said, a crooked smile lighting his square, wrinkled face. "We don't want to accept the fact that He's our father, and until we do, there isn't much He's able to do. God is a gentleman. Fortunately, He's also very patient."

Help me be patient, Daniel prayed silently and took his foot off the brake. He had work to do, after all, to prepare for the next semester. Maybe Kat would stop in at the theater offices, even though she was on break, and he could get her to talk. At the very least, he could let her know he was there, willing to help.

Chapter Eight

Monday, January 6

Lynette returned home to an empty house—empty of Mike Tyler and his clothes, his favorite pots and pans, the contents of the refrigerator and pantry, and all the furniture in the TV room. She was surprised he had taken so little. Her mother's lawyers had agreed to let him come back to Ohio and take his possessions and leave the house to her. There was still a lot of wrangling to do over the business, but Mike had been warned to stay away from all his female employees and have no contact whatsoever with Lynette and her daughter. He was advised to stay in the next county and warned that his phone records and Kat's would be monitored, to ensure he didn't harass and threaten her into silence.

She wanted nothing to do with the catering business, which had been Mike's pride and joy, his dream, but she refused to walk away and let it collapse. She had put just as much work into the business as her soon-to-be-ex-husband. She decided to see about either selling her half to Mike, or demanding the entire business be sold to someone else and taking the lion's share of the proceeds. Her mother and Jacob, the family lawyer, had advised her that the best weapon she could use to control Mike Tyler was to threaten his reputation by broadcasting the truth. Appearances were everything to him. Lynette acknowledged that with a sour sense of self-mockery. After all, he had married her for her connections and her experience with upper crust society, as well as her business acumen.

If she could have had her choice, Lynette would have come back to Ohio with Kat the day after Christmas. Unfortunately, all the stress of the battle on Christmas Eve had given her mother chest pains and a shortness of breath that the elderly woman hadn't been able to hide. Lynette had managed to convince Kat that it was just stress and excitement and put her daughter on the plane back to Ohio. Then rushed to the hospital, hating herself because she had allowed Patricia and Gloria to take her mother to the hospital instead of taking care of it personally. She had nearly wept when she got the phone call from Kat, saying that Bekka had come home from Florida early, and she wasn't alone in the apartment. Even if Mike had been stupidly vindictive enough to try to catch Kat at the apartment, Bekka would have been there to protect her. The older girl's presence in their lives had almost convinced Lynette that God did care about them and watched over them, and He had sent Bekka Sanderson to be Kat's guardian angel. She wouldn't have been able to get through the last two weeks, watching over her mother and assuring herself she was indeed out of danger, if Kat hadn't had Bekka.

Lynette was barely home an hour when a courier came with a registered letter. Mike had filed for divorce. Had he acted so quickly from his spoiled child mentality, thinking he was punishing her for not letting him abuse her daughter, or had he acted out of fear of her mother?

She supposed she should be grateful for her mother's power, but thinking how Mike had crumpled and complied in terror, despite all his bluster, made her think of Daniel. He had hung on for weeks, making a nuisance of himself, trying to persuade her that he could take care of her and their unborn child. That he loved her. How long had it been since Mike said he loved her?

Now that she thought of it, Lynette realized something. Whenever Mike tried to talk her into something, his reasoning had always been "because you love me." Never because *he* loved *her*. He depended on Lynette's love for him to always get what he wanted. The only person Mike Tyler really loved was himself.

She went to the apartment to talk with Kat. They had talked on the phone every day since her daughter flew back to Cleveland. That wasn't enough for Lynette. Kat assured her Bekka took good care of her, and despite how everything had exploded into the open at Christmas, she felt better than she had in years, but Lynette needed to see her daughter to be sure.

Kat wasn't at the apartment, and Lynette nearly panicked right there in the hallway outside the door. Had Mike done something? Just because he promised to leave Kat alone for the sake of keeping the catering business didn't mean he would keep that promise. Lynette had always thought he was too lazy to get violent, and Christmas had proved her wrong. After all, she had never suspected he was a lecher trying to get his hands on her daughter.

Then she thought about one of their few conversations about Kat's class schedule for the coming semester. School had started, hadn't it? She came downstairs and headed for her car to drive over to whatever classroom building Kat would be in. But that, she realized a few moments later, was ridiculous. Butler-Williams University sprawled across the entire town. It was a nice day, for January. She could just walk. If she could remember where all the buildings were.

Lynette checked her organizer in her purse. Sure enough, there was the schedule and map Kat had given her. She felt a moment of pure triumph. Mike had always mocked her for struggling to keep organized and on top of things, even as he relied on her to be his personal secretary and keep his life in order. That showed how wrong he was, yet again.

Work-study. Kat had work-study at the theater arts building. That was only down Main Street and up Sackley a block or two from the apartment building. She could hoof it in no time. The exercise might even do her good.

Lynette let herself enjoy the quaint storefronts, the houses turned into shops, the tiny strip mall someone had built that managed not to look out of character with the neighborhood. She made note of a few places she wanted to visit, just because Kat raved about them. The Penny Pincher, where her daughter had found clothes she preferred over the designer originals her grandmother sent her. The Perk and Perch coffee and sandwich shop. The Toy Box. The Bookworm. Lynette was almost disappointed to reach the corner of Sackley and Main and turn right to reach her destination.

She had seen a few signs in windows asking for part-time workers. A few hand-lettered signs even stated the hours. Four hours each, two days a week in one place, one eight-hour shift in another. She supposed that whatever college students had filled those spots had moved on, or were unavailable, thanks to their new schedules. Why not apply? Even if she came away with everything in the divorce and court battle, she didn't want to keep the catering business. Too much ugliness woven into the pleasant memories now. She certainly had enough free time, now that there was no Mike Tyler to pick up after. No social schedule to keep track of to support his business. No bookkeeping for his business. No pinch-hitting when one of his supervisors called in sick and a fancy dinner party needed to be assembled in two hours.

Lynette almost laughed as she realized she wouldn't have to put up with the horde of self-important people with whom Mike socialized. They were all his friends, never hers. She was his hostess and the decoration on his arm. Chances were good those people would turn their backs on her once the divorce was final. Especially if they chose to believe Mike's version of the story—that Kat was a tramp and came after him, and Lynette had chosen her daughter's lies over poor, misunderstood Mike Tyler. Well, she decided with a grin that grew wider with each step, she was better off without them all. Good riddance. Especially Judge Foggerty and his self-righteous, domineering clique.

"No, I won't be vindictive. I'm just lucky to get out of there with my mind in one piece and Kat unharmed," she told the damp breeze that kissed her face.

Kat was unharmed, physically. Mike may have glimpsed her in the shower a few times. He might have held her too long or too tight when he managed to steal a hug, and his kisses had been too wet, and his hands might have touched places where he had no business going, but he hadn't raped her. Hadn't bruised her before that fight on Christmas Eve or broken any bones or sent her to the hospital needing stitches. Some courts would declare Kat was unharmed.

In her mother's heart, Lynette knew Kat had been harmed enormously. No wonder the girl never dated a boy more than twice. She was probably afraid if he got any closer to her, the boy would want more, and would want what Mike had been pestering her to give him for years.

It was true what psychologists said. A girl's relationship with men was influenced by the type of father she had. Maybe Kat had been spared a good deal of damage because Mike hadn't come into their lives until she was ten, but the years since then had certainly left their mark on her.

Lynette stopped short with her hand on the door into the theater arts building. Two thoughts hit her simultaneously, and she didn't know if they terrified her or filled her with hope. Should she stay and face the music, or flee for her life?

First, Daniel was Kat's advisor, and she trusted him already. She admired him. Maybe she even had a crush on him. Lynette had done some investigating, and she knew he was respected and trusted throughout the university community. He was the soul of honor when it came to his female students. Kat had even told her Daniel never shut the door when there was a girl in his office. Everyone knew it.

Second, Daniel was probably there, right now, in the building. He was Kat's advisor and Kat was his student assistant and she was working with him right that moment.

What had Kat told Daniel about her Christmas disaster? Was Daniel waiting for her to show up, so he could lambaste her for neglecting and endangering their daughter?

Or would he be the knight in shining armor she had always dreamed, and enfold her in assurances of his protection and undying love and forgiveness?

Don't be silly, she told herself as she yanked the heavy metal door open and stomped down the steps into the theater faculty area in the basement. *How could he love you after all this time? After what you've done to him? He's only a man.*

He's not God, whispered through her mind, even as she tried to push the thought away. But would even God forgive her for the messes, the bad choices she had made?

The sound of Kat's laughter and the hum of office equipment in full use rose up the stairwell. Lynette felt a heavy weight leave her chest at the sound. Well, why not? Kat had always felt safe here. Why shouldn't she be happy and on the road to recovery?

She emerged from the shadowy stairwell into an oddly shaped room: six walls, none of them the same length, with three doors opening out of them, and a small anteroom crammed with old props and furniture and overflowing cardboard boxes full of costumes. A copy machine, two cafeteria-length folding tables, a scattering of mismatched chairs, a desk covered with books and papers that almost buried the computer perched on it, three bulletin boards covered with notices and posters, and three metal shelf units overloaded with papers and office supplies. Kat stood in the middle, sorting papers across both tables, helped by Bekka and a young man with spiky red hair and three rings in one ear. Lynette couldn't remember what the code was for men's earrings, and right now she didn't want to know. It was a sure bet the boy was here for Kat's sake, so that meant he was straight. At least, Lynette hoped so.

"Oh, hi, Mrs. Tyler," Bekka said, stopping in mid-turn with her hands full of a stack of papers from the copy machine. "Something wrong?"

"No." Lynette tried to laugh as she came into the crowded lobby. Amazingly, despite the chaos, it was organized chaos. It wasn't a mess, so much as it was in multiple use. Three professors used this little room? She was surprised it wasn't ten times more crowded and cluttered. "I got back to town this morning and thought I'd check in with Kat. How are you doing, sweetheart?"

"A lot better." Kat put down her papers and crossed the room. She almost had a skip to her step and hugged her mother. "How are *you* doing? How's Granny? Bekka's been praying up a storm for her since you called last week."

'The doctor said it wasn't a heart attack, exactly." She cast a glance at her daughter's roommate. Bekka just shrugged and offered a lopsided smile and went back to work. "Does Bekka —"

"Everything, Mom." Kat shrugged a little. "What do you mean, not exactly a heart attack?"

"Stress. Indigestion. Headache. She still got quite a bit of work done on... our little problem."

Her daughter's words hit her then. *Praying?* Why in the world had Kat said that?

"If you want to hide out at our place for a while, there's room."

"Thanks, honey." She couldn't resist another hug. Kat didn't seem to mind, but the boy—who still hadn't been introduced—gave them a frowning glance and busied himself at the copier. "I just got the paperwork today."

"The slime bag works fast."

"We're trying to do this quickly and quietly. The slime bag —" She snorted, enjoying the euphemism for Mike. "He's even more eager to get this over with, with as little fuss as possible, than we are. If we could keep you out of it, I would certainly make a bigger fuss, for the sake of all those girls who work for him."

Lynette felt a little guilty for putting Kat's comfort ahead of protecting those girls at the catering business. Some might have been targeted by Mike when he couldn't get his hands on his stepdaughter. What had happened to her ethics? Maybe they had gone the same way as her dreams of fame and romance and happily ever after.

"I know a couple of the girls who work for..." Bekka grinned, with a nasty sparkle in her eyes. "For Chef Creepo," she continued as she crossed over to mother and daughter. "I can pass the word along, that there was a fight over the way he *wasn't* treating Kat like his daughter. That's all we have to say. You keep quiet, we don't give any more details, and we let the rumor mill do its work. I've talked to some of the girls who work for him, and nobody can stand him. It'll all be bad for him, and the way people like to make up stories, they'll forget about Kat's part in it altogether."

"Bekka Sanderson, you have a devious mind." Lynette wished she had thought of that.

"I know. Isn't she the best?" Kat grinned.

"Who's the best?" a man asked, coming in from the stairwell door.

Lynette's heart banged against her ribs, pushed against her throat, then dropped down somewhere around her knees. She turned, nearly missing Daniel as he breezed into the room. He dropped a canvas tote in the first available chair, shed his bulky, rusty black wool coat and flung it in the general direction of a coat rack. Amazingly, it caught. Then Daniel turned to look at the four in the faculty lobby. His smile froze.

Then it widened. His eyes brightened. Suddenly, there was too much oxygen in the room.

"Hi, Lynette." He took a step forward, holding out a hand, then glanced at the three students, who suddenly all got very busy with their collating.

"Dr. Morgan."

"Oh, please," he said with a groan, and his eyes sparkled with that humor she loved and missed. "The kids don't bother with the formalities, why should you? Morgan's fine. I'll even answer to 'hey, you.' But around here, that covers a lot of people."

"Morgan." A ridiculous desire to giggle fluttered through her chest.

"What brings you to the dungeon? Is Kat already complaining about what a slave master I am?"

"I think you ought to give her more work. Keep her out of trouble."

"Mo - other!" Kat's cry of dismay didn't have quite the disgust and scorn it could have. She ruined the effect a moment later by sharing smothered giggles with Bekka.

"I have this feeling I interrupted something important." Daniel waved a handful of mail he took out of the canvas tote. "If I'm not being rude, I'll just retreat into my cave—"

"I was leaving, anyway," Lynette said. "I just got home from Chicago and wanted to make sure Kat wasn't starving or locked out of the apartment. The usual."

"How was Chicago? How's your mother doing?"

"She's... doing better. Christmas was stressful." She was suddenly painfully aware of the three students who appeared busy but were all too obviously straining their ears to listen. "She says hello."

"Uh — Mom?" Kat ventured.

"Your mother and I had a class together at Northwestern," Daniel explained.

"You didn't tell me that before."

"We remembered after we met up at Thanksgiving," Lynette hurried to say.

"Theater experience class, they called it," Daniel continued, with a nod to her. "We went to professional productions and got all dressed up. Your grandmother had us over to the house afterwards, once. Quite impressive. Tell Mrs. Teague I'm glad she remembers me." That laughter died from his eyes. "I certainly remember her." Nodding abruptly, he shouldered his office door open and vanished into the darkness. The door latched firmly.

"Why didn't you tell me you went to school with Morgan?" Kat blurted. She nearly danced with excitement.

At least she wasn't angry.

"I thought we did, when we met up at Thanksgiving," Lynette murmured.

"Did he know my dad?"

"Yes." She paused, the rest of her long-prepared story forgotten when she got the strangest look from Bekka.

Almost as if Kat's roommate knew the truth.

But that was ridiculous. Why would Daniel tell Bekka about their relationship and past, but not his own daughter? Certainly, Bekka had been his assistant for several years, as close to him as a daughter. As close to him as Kat was already. But he wouldn't tell Bekka, would he?

"Yes, he knew your father... very well," she continued and prayed the pause wasn't that noticeable. Lynette realized she had been doing a lot of desperation praying lately. Was there any chance God had started listening again, after all these years? "But Kat, do me a favor?" She waited until her daughter nodded. "Don't ask him. That was a painful time for all of us."

"Okay."

The exchange, especially Bekka's look, stayed with Lynette as she finished her errands and went home to her strangely empty but peaceful house. Maybe she needed to spend more time with her daughter's roommate?

Kat called less than an hour later, and it was then Lynette learned Bekka had been there for Kat when she fled back to Tabor. Bekka had suspected for a while about Mike, but had been afraid to say anything and start trouble if there was nothing really wrong. It was the main reason she had asked Kat to share an apartment with her when the opportunity came. Lynette whispered another "thanks" prayer and went about her few chores. The house was certainly easier to take care of without Mike's constant mess. But her mind kept busy, thinking of ways to maneuver to spend more time with her daughter and her roommates.

"Sunday? Sure, Mom, that'd be great," Kat said, when Lynette called her the next day. "Smoking credit card time?"

"Not quite. Shopping therapy, certainly." Lynette chuckled, and it amazed her how strange it felt. "I'll pick you up around ten and we can get a late breakfast and hit Kingsbury Mall. Sound good?"

"Sure... but make it around 12:30, okay?"

"You don't sleep in *that* late, do you?"

"No. Bekka asked me to go to church with her again. And Morgan's teaching the Singles class this week, so I really want to go."

"Don't you get enough of him during the week?" slipped out before Lynette could censor herself. "I mean, you have two classes with him and you run his errands and pick up his breakfast coffee and... Oh, I don't know why I'm worried. Danny Morgan's the last person to ever hurt you."

"Mom?" Kat's voice cracked a little. "Mom, you don't have to worry that much. I mean, sure Mike saw me through the shower door and he kissed me really slobbery but he never hurt me."

"He hurt your spirit. I'm surprised you have anything at all to do with men because of him."

"Well... don't think I'm being weird, because I don't really understand it myself, Mom, but..." Kat sighed, the sound coming through the phone with a whistle in it. "Bekka said she's been praying for me ever since she met Mike. And she says she knows Morgan prays for all his students, and Mr. Randolph, our tech teacher goes to Bekka's church, too, and Dr. Holwood, and they all get together to pray for their students. And I don't know, maybe all that praying kept it from being so bad. Maybe all that praying... I don't know, maybe God kind of made Mike mess up and drop the mask he always wore for you and Granny. Before something really awful happened."

"I hope so, sweetheart." Lynette closed her eyes, put her back to the wall next to the phone table, and slid down to the floor.

She had held thousands of phone conversations in that position since high school, slouched against the wall with her knees level with her head. If only she could go back to those carefree days.

Would she have fallen for Daniel Morgan's charm, almost from the first day of school? Would she have aimed herself at him, determined that he was "the one," to belong to her for the rest of their lives? If she could change any part of her life, what would it be? Would she have cancelled their date, the night they had sex in the furniture prop room and conceived Kat?

No, she wouldn't cancel her daughter's life. Even if that sacrifice meant keeping Daniel and following all those beautiful, bright dreams they had woven together. But couldn't she have pushed aside her fears and trusted him more, and let him take care of them?

Where would they be now?

"You go on to church, Kat, and I'll pick you up at 12:30, all right? Why not bring Bekka and Amy with us? Wouldn't that be fun?"

"Sounds great. I'll ask them."

Tuesday, January 21

"Morgan?" Bekka dashed into the theater lobby, almost skidding on the water that had seeped from the pitiful doormat where everyone stomped slush off their feet. This late in the afternoon, the scrap of material wasn't able to absorb any more and the water made the bare concrete floor slick. "Big emergency over at the *Picayune*."

"Joel isn't here," Daniel said, getting up from the table where he and the General had been looking over the three-dimensional cardboard mockup of the set they wanted to build for the spring production. His first thought when someone mentioned the town newspaper was an emergency having to do with Joel's daughter, Max.

"I think you'd better call the church, the prayer chain, the trustees." Bekka inhaled deeply a few times, making him think her red cheeks were from running all the way from the newspaper office, rather than the cold weather. "Did you read today's paper? The story Curt and Toni wrote about the White Rose?"

"Heart-breaking," the General rumbled.

"The scuttlebutt is that the White Rose went after Toni at her house, to punish her for what she said about him killing her sister twenty years ago. Curt was there, so he scared the guy off, but they're both in the hospital." Bekka sank down on the edge of the table and wiped her face with her gloved hand. "I was over there, talking with Max about—it doesn't matter about what. But I was there when the fireworks started. Chief Cooper is frantic about Angela. He just about tore the place apart, looking for her, before it got through to him that she wasn't there."

"Angela?"

"Angela Coffelt, the senior editor," Daniel said. "I don't understand—

"

"She's the White Rose's newest target, but Chief Cooper made a big statement to his men today that they have to end this now, because he's in love with her — and as far as everybody knows, the White Rose was there and heard." Her eyes were wide and somber.

"Please, Lord, protect them. End it now," Daniel whispered, and reached for the phone. The more people in the prayer chain who knew, the more prayers there would be, adding weight to the protection that would wrap around Angela. Maybe later he would marvel at the concept of the chief of the Tabor Heights police being secretly in love with the newspaper editor. Right now, he had bigger concerns on his mind.

Bekka was still in the theater lounge, which was crowded with students and faculty who belonged to Tabor Christian, praying and making phone calls to other concerned parties, when Max called her father with the news. Angela Coffelt was safe, and the White Rose had been captured. She couldn't pass on any more news than that, not until the police approved the release of details, but as far as Daniel was concerned, those two details were all that mattered.

Thursday, January 30

"Morgan?" Kat burst through his open office door almost before he could finish hanging up the phone that morning. "We really need your help."

All Daniel could think of was that Lynette was in trouble and had asked for him. He had driven by her house more times than he could count in the last three weeks, looking for some sign of her, trying to screw up his courage to ring the doorbell and ask if they could talk about Kat. He wanted his daughter to know who he was and become more than just her teacher and advisor.

He wanted a small piece of Lynette's life again, even though she was married. Was that so wrong? They had a shared past. In a sense, in the entirely biblical sense, she *was* his wife from the moment they had first had sex. Yes, she had pushed him out of her life and married someone else, but Kat's existence bound them together. Didn't he have any rights?

But he kept thinking of those miserable days when he haunted her dormitory and then her mother's house, begging just to talk to Lynette. He relived his anger and hurt, guilt and sense of betrayal. With so many years behind him, he could look back and honestly assess the situation. With their irresponsible actions, they had betrayed each other. Yes, she had forced him to go away, wronging him irreparably, denying him his rights as Kat's father. But in all honesty, Daniel knew he had wronged her by giving up so easily.

He refused to give up now where Kat was concerned. He vowed a dozen times already he would be there for Kat whenever she needed him, whatever she needed. Whatever Kat needed right now, he would do it for her, get it for her, no matter what. And he would be patient, giving Lynette time and space to get used to him being in their lives now, so they could work together to tell Kat the truth.

"What's wrong?" He shot to his feet, reaching out a hand to Kat.

"It's Bekka. You know that book she was so excited about? The one that guy she met in Florida wants to publish? It's all a scam. He's a major crook and he's trying to extort money from her grandparents and I know she needs to lean on somebody and she won't cry but I bet she wants to and... can you talk to her?"

'Sure." Daniel almost dropped back down into his creaky chair again. He felt blindsided.

Kat didn't need him, but *Bekka* did. Yet Bekka never seemed to need anybody. Whenever she asked for advice, it was mostly to check out what she'd already prayed about and decided for herself.

"Great. I knew you'd help." She started backing through the door, then paused. Daniel wondered if she was about to finally reveal what had been a shadow at the back of her eyes since she got back from Christmas. "It's... it's really nice to..." Kat shrugged, and Daniel could have sworn she blushed a little. "It's great to be able to... depend on... well, if we could pick our own fathers, all three of us decided we'd pick you. If you were old enough to be somebody's father," she added, hastily, and vanished through the door.

Daniel stared at the empty door for at least five minutes, his mouth hanging open. Then he laughed. He turned and propped his elbows on his desktop and hid his face in his hands and laughed until the tears came.

Bekka's problems were no secret to him. She had gone to the Randolphs for advice when her miracle book sale started to go sour. Joel immediately told Daniel, because he knew how important anything affecting her would be to him. Daniel and Dr. Holwood prayed hard and the Randolphs got to work, pulling strings and calling in favors. They had hooked Bekka up with Chuck Winters, who seemed to know everyone in Hollywood and the publishing industry. According to Winters, when this whole affair was cleared up, Bekka would be instrumental in helping to close down a shady business that had robbed and intimidated scores of hopeful young writers.

Kat coming to him and asking him to help was a good sign. No matter what her stepfather had done to her, she still reached out. She still wanted a father.

"If I were old enough to be somebody's father," Daniel muttered, and laughed a little more.

He wished he could tell Lynette what Kat said. Would she laugh, too, or would she be hurt? But why couldn't he call her? He seemed to have missed her every time he drove past the house. That slob husband of hers couldn't be around during the day, could he? It wasn't like he could leave a message on the answering machine.

Daniel picked up the phone and dialed. After all this time, so many instances where he intended to call and then gave up, he knew Lynette's number by heart. The phone rang five times, then the answering machine picked up, with Lynette's gentle voice. Daniel hung up before the greeting ended.

Chapter Nine

Saturday, February 1

"I don't know if they're crazy or not, Mom." Kat sighed as she settled into the couch and stared at the dancing gas flames in the fireplace of her mother's house.

"Somehow, I doubt Danny—your Dr. Morgan is crazy. Of course, working with crazy drama students every day could push him close to the edge."

Lynette's knees wobbled as she made that slip, but Kat didn't seem to notice. She put down the tray with their afternoon snack of hot chocolate and "sloppy nachos" on the coffee table in front of Kat, and stayed standing. She couldn't blame Kat for being rather introspective after what happened more than a month ago, but why bring up this particular subject?

"But Morgan and Bekka both keep talking about how it all worked out for the best, that God was in control even when it seemed like that crook was going to hurt her grandparents. I heard some of those messages he left on our answering machine. He was almost threatening her life because she wouldn't sign the contract and fork over a lot of money. She should be furious. But she just keeps talking about trusting in God and... I mean, she's even got Amy talking about how maybe God really does care and... I don't know." She rested her chin on her clenched fists. "Where was God when Mike was drooling at me?"

"Most of the time, you have to *ask* God. Like I wish you had asked me for help. You didn't tell me what was going on because you thought I wouldn't believe you. Maybe it's the same with God. He didn't do more because nobody asked. But maybe that *was* God, keeping Mike from doing anything worse," she offered almost on a whisper. Lynette settled down on the arm of the couch and squeezed her daughter's shoulder. "I turned my back on God when you were a baby. If He hasn't been taking care of us, it's because I told Him to go away."

"You can't do that to God. I mean, He's everywhere, isn't He?"

"Yes, but God is... God has wonderful manners. He's always waiting, but if you tell Him to leave you alone, eventually He does." Wasn't that what she had done to Daniel? If she asked Daniel to come back into her life, would he, quietly and gently and kindly, just like God seemed to be easing into Kat's life?

"God sounds great, but a lot of the people who say they know Him sure make me sick."

"I know." Lynette felt a heaviness that made it hard to breathe for a few seconds. Was that guilt? Had she done this to her daughter, by turning her back on God just because the legalists in her mother's old church punished her for her mistakes?

She wished she could talk to Daniel like Kat and Bekka did. Would it be so bad to call him, ask him to come over, pour everything out to him like she used to when they were in school?

No, she couldn't. Not while she was still living in Mike's house. The legalities of the divorce were due to be over any day now. Then she would sell the house and everything that reminded her of him and start over.

Maybe then she could call Daniel and they could talk.

Finally.

Even if he hated her.

He certainly hadn't shown her any hatred those few times they ran into each other before. But he hadn't known what Mike was doing to their daughter back then.

What was she going to do?

Monday, February 24

There was something about late February that made Daniel want to curl up and sleep until Easter. Every year, he vowed he would insist that the Powers-That-Be give him no classes before third period during the winter semester. Every year, he let them schedule him for first period classes. Which wasn't fair for all the theater students who worked on sets and rehearsals and costumes until midnight or later. Somehow, when he voiced that complaint to his fellow professors, they groaned and commiserated, but never volunteered to march with him to Dr. Holwood's office to institute a change.

That morning, Daniel wished he had an older student assistant to take over his Theater as Literature class, so he could sit in the back of the room, put his feet up, maybe pull a slouch cap over his eyes, and pray he didn't snore or drool if he fell asleep. Or worse, fall out of his chair.

He couldn't do that, though. Even the double cinnamon cappuccino Kat brought him before she ran off to her history class didn't help. He wondered if he should switch to double espresso or start carrying a bag of those chocolate-covered espresso beans Vic Thomas swore by. Speaking of Vic, maybe he should sign up for a membership at Gold Tone Gym and get into shape. That would give him some energy, wouldn't it?

Whatever was dragging him down this morning, Daniel almost

didn't realize the classroom hadn't emptied immediately when class ended. He barely paid attention as his students filed out to catch the last fifteen minutes of breakfast at the cafeteria or rush to their next class. Daniel reached to hit the light switch as he headed for the door, and looked back like he always did, to see if there was any clutter he should pick up as a courtesy to the next class. Being so early, most of his students brought donuts, sausage biscuits and other assorted junk or fast food, and often dropped the wrappers and left them on the floor.

Daniel didn't see any wrappers, but Amy drooped over her desk and Bekka moved in slow motion as she slid her books into her backpack. He cleared his throat. Amy didn't move, just kept staring at some point two feet off the ground in front of her.

"The next class isn't until noon," he finally said, when she didn't move for several seconds more. Amy startled and looked around the room, drawing a chuckle from him. "Are you all right?"

"Yeah. Great," she said on a sigh.

Daniel felt a sympathetic throb. She sounded like she had been wounded in her never-ending cycle of silly quarrels with Joe. He wished those two would see how much they loved each other and get over the petty bickering.

Hadn't Kat mentioned something about Joe taking Amy out last night, and her roommate being a little too quiet? Amy was never quiet when she broke up with Joe.

Stop it, he scolded himself. *You're not their father.*

Still, anything that affected Kat's roommates eventually affected her. Maybe Amy just needed someone to talk to who didn't know what she looked like first thing in the morning. Daniel put down his briefcase, perched on the front of his desk, and offered what he hoped was a sympathetic smile.

"You don't sound too sure. How's the poetry business?"

"Bankrupt."

That was a change, Daniel admitted. Amy was always so adamant about the quality of her work and the superiority of poetry over every other art form. What had brought on this change of heart?

"Another rejection?" He crossed his arms over his chest and settled in to listen with undivided attention. "Kat told me you've been having a bad run lately."

"Kat told you? Why?"

"Kat talks about you and Bekka quite a bit. She says if it weren't for you two, she would have given up writing screenplays long ago."

"She never told us that," Amy said slowly.

"That's how Kat is. She can't tell anyone how she feels about them. She has to put it into a script or tell someone else."

Daniel wondered if that was how he should approach Lynette about telling Kat the truth. Yeah, that sounded good. He would write a script about their family and ask her to read it. They were a family, he vowed yet again. Fractured, separated by stupidity and fear, but still a family.

"I thought I had problems." She sat up a little more and a tiny smile put some color back into her face.

"You do have talent, Amy. Sometimes the hardest part of being a writer is the staying power."

"Got that right."

"So, was it another rejection?"

"Worse. Joe just sold a song. He got a contract for five more, and a check for a thousand dollars!" she wailed.

"Jealousy is a green-eyed monster, huh?"

"If I see Joe's grinning face today, his eyes will be black." Amy sank lower in her chair.

"I know you two argue over whether poetry or song writing is better —" he began.

"But it was my poem!"

"What?" Daniel shook his head. Surely he hadn't heard that right.

"One of my rejects." Amy's voice cracked. She hid her face in her hands, her elbows on the desk. "I worked on this poem for two months and it was trash. Joe wouldn't let me rip it up. I gave it to him and told him I never wanted to see the stupid thing again. And then we broke up."

"Makes sense, I suppose." Daniel managed to smother a grin, but the longing to laugh made his voice rich. He crossed his legs, rested an elbow on his knee, then rested his chin against the heel of his hand, his fingers curved just enough to cover his mouth, in case he lost control of himself.

"I think we spend more time making up than arguing. That's an improvement, isn't it?"

"He changed your poem, set it to music, and sold it. Is he making you eat crow?"

"He gave me half the check without my even asking, bought me a whole ream of my favorite paper and roses, and took me out to dinner. How can I be mad at him?"

"I wish I had your problems," Daniel admitted on a sigh.

"I sound pretty stupid, huh?" Amy shrugged, rubbed at her eyes, and managed a cockeyed grin.

"No. Young, idealistic, creative, in love, impatient with the entire process of success. Sounds like someone I loved a long time ago."

"So..." Amy looked around the room, blushing a little, as if she could see into his thoughts.

She flinched, and Daniel followed her line of sight to see Bekka standing by her desk, trying not to look like she listened. To leave the room, she would have had to walk between them. Obviously, she had chosen to try to stay inconspicuous. The other girl shrugged and offered a sheepish grin, then bent her head over her backpack, which was obviously packed and ready to go. Daniel wondered why she was still there. It wasn't like Bekka to eavesdrop. Unless she was worried about Amy, too?

"So, how did Kat do with the soap scripts?" Amy blurted, in an obvious attempt to change the subject. "She absolutely hated doing them."

"It doesn't show. Anyone can write a good script for a TV show they love. It takes a real artist to write a great script for a show they hate."

"Kat just got rejected by—Oh, I can't remember the show. It's on SyFy. It's her latest infatuation, and she's been rejected three times by them. Tell her what you just told me, and she'll either scream or kiss you."

"You think so?" Daniel rocked back a little on his tailbone, feeling a jolt pass through him at the suggestion. He couldn't fight a smile, at the mental image of a hug and kiss from his daughter, no matter the excuse.

"She's between boyfriends right now. Why not?"

"I don't know if it would be—"

"Appropriate? Heck, considering the gossip going around about you two, what harm would it do?" Amy tried to laugh.

"Gossip?" He stood up, fists clenched, ice filling that place inside that had been warm and wistful a moment ago.

"If you eat lunch with your assistant at least once a week and you give her rides home from school and you loan her your books, when you won't loan books to anyone else, rumors are going to start."

Amy closed her books with a snap for punctuation. Slipping into the role of one in-the-know seemed to have returned her equilibrium. Daniel told himself to be happy for her, even as he tried to regain his own balance.

Who spread rumors about them? He always did those things for his student assistants, so why did it feel dangerous to follow that practice with Kat? Nobody knew she was his daughter. Did they? Had the rumors been there for Bekka and previous assistants? Why hadn't he heard about them? He could just see Lynette's face if those rumors ever got back to her.

"I didn't realize," Daniel finally said.

"Yeah, we know. Bekka and I have been keeping an eye on you. If we thought there was something filthy going on, we'd bring the roof down."

"Thanks for the vote of confidence. I thought I was—" Daniel looked up and his gaze met Bekka's. His face got warm when she offered a lopsided grin and waggled her fingers at him. "I thought I was more discrete than that," he finished on a sigh.

"There isn't something funny going on between you, is there?" Amy paused in sliding out of her chair.

"Of course not! What kind of man do you think I am?"

"Don't ask me to judge men's character right now, after Kat's stepfather molested her—"

"He what? When?" Daniel nearly roared, and Bekka echoed the sound with a groan.

"When she was little. Everything came out at Christmas. He was all over her. In front of her mother, to make things worse."

"I'll kill him. If he ever lays a hand on her again—"

"Kat sure doesn't tell you everything." Amy's exasperated tone and her smug grin put a halt to the fury boiling through him, as surely as a dip in an icy pond. "Her mom divorced the pervert in January." She was obviously delighted to be the bearer of such news.

"Really?" Daniel sank down on the edge of the desk again, breathless from the lightning-fast change of emotions. From worry to killing fury to—hope? Relief? A sense that all his prayers were about to be answered?

What kind of a man was he, really? He should be furious for his daughter's sake. And for Lynette's, too. What had they endured, living with Mike Tyler all these years, and nobody ever knew?

"She got everything. I'd have thrown him in prison for the rest of his life. I mean, no wonder Kat won't keep a steady boyfriend. She can't trust guys," Amy rattled on.

"She can trust me!"

"Yeah, but you're different."

"I hope so." Daniel swallowed hard. "Amy, do you believe in second chances?"

"If I didn't, Joe and I would have split forever years ago."

"That's all I needed to know." He snatched up his briefcase and headed for the door.

He paused there and looked back at the two of them. Amy was busy gathering up her books and didn't see him. He fumbled with his briefcase, freeing his hands just long enough to form a praying hands gesture, and nodded to Bekka. She nodded back. For a second, he wondered if she had been waiting to talk to him about something. Daniel knew if it was really important, Bekka would have flagged him down.

"Turn the lights off, would you?"

He was running by the time he reached the faculty parking lot. Daniel suspected more than a few students saw and laughed. He didn't care. He wore sneakers and splashed through a dozen slushy puddles but didn't care about that either. That was what car heaters were for, weren't they?

The important thing was remembering where the nearest florist was. He didn't have to think about how to get to Lynette's house. He could drive the route blindfolded.

~~~~~

The only witnesses that late morning were a few birds exploring the side yard of the expensive, upper-middle class, immaculately landscaped
~~~~~

house with the For Sale sign in the front yard.

Daniel drove up the driveway and parked halfway between the street and the sidewalk leading through dead flowerbeds to the front door. He sat for several seconds, staring at the closed, gold-trimmed front door. A shadow moved against the sheers in the big bay window of the living room. He flinched and put his hand on the steering wheel, half-ready to jam the key into the ignition and get out of there.

What was he doing here? Lynette would be furious. She hadn't told him what happened. Kat hadn't come to him for help or comfort. What in the world made him think either of them wanted him here? They certainly didn't want him to know.

Anger slid a hot thread through his honestly acknowledged panic. Wasn't it his right to know? Wasn't Kat his daughter, even if she didn't know it? Lynette should have known he'd want to help, that he had a right to be involved.

"Whose fault is it, anyway?" Daniel whispered, staring at that front door as if it were alternately the gates of Alcatraz and Heaven. "You should have kicked down her mother's door instead of letting her fancy lawyers scare you away. You should have contacted her when you got the job here, when you finally had something to offer them. But *nooo*... you had to stick to your pride and curl up in a corner and lick your wounds. Lyn probably thinks you hate her."

He closed his eyes and rested his fists on the top of the steering wheel, his forehead on his fists.

Whose fault was any of this? Well, Mike's, certainly. Who did that arrogant slob think he was, molesting Lynette's daughter? Daniel had never been one for solving anything with his fists, but he admitted it would give him great pleasure to drive over to that catering business and do some tenderizing on Mike Tyler's face. Let the police come. The whole truth would come out, and he'd probably be hailed as a hero.

To the world at large, maybe. Not to the social elite of Stoughton who called Mike Tyler their friend. And certainly not to Lynette and Kat, because didn't he have enough evidence they wanted the whole situation kept quiet? He wouldn't endear himself to either one of them if he brought Kat's problems out into the open, where the newspapers might pick it up. And he wouldn't be doing BWU any favors by creating a news item about a tenured professor being hauled off to jail.

"Not going to work that way. Please, Lord..." Daniel wasn't sure what he wanted to say. All he could do was offer the ache and terror and anger and hunger to God and hope for the best.

Taking a deep breath, he finally reached for the door handle. The birds paused a few seconds when the door of his six-year-old Beretta creaked open, then they went back to looking for bugs. Daniel took twenty feet of sidewalk slowly, fists clenched, gaze fastened on that closed front door. Not a sound penetrated the thick walls of the house. The entire neighborhood was quiet with that chill sense of waiting, balanced on a razor's edge, either falling back into more winter ice and gloom, or spilling forward into early spring. Daniel chose spring. It helped to realize there were probably no witnesses around, early enough in the day for the children to still be at school and most adults to be at work or out shopping.

At the front door, he took a deep breath, bracing himself before he reached out to press the doorbell. Daniel yanked his hand back just before he touched the button and sprinted back to his car with his heart racing. He dove halfway into the back seat, emerging a few seconds later with an enormous paper-wrapped bouquet of hothouse-grown wildflowers, wrapped with a satin ribbon. He cradled it as if it were made of glass as he strode back up the driveway and nearly punched the doorbell.

He shifted his feet a few times, waiting for the door to open. Seconds ticked by. Daniel glanced around the neighborhood and took one step backward to his car when the heavy panel flew open.

"Daniel?" Lynette gasped. She blushed and immediately yanked the blue bandanna off her hair.

She had a smudge of dirt along her nose, and another longer smudge on her cheek. Her sleeves were rolled up and her baggy blue sweatshirt was spotted with water and dust and smears of more stubborn dirt.

No fancy designer clothes and just-from-the-shop hairdo. Daniel wondered if she had decorated herself that way for Mike, and this was the real Lynette. It struck him that she was no longer the girl he loved at the university, with those shadows under her eyes and the fine wrinkles around her mouth from worry and anger and stress.

He stared at her for a few more seconds, deciding she was the most beautiful thing he had seen in a long time. Especially when it finally sunk in that she was in the middle of packing or cleaning the house or doing something related to that wonderful For Sale sign in the front yard. She wasn't dressed up as Mike Tyler's trophy wife. She was leaving this house.

Thank You, Lord, Daniel shouted deep inside. He offered a grin. Telling Lynette she was beautiful was probably not a smart move. She probably felt grubby and awkward right now. How many times had Mike had the intelligence to tell her she was beautiful when she didn't feel that way?

Probably not often enough, maybe never, Daniel decided.

To his wonder, Lynette smiled at him, and her smile grew with each second of silence that passed. Her blue-gray eyes widened a little, and there was a glow to her makeup-free face that Daniel swore grew a little brighter the longer they looked at each other.

This was going to work. She wasn't going to throw him out a second time.

Daniel finally remembered the flowers, jerking a little as if waking from a dream, and handed them to her. The man who could do improv in the worst situation on stage couldn't think of a thing to say. Lynette blushed, but her eyes sparkled as she held out her arms and took the flowers. Then she stepped back, inviting him into the house.

"It's kind of a mess," she murmured as she led him down the short hall into the kitchen. "Everything is," she added, tossing the bandana into a cardboard box marked *apples*.

"Need any help?" Daniel swallowed hard when she stopped short, her back to him. He could almost see her shoulders hunch with tension. "With anything. Whatever you need, Lyn."

"You heard." No inflection at all in her voice.

"It wasn't easy finding out anything. I knew Kat was upset just after Christmas, but... Those three have a pact of silence... Kat didn't tell me, if that's what you're wondering."

"Why wouldn't she go to her — to her father?" She finally turned, and the glimmering threat of tears made her eyes bigger.

Daniel knew then, she had cried too many tears by herself.

"I'd be lying if I said I wasn't ecstatic when I heard you finally dumped the scum ball."

"No, actually, he seems to think he dumped me." She choked on what sounded like a bark of hysterical laughter and an effort not to sob.

"The guy is a total jerk. A loser of the hundredth magnitude." Daniel jammed his hands into his pockets to still their trembling. "Would you get mad if I asked why?"

"He — he thinks he didn't do anything wrong. Like, it's his right to — to drool over my little girl and try to touch her and —" She shook her head and dropped the flowers onto the table half-covered with dishes and newspapers and boxes. She reached into the apple box and dug out the blue bandana to wipe her face. "When he started sobering up, he thought he'd scare me into accepting what he's been doing, if he threatened to divorce me. As if my life would fall apart without him, the jerk! Mother launched her lawyers at him before the police got him to the front door."

"How's Kat?" Daniel scolded himself not to ask how bad it had been that the police were involved. He would let Lynette tell him when she was able — when she trusted him enough to confide such painful details to him.

"He never actually *did* anything. Nothing that would stand up in court, up until he got drunk on Christmas Eve and..." She shook her head and slammed her hand down on the table. "But he came between me and my daughter! He had her convinced I wouldn't take her side! I will never forgive him for that."

"I know a couple guys on the football team who'd be glad to drag him into a dark alley. As a favor to me."

Lynette snorted, bitter laughter mixing with the tremors of anger and pain that wracked her. She shook her head, stumbled back two steps to lean against the counter at the sink, and wiped her face again.

"Danny—"

"I mean it. Whatever you need, I'm here. I'd be lying if I said I never stopped thinking about you. And I'd be lying if I said I wasn't ready to jump over the moon when I heard you were finally free. Kind of shows what a selfish jerk I am. Thinking about myself, when I should have been worrying about you and Kat."

"No. I think it's sweet." She offered a trembling smile. "Do you know how long it's been since someone felt that way about me?"

"The world is full of jerks. Me at the top of the list." Silently praying, Daniel crossed the two yards of empty space between them and reached out to take hold of her free hand. Lynette went still, but he thought, hoped, her mouth relaxed a little. "This is probably the wrong time, but I want to be part of your life again, Lyn. Maybe I don't want to take the chance somebody else will step in while I'm waiting for the right time."

"You don't see a line at the front door, do you?" she whispered, looking at their joined hands. A hint of a smile touched her lips.

"Let me help?" What he wanted was to wrap his arms around her and never let go, but that was the wrong move for right now. "I mean it. I don't have any classes for the rest of the day." It was a lie, but he knew he could call Joel Randolph to fill in for him. He hadn't the foggiest idea what to tell Kat and the new student assistant she was training.

That was a question for later: what to tell Kat, and when?

"What? Wash windows and move furniture and..." Lynette looked up into his eyes again, and Daniel saw a melting and relief and easing of pain that made him want to pound Mike Tyler into the ground. She should never have been that hurt, by anyone. Ever.

"Yeah. Anything you need. Just tell me what you want."

Tuesday, March 11

She wasn't quite sure why she did it, but Lynette asked Daniel's opinion on the condominium she wanted to buy in Tabor Heights. Did he think she was just trying to be a "smother mother" and live close to Kat? Or was it for sensible reasons, like the part-time job she lined up at the Blooming Miracles florist, the low cost of the high-quality, nearly new condominium itself, and the close proximity of the bus lines? She planned to simplify her life, to totally cleanse her style, her habits, of all the elegance and luxury that had been foisted on her by Mike Tyler and his pursuit of high social standing and influence.

He looked over the condo, checked the seals on the windows and the condition of the pipes, the age of the water heater — when had he become such a handyman? — and called the builder, who turned out to be a friend from church. When he presented her with the background of taxes and utility bills and the repairs made to the condominium since it was built ten months ago, he also gave her a piece of news she didn't expect.

"I live two blocks over," Daniel said, hooking his thumb over his shoulder in the direction of Kiln Street. "You ought to consider that before you sign the lease."

It was on the tip of her tongue to ask him why he thought she would change her mind if she knew he lived so close. Then a wave of heat flooded her, scrambling her emotions and thoughts for several seconds.

Daniel thought she wouldn't want to be that close. Either he was being considerate, or he was afraid she would be angry. He gave her warning, so if this comfortable, comforting relationship turned sour, she could be prepared to see him everywhere.

She would see him everywhere, wouldn't she? At the grocery, the hardware store, the bakery, the coffee shops and bookstore. A dozen other places. And every time she came to see one of Kat's productions at school.

That brought up another thought she had been playing with since he strolled back into her life like a slightly dusty, relaxed white knight.

"I don't think Kat should know we're... seeing each other." She blushed. How could she call it dating, when they had only gone out for pizza once, and the rest of the time Daniel had been helping her pack and tote unwanted things to resale shops, and look for a new place to live?

"How does that lead into us living two blocks apart?" Daniel smiled, but she could tell her words had knocked him off balance.

'I want us to get used to being together before Kat sees us together. I mean, it's not like she's upset about Mike leaving us." That earned a snort from him, and he had the good grace to look away so she wouldn't see his wry grin. "If we live in the same town and Kat happens to see us together, she'll think we just ran into each other. I want to make sure she likes us being friends before we tell her there's something more."

"More as in dating, or more as in I'm her father?" His smile was more bared teeth than humor. At least he wasn't furious with her.

Could Daniel get angry with her? The only time she could remember was when she shoved him out of her life, and then there had been more hurt and confusion than real anger.

"It's going to be awkward enough when we do tell her."

"Especially since she thinks I'm dead."

"You know about that?"

"It's okay, Lyn." He shuffled the condo statistics papers around on the counter of what would hopefully be her kitchen.

No, Lynette decided then. It *would* be her kitchen. She was taking this place. She wanted to become part of the town where her daughter lived and had dug in roots that let her heal. She wanted to become part of the town where Daniel lived. There had to be something about Tabor Heights that helped him be the man who would reach out to help her instead of crucifying her and gloating over her pain.

"I understand why you told her that. It covered a lot of problems." Daniel shrugged. "I decided to be flattered."

"Flattered?" It took a few seconds to catch up with what he was saying.

"Kat said you always looked sad when you talked about her father. I kind of hoped that meant you missed me, that you didn't hate my guts."

"Never," she whispered.

Chapter Ten

Friday, March 28

It was cowardly, and Lynette knew it, but that didn't stop her from scheduling moving day for Daniel's busiest class day. It meant losing Kat's help for several hours, but Lynette didn't mind. To her delight, Bekka and Amy volunteered to help, and the moving company took care of a large part of the grunt work. Kat was there to help with unwrapping newspaper-wrapped dishes and running them through the dishwasher, and to help put out rugs and hang pictures at the end of the day. When Kat left for rehearsal, Daniel showed up with a Chinese banquet and helped her set up her TV, DVD, and stereo system.

Maybe he was just as relieved not to have Kat see them together. She hoped. This was all going to take some time to get used to, but she wanted it, with an ache like a leg regaining feeling after being asleep for hours.

Maybe years.

They met for lunch at Stay-A-While or the Bluebird Café once a week. Never on the same day. Making a routine implied more than Lynette was willing to admit, even to herself. And always at the restaurant. She never met Daniel at his office and he never came up to Blooming Miracles or her condo to pick her up. Daniel never suggested it, though such a practice would have been easier on them both. Lynette chose to believe he felt the same as she did. Uneasy about Kat seeing them and asking questions they weren't prepared to answer.

That was a comfort.

So why did she feel a little disappointment, every time he gave in to her wishes without a murmur?

Saturday, April 5

Just before Easter, on the spur of the moment, Daniel suggested they drive up to Sandusky and take the ferry to Put-in-Bay on South Bass Island. Lynette laughed with him after they both confessed they had lived in Ohio so long and never visited the Lake Erie Islands before.

"Probably half these places are closed this early in the season," Daniel said, as they looked through the guidebook for the island, which he had purchased just before they boarded the ferry. The stiff lake breeze tried to snatch the book from his hands several times, but neither one suggested they leave their vantage point on the upper deck of the ferry.

The lower deck had been commandeered by a troupe of noisy, delightfully lively children. Lynette estimated they ranged between third and seventh grade. She saw at least ten adult bodies towering over the miniature tornadoes, but the adults were moving so quickly, and in so many directions, she couldn't be sure how many there were or even get a good look at their faces. She was just grateful Daniel found the stairs and the children stayed below decks. It gave the two of them a semblance of privacy and muffled the uproar from below. They had a wonderful view of the lake as they slid across the waves. They had the day's itinerary mapped out before the ferry touched the docks, and then abandoned it entirely.

They rented a golf cart instead of bikes to get around the island and spent the first three hours visiting Perry's Monument and Perry's Cave. Supposedly Commodore Perry set up his headquarters in the cave during the Battle of Lake Erie. Lynette clutched Daniel's arm as they walked down the steep, damp cement steps from the gift shop to the cave and kept her grip as they crossed the uneven stone floor, worn smooth by water erosion. She marveled at the stone straws formed by drip water, and listened to the short, simple tour given by the guide, pointing out the underwater stone formations and the pipes that once fed underground water to a hotel that no longer existed. She flinched just like the other four women in the tour when the guide pointed out the few bats and several birds that came in through the crevices and made their home in the cave.

The maritime museum was open, but not the aquatic studies laboratory or the wildlife museum. Lynette was glad to just walk around the exhibits, reading the placards identifying the models, the bits and pieces of Lake Erie maritime history, and to steal glances at Daniel from time to time. He wasn't the boy she had fallen in love with in college, and she thought maybe she liked him better. There was something solid and reliable about him, something more real, so she didn't feel quite so sad when she thought of the dreams he had given up, and the brilliant light of energy that had faded. Daniel could have been a star on stage and screen, but he had chosen to spend his time giving others the training to follow their dreams. No wonder Kat adored him like she did.

They indulged in giant onion rings, fried mushrooms and milkshakes for lunch, reminiscent of college dates, strolled down the tiny merchant's district, examining all the kitschy souvenirs with maps of Ohio or Lake Erie or lighthouses, and ate ice cream cones. And held hands.

Several times, when he leaned close and they got quiet and looked deep into each other's eyes, Lynette thought Daniel might try to kiss her. Especially when they had been laughing or just silly a few moments before. They had laughed and kissed so often in school. Or were those just selective memories? Either way, Daniel didn't try anything. Maybe because they hadn't been officially dating for very long. Or because he still had some bruised feelings, or even resentment?

Lynette hoped not. Maybe he was simply more restrained and cautious in some areas. She wondered if she had brought the change in him, or his clear, simple, strong faith had done that.

She envied him. Daniel hadn't been brought up in church, but his version of God certainly seemed more real and personal and friendly than the God who had looked down from somber paintings and stained glass windows since her church nursery days. Not that they had talked much about church or faith. It just seemed to come up regularly in conversation about the things they had done since the last time they were together.

With all the extra time he gave to his students outside the classroom, Lynette wondered how Daniel could find so much time for church, serving on committees, teaching a Sunday school class or helping out when the youth used the Gold Tone Gym. Tabor Christian seemed such a natural, integral part of Daniel's life, it always came up in conversation. So, God always came up in conversation, even if only for a few seconds.

The idea that Daniel had a spiritual life, and she didn't, depressed Lynette. She put it aside to brood over later and set herself to enjoy every minute of the day. It was enough to know she brought that smile to his lips, and he focused on making sure she had a good time. It was enough to walk down the street holding hands with him and talk about anything that came to mind.

They played mini golf at the War of Eighteen Holes, and she laughed as he related a fundraiser mini golf tournament the theater department held four years ago, where everyone had to wear costumes and maintain the character that went with the costume. If they broke character, they lost points. She teased him until he relented and finally admitted what costume he wore—Caliban from *The Tempest*.

"Have you ever tried to play mini golf while you're bent over with a fake hump in your back and a fright mask that makes you blind in one eye?" he said, twisting his body sideways and bending over to demonstrate his position. "I found out the hard way, you do need two eyes to play this game!"

"But you won anyway, right?"

"It was a matter of honor—it was the faculty against the student assistants against the techies. How were we going to keep order in the classroom for the rest of the year if we didn't win?"

"Uh huh." Lynette eyed him for a moment as he straightened up and made his putt. From the twitching of his mouth, she could guess what he didn't say. "So, how badly did the kids beat you?"

"I'm not saying—except that I'm glad I didn't make any bets with grade point averages on the line."

"You're kidding me!" She burst out laughing. She could guess which member of the faculty was arrogant, flamboyant, and lovable enough to do that. "It's a good thing the General is the head of the department, I guess."

"It's a good thing the student assistants who got guaranteed B's earned them legally." Daniel waggled his eyebrows at her, destroying his somber expression. Then his eyes sparkled and he grinned, and they both laughed like idiots, standing there in front of the wooden statue of Commodore Perry. It was a good thing they didn't have anybody waiting behind them, because it was very hard to play mini golf while laughing.

No dark cloud of depressing thoughts or worries hung over Lynette's head as she boarded the ferry at the end of the day. Even the boisterous children, who seemed to be everywhere on the island, following them around every place and now back to the ferry, made her laugh. Especially when Daniel hooked an arm around her waist and swung her out of the way of a stampede. They laughed together and scrambled for the stairs up and out of the way.

The laughter caught in her throat as she looked back to watch the adult leaders scramble to corral the children, and one of them was Bekka.

Lynette followed Daniel up to the top deck and took a seat at the prow of the ferry. The wind whipping at their faces and the blast of the ferry's horn made talk impossible. She couldn't have spoken even if he tried to carry on a conversation.

Had Bekka seen her?

More important: Would she tell Kat she had seen the two of them on the boat?

Lynette was fairly sure it wasn't illegal or unethical to date her daughter's advisor.

If it were, she had a perfectly reasonable defense: "He's her father and we're getting back together."

Were they? Lynette looked away, in case Daniel read her thoughts in her face. She thought Daniel wanted to be a permanent part of her life. But what if she were wrong?

There were so many obstacles. Kat's reaction to hearing they were dating, being the first.

Learning Daniel was her father and her mother had lied to her, obviously the largest.

Much as she wanted the assurance that Daniel would always be there, Lynette had to be honest about this. She had no idea if they had any more of a chance of being and staying together now than they did in college.

She didn't tell Daniel she had seen Bekka. Maybe Bekka hadn't seen her, or even better, that wasn't Bekka at all, but an unreasonable facsimile.

~~~~~

"We can't go on much longer like this," Daniel said.

They had stopped for dinner at a place that boasted the best ribs this side of the Canadian border.

Lynette choked and almost spat out her mouthful of cornbread. She closed her watering eyes and prayed he blamed that and her flushed cheeks on the choking.

Had she subconsciously already known he was ready to dump her?

"Sorry. Bad timing," he said, when she got rid of the tickle by drinking half her glass of water. "Our luck's going to run out, Lyn. Kat's going to see us together sooner or later and start asking questions."

"Oh. Right." She fought a giggle of relief.

"Once or twice, she'll accept as coincidence. But our daughter is way too smart not to notice something's going on."

"Is something going on?" Lynette batted her eyelashes at him to cover the sudden terrified thumping of her heart.

Please, God—I'll even go to church every time he asks me, from now on!

"I sure hope so." Daniel reached across the table with both hands and held both of hers. "We really should let Kat know what's going on."

"She'll be shocked."

"She'll be more shocked if half the town knows before she does."

"True." She looked down at her barbecue chicken. Suddenly, it lacked all flavor. "I should probably tell her tomorrow."

With luck, Kat would still be in bed before Bekka went to church. Lynette thought she could call her daughter and take her to a late breakfast. The hysterics would be over before Bekka got a chance to mention—casually, because Bekka never gossiped—that she'd seen Kat's mother and Daniel on the ferry coming from Put-in-Bay.

"I've got a great idea. Why don't both of you come to..." For a moment, his smile faded. Daniel shrugged. "How about I meet both of you for lunch after church, and we can tell her then?"

Lynette thought she would burst into tears for a moment. She knew as if she'd written the script, Daniel had meant to suggest she and Kat go to church with him.

Like a real family.

"I don't think so. The girls usually have plans of one kind or another on Sunday afternoons." She caught hold of his hands when he started to withdraw them. "Why don't you pick me up for church, and we'll work on our strategy over lunch?"

If there hadn't been a table between them, Lynette knew Daniel would definitely have kissed her this time. He squeezed her hands so tightly she lost all feeling for a moment. His face glowed with such joy, he
~~~~~

could have lit the entire shadowy restaurant by himself.

Just because she said she'd go to church with him.

Please, God—why can't I love You like Daniel does? Why does he get so much from church, and I can't even stand to listen to a Christian radio station?

~~~~~

Despite falling asleep on the long drive back to Tabor Heights, Lynette buzzed with energy by the time she stood in the doorway of her condo and watched Daniel drive away. She sorted through the mail that had come, washed up and changed for bed, studied the TV listings and found nothing worth her time or attention. She wished she could go to sleep, just so she could bring the morning that much closer, sooner.

What would Kat say? What would her daughter do? What was the best approach for telling her that her mother and advisor were dating? If she was receptive to that—Lynette suspected Kat would be overjoyed—maybe they *should* move full steam ahead and tell her the rest of the truth.

Lynette glanced at the clock on her range as she contemplated making a cup of tea. Kat had given her dozens of sampler packets of herbal tea as a housewarming gift. There had to be something among them to soothe instead of keep her awake.

Nearly ten. It was still early for the girls to head off to bed, despite Bekka's very responsible example. Lynette smiled, feeling once again that warm, helpless wave of gratitude that Bekka had sensed something wrong and stepped in to help Kat without making the problem worse with her suspicions. She suspected her words to Kat just a little while ago had been true, and God had sent Bekka even before they thought to ask for help.

Then Lynette's smile stopped. Yes, and if Bekka was that perceptive, to know Mike sexually harassed Kat without actually seeing anything, then she was perceptive enough to see Daniel and her together and know what was going on.

Why hadn't she heard anything yet? Surely Kat would have called the minute Bekka mentioned what she saw?

"I've wasted enough time waiting for something to happen in my life," Lynette growled as she stomped over to the phone hanging on the wall and lifted the receiver. It took seconds to dial. She could have taken less time to step outside and shout. The girls' apartment was only a ten-minute walk away, after all.

"Hi, Mom!" Kat sounded excited about something, but not upset. Lynette hoped that was a good sign.

When she hung up nearly half an hour later, she was more bemused than anything else. Kat had spent most of the day alone and enjoyed every minute of it, because she had a brainstorm about a script she had to write for Daniel's class. Amy had been out all day with Joe at the Rock Hall and then the Science Center, still celebrating Joe's contract. And Bekka had just
~~~~~

arrived home half an hour ago, exhausted. She had been drafted to help with a trip to Put-in-Bay the Middlers class from church had taken. Three adults had come down with the flu at the last minute. According to Kat, Bekka had been kept so busy she didn't take a single picture and barely got to eat half her hamburger at lunch.

Bekka hadn't said a word about seeing them on the ferry. Lynette wondered if *anything* would be said. At least now she knew that was indeed Bekka she saw on the boat, and it explained why she was with all those children. It also meant chances were good Bekka hadn't seen her with Daniel.

"I'm a coward," she whispered in the silence of her kitchen.

That thought stayed with her the next day, as she sat through Pastor Glenn's sermon and received warm greetings from people in church who recognized her from around town. It seemed half the customers at Blooming Miracles attended Tabor Christian.

And that, in turn, affected their lunch discussion about when and where to tell Kat. She finally told Daniel about seeing Bekka on the ferry, and the terror that gave her.

"If we tell Kat, then we don't have to be afraid anymore," he said, with that lopsided smile that as far back as college meant he was hurting and trying to understand.

"I know. My head says that. My heart is—What if I mess this up again, Danny?"

"What's to mess up? We're older and wiser, and we finally have a chance to fix what went wrong when we were kids." He reached across the table, carefully avoiding their half-empty bowls of hot and sour soup and shrimp chips. "I'm willing to do everything it takes to make this work," he said as he clasped her hands in both his.

This was becoming a habit, Lynette decided. A very good habit. One that made her feel cherished and protected. So why wasn't she shouting it from the housetops of Tabor? She allowed herself the greedy pride that Daniel wanted *her*, instead of the dozen other women in town he could be involved with. Why couldn't she tell their daughter?

"And if you're feeling uncomfortable or scared... I'm kind of worried about the reaction from Kat, too, since we're making deep dark confessions," he continued.

"I guess I'm ashamed," she whispered. "Of what I did to you, to us. To Kat," she hurried to add, when his eyes got wide and his hands squeezed tighter for a moment. "How do you explain all those mistakes and the fears in fifteen seconds, before Kat explodes like an atomic bomb?"

"True." After a moment, that strained smile warmed and softened. "Okay. I won't push you for full disclosure anymore. When the time's right, we'll both know."

"You... won't?" Lynette felt like someone had just emptied a tank of oxygen into the room. She felt as if she could breathe clearly for the first time in days.

"It's kind of fun, I suppose. Seeing how long we can keep this secret. Kind of like kids sneaking around in the back seat of... wrong analogy." He shuddered as he released her hands and settled back in the booth seat.

"I know what you mean. I'm glad you're nervous about Kat, too."

"Nervous isn't half of it. I've written a dozen scripts for what happens when she finds out. Do half the girls in the theater program suddenly become her best friends instead of hating her guts, now that they know *why* she's teacher's pet?"

"You're terrible!" She contemplated kicking him under the table.

"I know." Daniel dug into his pocket and pulled out his wallet. "I also have box seat tickets for the next Guardians home game. If you can stand being with the General..." He grinned and showed her the tickets.

"Let me guess. He's a very dramatic fan?" Lynette chuckled with him when Daniel simply rolled his eyes.

It was going to be all right, she knew then. Everything was going to be perfect.

She might even think about going to church with him every Sunday. Maybe next week, she'd even be able to hear most of the sermon. If thinking about God more and praying without always saying "gimme" made that much of a difference, and if it made Daniel happy to have her sitting in the pew next to him, she would certainly keep doing it.

Tuesday, April 8

"Crowds," the General growled.

Daniel muffled a snort of laughter, but not his grin. Only a sell-out game at Progressive Field could muffle his co-worker's stentorian voice. He glanced over his shoulder at Lynette, who held onto his jacket sleeve for dear life, so they wouldn't be separated.

"You were right," the leader of their little caravan pronounced, ending with a loud sigh that Daniel swore blew a couple caps off the heads of the fans in the long, slow-moving line in front of them. The General turned to meet Daniel's eyes. "We should have left an hour earlier." At ten minutes until the game was scheduled to start, Cleveland against Atlanta, they had barely made it through the gate.

"Traffic was worse than I thought, that's all," Daniel offered. One nice thing about August DeFiore—he always admitted when he was wrong, and no one ever had to say, "I told you so," to him.

"Might as well enjoy the scenery while we're here," Lynette offered. She moved up a couple inches, pressed against his right side. If Daniel dared move his arm, he could have put it around her.

He glanced around at the crowd, feeling a tiny quiver of guilt at the thought. Lynette's paranoia about Kat, about being seen together and discovered, affected him now, at the oddest times. What was wrong with him that he felt guilty about wanting to put his arm around her in a public place? True, he hadn't tried to kiss her yet and she hadn't offered, but wasn't it about time to move past the handholding stage? Without feeling like half the world was watching and ready to condemn? Yes, they had been wrong twenty years ago, but they were trying to make it right. Didn't that count for something?

Daniel's gaze slid over the crowd. He wished the box seats had a different entrance from the rest of the seats in the stadium. Then he grinned, scolding himself for being an elitist. He hadn't planned on attending any Guardians home games this year because he didn't think he'd have the time. Funny, how finding someone to spend time with helped him find time to spend.

His heart skipped a beat and he swung his gaze back over the crowd again before the image he had caught fully registered. That floppy faded denim hat with the purple flowers looked awfully familiar. It had stared him in the face during his first period class for the last week — every time Amy Whittier bent her head to take notes. Daniel looked straight at the spot where he thought he had seen it. Next to the hat, and six inches up, was the long, lean face of Joe Kriegan. The hat shifted, revealing a long blonde ponytail, then Amy turned her head. Daniel looked away before their gazes met.

Just great. Amy's got the biggest mouth of the three. Daniel grinned as he recognized the chagrin in his thought. If Amy hadn't been a blabbermouth, would he have ever known about the divorce and Lynette finally being free? Probably not. Kat hadn't wanted her roommates telling anyone.

Daniel glanced back, bracing himself to face the music. He saw the crowd around Amy and Joe marginally clear, and the couple moved up the steps toward the nosebleed section. Joe had hold of Amy's arm, and she seemed a little stunned. At least, she wasn't talking a mile a minute and gesturing back toward where Daniel was still stuck in traffic, between the General and Lynette and 5,000 other fans on an unusually warm April evening.

He debated warning Lynette during the first three innings. Then Daniel mentally shook himself. What was he doing, carrying her fears? The sooner Kat knew they were dating and got used to the idea, the sooner they could tell her he was her father. He had visions of a summer spent as a trio, getting to know his daughter better than class and work-study allowed. Maybe weekend camping trips? More excursions to Put-in-Bay or the Metroparks Zoo and Rainforest, or Cedar Point amusement park? All the things he hadn't been able to do for her as a little girl.

Amy was sure to tell Kat what she saw as soon as she got home. Of course, knowing Amy, she might just borrow someone's cell phone and call the apartment to shout the news.

Daniel relaxed in his chair and settled down to enjoy the game. He wouldn't take Lynette's enjoyment away from her. Even if the Guardians didn't smear the Atlanta Braves, it was entertainment enough just watching the General act as a one-man cheering section.

Wednesday, April 9

"So, how'd you like that game?" Bekka said, when Daniel stepped out of his office to refill his coffee the next morning. She perched on the worktable that doubled as the work-study students' desk, reading the syllabus for summer session Kat had been assembling yesterday.

"Game?"

"Amy was in absolute hysterics yesterday all through the game. You were there with the General, weren't you?"

"Uh... yeah. Were you?" Daniel put down his mug. It was his favorite, heat-sensitive with Captain Picard from *Star Trek* appearing and disappearing on the transporter pad. He didn't want to risk dropping it on the cement floor. He planned on holding onto it until it was worth about $3,000 on eBay.

"Yep. I just had to get out of the apartment, and Joe had an extra ticket and..." Bekka sighed. "I know I shouldn't be jealous, because Kat won't hold onto a guy past two dates, but they won't even give me a second look when she's around."

"Jealous?" Daniel wondered if he should sit.

Just how had they switched from the baseball game to Bekka's jealousy of Kat's romantic life?

"Shane Hopkins was taking Kat to the game last night, and I just had to get out of the apartment before he showed up." She raked her fingers through her hair and groaned, then gave him a sheepish look. "I've been so busy, I've never really paid attention to a guy before, except as a co-worker or Kat's flavor-of-the-week, to feel sorry for him. Once she dumps him, he's never going to come near the apartment again, so what chance do I have of Shane ever noticing me?"

"Shane Hopkins." Daniel searched his memory of students, trying to place Shane. He knew the name, and a moment later, the face and some details slid into his memory. Shane was one of Dr. Holwood's honor students, taking extra-credit classes, working toward his master's in English at John Carroll University while he finished his second degree, theater, at BWU.

He also rode a motorcycle in every weather and never went anywhere without his dusty brown Stetson. Dr. Holwood had joked he thought the hat was sewn onto Shane's scalp.

"He's a good student," he offered, wondering if that was the wrong thing to say to Bekka. Shane was a perfect match for her, and Daniel grinned as he realized he made that assessment. Was he getting old, playing matchmaker for his students?

"Yeah, and Kat's got him. One date down, one to go." Bekka shrugged. "It was a fun game, once I could get my mind off Shane. Amy was nearly falling out of her seat through most of it. She didn't care if the Guardians won or lost. I mean, the General? A baseball fan? Even Kat thought it was funny."

Daniel chuckled with her and picked up the Picard mug with slightly shaking fingers. Kat had been at the stadium, too. Talk about close calls.

The next moment, he felt disappointment slide through the relief. If Kat had seen him and Lynette together, that uncomfortable confrontation could have been faced and finally put behind them.

"I know it's a cliché, Bekka, but you could try praying about it. Maybe Shane isn't the guy for you. Or maybe God pointed him at your apartment and he got distracted by Kat."

"Yeah, she's a distraction all right." But Bekka smiled as she said it.

Thank You, Lord, she was there when my little girl needed her, Daniel prayed as he watched Bekka saunter up the stairs a few minutes later. *Bekka's a good girl. She deserves someone who wants to take care of her for a change, instead of her taking care of everyone else.*

Sunday, April 20

'Lyn?" Daniel's voice sounded strained, coming through the speaker on the answering machine. It startled Lynette, so she stumbled as she stepped out of the shower.

What was he doing, calling at only 6:30 on Sunday morning? He wasn't supposed to pick her up for breakfast at Stay-a-While and then on to church, until eight.

"I'm sorry. I have to cancel." He took a long, shaky breath. From the sound of it, he fought not to cry. "You know the Randolphs? Joel and Emily—from Homespun. There was an accident last night. I'm spending the day at the hospital."

The answering machine cut him off before he could go any further.

Lynette stood in the hallway, dripping on the tile floor, listening to the answering machine hum as it processed the message. A shiver went through her, and she wasn't sure why. There were so many reasons. The grief that thickened Daniel's voice. The thought of something bad enough to affect him so. His fear for his friends.

She had met the Randolphs only recently. It still amazed her a little that a former movie star, Emily Keeler, lived just a few streets away, ran the community theater, and was as sweet, genuine and friendly as she had appeared in her films. Lynette had seen how devoted Joel and Emily were to each other, and to their children, and had to fight a sick twisting of envy and guilt—would she and Daniel have been like that, after twenty years, if they had stayed together?—so it wouldn't spoil their time together.

Joel and Emily, in the hospital. Their three children were probably paralyzed with the shock. There was a production coming up in just another week at Homespun. Was it *Taming of the Shrew*, or something else Shakespearean? And what about Joel's responsibilities at BWU? Who would teach his classes while he was in the hospital? It was a good thing BWU's final production of the year was finished and the set dismantled, or there would be that to think about.

It suddenly made sense for Daniel to go to the hospital. He would confer with Max and probably the General, and figure things out.

Lynette paused on her way back to the bathroom as another thought made her ache, and tears touched her eyes.

Daniel was there for the Randolph children, as he had never been *allowed* to be there for his own daughter.

Lynette barely dried herself before she got dressed and headed for the hospital. The Randolphs were new friends, but they were still her friends, and she could be there for Daniel, at least.

Chapter Eleven

"So, she's the lady Dad was smirking about?" Max asked. She raised her head from the stack of notes she and Daniel conferred over, and tipped her head, gesturing to the other side of the long hospital waiting room.

For a moment, Daniel just stared, wondering what she was talking about. Then he followed her line of sight and saw Lynette sitting with Jeanette Marshall, Pastor Glenn's secretary. Both women had cell phones, and they worked through a checklist Max and her brothers had scribbled down during the long night of waiting, calling people who needed to know about the accident.

Daniel allowed a weary smile, just for a moment, and turned back to meet Max's dark, knowing, weary eyes. He nodded, and they went back to deciphering Joel's handwriting so Daniel could take over his classes for the rest of the semester.

"Mom really likes her," Max commented a little later. Her voice cracked a little on the first word.

Emily was already upstairs in ICU. Thanks to head injuries when a drunk driver plowed into their car with a semi truck last night, she was in a coma. Joel's leg was shattered and he had required nearly eighty stitches from numerous lacerations all over his body. His outlook was better only because the doctors just didn't know anything yet about Emily.

Daniel remembered what Joel and Emily had told him about Max at Christmas. Did she wish her real father was here to help out? Or did she resent him? Did she blame him, in that twisted way that came with grief? Did she think that if he had stuck around and married her mother, none of this would be happening? What if Kat were in the same situation? What if something had happened to her and Lynette before he found them again? Who would have been there for Kat, when she really needed her father?

Lynette went with Jeanette to run a few errands: food and fresh clothes for the Randolph children and to pick up Jeanette's little boy, BJ, now that Sunday school was about to end. She wasn't there when the wave of university students invaded the hospital just before lunch. Daniel laughed at the irony and wondered if that was God's mercy or His sense of humor, that Kat just missed her mother. She would have been totally confused to see Lynette there, helping out. For all Kat knew, her mother didn't know the Randolphs, didn't go to Tabor Christian, and certainly didn't spend time with her advisor.

The roommates came in together, which was expected. Bekka hugged Max, and Amy gave her a big basket of cookies and apples. From the aroma, the cookies had just come out of the oven. Max's two brothers drifted over, probably drawn by the smell. Daniel smiled, watching the little exchange. Amy might have a whiplash tongue sometimes, but her heart was in the right place.

Kat hung back, watching, offering shy little smiles, not saying much to anyone. Daniel wasn't surprised when she drifted over and just stood with him.

"He's going to be okay," he offered after a few minutes of silence. She had only greeted him with another crooked little smile. "We're still waiting for word on Emily."

"It's not fair," Kat muttered.

"No, it probably isn't. Who ever said life was fair?" That earned him an exasperated look, which was an improvement. Daniel dared to rest his hand on her shoulder. Kat flinched, then the shattering tension fled under his touch. "They're in God's hands, Kat."

"Is it that easy for you?"

"It's never easy." He offered her a smile and wished he could put his arms around her and let her lean against him.

Daniel wished she would cry on his shoulder and say she was glad it wasn't him, her father, in that operating room right now, having his leg put back together like a jigsaw puzzle.

"Mom talks about God a lot more lately. I guess that's good. I wish I knew God like Bekka does. I mean—" She cleared her throat nervously and shrugged. "With all the garbage she's gone through lately, if she didn't have God, she'd be crazy."

"You can know God just as closely. Just ask. He's been waiting all your life to be the father you never had."

Kat stiffened and really looked at him for several seconds. Tears made her eyes appear huge. Daniel mentally kicked himself for that slip.

"If that was my dad in there," she whispered, "I'd be falling to pieces. Does God help that much?"

"When we let Him."

"Morgan!" The General bombed through the doorway, nearly knocking aside several students from Joel's advanced stagecraft class. "I just heard. What can we do? Where are the children?"

Kat offered him a shaky little smile, rolled her eyes in exasperation, and danced out of the way. Daniel didn't get to see her or talk to her for the rest of her visit. He didn't even see her leave.

Please, Lord, was it enough? Daniel let himself speculate that God had allowed the Randolphs' accident to bring about this conversation, to prompt Kat thinking in that direction.

Was that arrogance? He prayed not. He prayed this was all part of a larger plan, and the suffering everyone endured today would be well worth it; the results and blessings worth the price paid.

When Lynette returned later that afternoon, he made sure she stayed with him and held her hand the entire time.

What if that was Lynette in the hospital, suffering from a catastrophic accident? Would he have this foundation of peace under his grief and concern?

Lynette had grown up in church, but she had fallen away. Would she be able to face all this pain and uncertainty if it was happening to her? Daniel vowed to get her to talk with Pastor Glenn, soon, and make sure.

Tuesday, April 22

"You're kidding." Daniel looked down the long hospital hallway, waiting for someone to jump out and say "gotcha." He really expected Joel to pop out, despite the cast encasing him from hips to toes—and asleep when Daniel checked on him five minutes ago—and laugh at his reaction.

"Please?" Max twisted her face into what Emily called the "pitiful puppy-dog" expression.

It worked better with Jeremy and Joe. Max had too much mischief in her, under normal circumstances, for anyone to believe her innocent act. It was even less effective today. Her color was better, and she looked like she had managed to get some sleep last night.

"Me? Play Petruchio?" Something deep inside him started cheering, jumping up and down excitedly. Like he had felt when he was still a student and got the plum part in a production.

"Dad agreed with me that you're the best bet."

"Yeah, but I'd really examine any decisions Joel is making lately. Especially since he was probably half-asleep and doped up when you asked him."

"Morgan... " She crossed her arms, took a step back and waited. Max knew him too well. She knew he was dying to get back on the stage, even if it meant less than a week to learn his part and fit into the pacing and by-play the rest of the ensemble had already established.

"You know I'll do it." Daniel squeezed her shoulder, giving her a little shake before he released her. "You can always depend on my ego."

"Ego schmeego. You're a sucker for people in a bind. Can you come by early tomorrow for rehearsal, so Della and Gretchen can get you fitted for the costume? Dad's built a little wider than you are, but the height is a good match, so there shouldn't be that much work to alter it."

"You were really sure I'd say yes, weren't you?"

"With suitable groveling and inducing guilt, yeah."

They laughed together as they walked down the hall to the elevator. Morning visiting hours were over. Daniel had tried to slip in between classes, hoping to catch Joel awake. Life was going to be hectic, his schedule tight, until Joel was out of the hospital and up to speed on life. It was already accepted that until Joel was allowed to drive, he wouldn't come back to teaching. Daniel and the General would have to cover all his classes and administer his final exams. Fortunately, Joel Randolph was so super-organized, he made his colleagues look bad. Thank goodness there were only three weeks left to school and *Taming of the Shrew* would only last two weeks.

When Daniel got back to his office, he called Lynette to tell her he was taking over Joel's part in the play. She was delighted for him. For a short while.

"There's something in your voice," she said. "Like you're hiding bad news from me."

"Not exactly hiding. Just not too happy to tell you about it." He took a deep breath and let it out as a slow sigh. "That means my evenings are tied up until the run is over, and my weekends, studying the part, and probably my lunch hours. The ones I don't lose to Joel's classes, that is. Not much time for us."

"Oh." Silence for a few seconds. "Well, don't you need someone to prompt you and read the other parts? I played a mean Katarina when you took that directing class, if you can remember back that far."

"You'd do that?"

"For Joel and Emily? Of course." Lynette managed a chuckle. "Besides, I have this great fantasy of spending the afternoon in the park with a picnic lunch, performing Shakespeare for the birds and deer. Sounds kind of... romantic. Don't you think?"

"Lyn, you are the greatest. I owe you. Big time."

"Well then, you can make the picnic lunch, how about that?"

"It's a deal."

Tuesday, April 29

Lynette shivered and wrapped her arms around herself to keep from falling down. Or bursting out in nervous giggles. Tonight was opening night for Homespun Theater's *Taming of the Shrew*, and she could hardly breathe for excitement. Daniel would be the star again, just like he deserved. Their lives hadn't taken the paths she imagined all those years ago when they had dreamed together, but tonight, Lynette willingly agreed with Daniel that things had turned out far better for both of them. He was happy doing what he was doing, helping others reach their dreams. She wouldn't give up Kat for the brightest lights on Broadway or Playhouse Square, or top billing in a multi-million-dollar epic.

Tonight was Daniel's night, and he wanted her there with him. Backstage, sitting next to the director's booth where she could see everything and everyone and not get run over by exits and entrances. Lynette scooted her folding chair over a little more and clutched her red rose a little closer. She prayed no one could see her clearly in the shadows, because every time she looked down at the rose, she blushed.

Daniel had been watching for her when she arrived, gave her the rose and kissed her hand when she took it. He said nothing. He didn't need to, with the love and joy and excitement glowing in his eyes. It was his opening night, but it was her moment of triumph, too. That was what she read in his eyes.

Please, God, don't let us mess up this time.

"How are you doing?" Max asked as she stepped into the tiny director's booth and put down her ever-present clipboard. She reached for her headphones and attached microphone and plugged them into the system but didn't put them on yet.

"How am I? I should be asking you," Lynette said with a chuckle.

"It's a relief finally getting to this point. Once we get over the hurdle of opening night..." She sighed and turned when someone called her name from the doorway to the Green Room. "Never ends."

Lynette nodded and laughed with her and watched Max hurry off to handle yet another catastrophe. She honestly didn't know how the young woman did it: manage the theater, keep a production from falling apart, visit her parents at least twice a day in the hospital, take care of her brothers, handle the printing company and work on her writing career. All without yanking her hair out or collapsing in exhaustion.

In the last week of crammed rehearsals and lending a helping hand with costume adjustments and repairs, she had come to know all three Randolph children. Enough to regret never having given Kat at least one sibling. What if something happened to her, and her mother wasn't there for Kat? Who could her daughter turn to? Joel's sister, Rose had arrived from out of town and had pitched in. And half the church seemed to be there day or night, like an extended family.

Family was important, and the church family just as important. What had she deprived Kat of, by turning her back on Christians in general, just because her mother's church had been so cold and judgmental? Lynette's spirits drooped as she fell back into the circle of thoughts that seemed to be old habit now. It still amazed her at times, to know Daniel had forgiven her and wanted a future with her. She thought she knew her daughter well enough to expect Kat to forgive her. Eventually. But what if it took twenty years? Could she survive the pain, the emptiness, the waiting?

At times like this, Lynette seriously considered asking Daniel to step back. Leave it at just friends. Promise never to tell Kat he was her father. She was afraid. She wanted the status quo to remain. Forever, if possible.

"Guess who volunteered to help usher tonight?" Daniel appeared out of the darkness behind her. He laughed and squeezed her shoulders when Lynette yelped in shock.

Then she turned and looked at him and burst out laughing. Daniel wore his boots and hosen for Petruchio's costume, and the long shirt that went under his doublet. He had a long, stained towel draped around his shoulders, and half his makeup applied. Even in the shadows, he looked like an escapee from a brothel, all his features exaggerated.

For a man his age, he still looked good in tights, too.

"Yeah, laugh all you want. Just don't laugh during the performance, that's all I ask." Daniel scowled at her, but she was close enough to see the laughter dancing in his eyes. He caught her by her elbows, lifted her from her chair, and guided her over to the side of the proscenium, where they could pull back the heavy red velvet curtain and peek out. "Take a look."

Mystified, Lynette obeyed. It took a few moments for her eyes to adjust from the backstage shadows to the bright lights above the audience. Then she saw, and nearly dropped her rose.

Kat led a gang of friends from school down the side aisle, showing them to their seats. She handed them programs and neatly danced out of the way of a group heading for a block of seats on the inside center section.

"Seems like half the theater students volunteered to help out any way they can," Daniel said.

"They all love Joel," Lynette managed to respond without sounding too wooden.

Her earlier giddy feelings returned but chilled with panic. She could only be grateful she had a backstage seat. What if Kat saw her there? How could she explain to her daughter why she was here? How could she explain being on a first-name basis with the entire cast and tech crew?

Lynette managed to smile and wish Daniel luck the backhanded theater way—*break a leg*—and settled down in her seat again when he hurried back to finish getting dressed. Her head felt light and her legs wobbled, and she was glad Max hadn't come back yet.

When was she going to tell Kat about her relationship with Daniel? Like he said, they had to tell her soon, before someone in town dropped the news on her like a bombshell. Kat would never forgive either one of them.

But she was afraid. How could she ever explain the whole cruel, unhappy story to her daughter? She wouldn't have to, if she left Daniel again. But she didn't want to do that, either.

God, please, I'm a coward and I'm selfish and I'm ashamed of what I did to all of us. Please. Fix things?

Friday, May 2

"Where are the girls?" Lynette asked as she lugged her sewing machine through the door of the apartment.

"At the theater." Kat barely looked up as she dumped the armload of curtains and hardware on the sofa, then staggered over to close the door.

After six months, the roommates had decided it was time to exchange the threadbare sheet over the sliding door to their miniscule balcony for a real curtain. Lynette had several sets of curtains salvaged from the house in Stoughton, which she was glad to donate. They needed major adjustments, though. Kat had been delighted to spend Friday night sewing with her mother, which made Lynette suspect boy trouble. Either another young swain refused to take no for an answer and go away after two dates, or Kat was caught between new heartthrob and old. Either way, it meant she could spend some precious time with her daughter. Lynette felt just guilty enough about her secret relationship with Daniel, she would have gladly given up more than a Friday night to help her daughter.

She really should tell Kat. There had to be some way to work up to it. But just how did one casually work into the conversation that she was dating—seriously, eagerly—her daughter's favorite teacher?

Maybe she should start with "Daniel's your father," and while Kat convinced her heart to start beating again, mention that they were dating.

"What are they doing up there?" Lynette asked instead. "It's finals next week. Don't they have to study?"

"Half their classes are term papers instead of finals." Kat grimaced. "The rats already have their papers finished and handed in. They're kissing up to the General right now."

"Kat!" Still, she had to laugh at the smug tone in her daughter's voice.

"They're desperate for lab hours and work-study money, and the General agreed to send some sacrificial lambs over to the summer drama program for Hyberg's rec department. He already picked the script, so they're spending the weekend getting the costumes and props organized." She snickered as she snaked the extension cord under the rickety dining room table so they could set up the ancient sewing machine. "I bet Bekka's wishing she never gave up working for Morgan."

"She needed more flexibility and you know it. Are you going to help them out tomorrow?"

"No way. I have a date with Roger." Kat frowned. "Or is it Shane?"

"Kat! Please don't tell me you're dating two boys at once." Lynette bit her tongue before she added "you know what happened last time."

Last time, Mike had threatened both boys when they showed up at the house at the same time. It had seemed cute and fatherly to Lynette back then. Knowing about his unhealthy interest in Kat now, she could only shudder. Protectiveness looked more like jealousy and possessiveness, in hindsight. She refused to remind her daughter of that time in their lives.

How would Daniel handle this?

"What's so funny, Mom?" Kat asked, pausing in dumping out the storage boxes of hooks and pins and other curtain hardware.

"Nothing. Just remembering something from work."

Truthfully, she had laughed at the mental image of Daniel getting both boys to play basketball or something else, to deflect them from their anger, and Kat left dumfounded on the sidelines.

She really should tell Kat about Daniel. He was right, after all. How much longer could they spend time together without being discovered? Everybody in town seemed to know and like Daniel, and as she spent more time working at Blooming Miracles, she came to know more people on a first-name basis. Sooner or later, someone who knew Kat and knew Lynette would make the connection, whether in looks or last name, and then it would all blow up in their faces.

Somehow, though, the opportunity never came up that night while mother and daughter sorted through the curtains to decide on the color, then tried to figure out what hardware would work on the antiquated rod over the balcony door. They could have just started fresh, but Lynette wasn't up to taking down the rod and buying a new one. She didn't trust Kat with power tools and was very thankful her daughter had the sense to stick to costuming and painting rather than set construction for her lab requirements. She had panicked when she heard Kat built the rigging for BWU's production of *H.M.S. Pinafore* last year, but that was before she found out it entailed tying knots and using super-bonding glue, and nothing more.

Then Bekka and Amy showed up, with boxes and boxes and more boxes of dusty wooden swords and boots and costumes and crowns and other paraphernalia to stage a massive children's theater production of *The Princess and the Pea*. They went back and forth between the apartment and the parking lot five times, which explained why they didn't walk from the theater as they usually did in good weather. The last time they returned, there seemed to be some feud going on between Bekka and Amy over the mail. Lynette chose to stay out of it, but she did notice Bekka stashed a large envelope in her room rather quickly. Then both girls collapsed into the nearest chairs.

"That's the last of it," Amy sighed.

"Now we have to sort everything," Bekka added with a groan.

"I have to admire you girls, taking on a big project like that," Lynette said, pausing to bite a thread.

"They need brownie points with the General. I wouldn't do summer drama with little kids to save my life." Kat wrinkled up her nose at them.

"You're just gloating because you get paid to help Morgan do research all summer in a nice, air-conditioned building." Amy couldn't seem to get up the energy to snarl.

Lynette doubted it was simply exhaustion from carting those boxes around. Daniel had mentioned some big change going on in Amy's relationship with Joe, mixed in with the sudden break in his music career. Lynette rather hoped the two of them were growing up. They made a cute couple, and she hoped they stayed together. She smiled, deciding that Daniel's concern for his students was just one more thing in her constantly growing list of *Why I have to keep Daniel in my life, or die trying*.

"Don't you wish you were?" Kat batted her eyelashes at Amy. That seemed to dredge up energy from unknown depths.

Amy leaped from her chair and reached for Kat's ponytails with both hands. Kat squealed and ran for their room. Bekka just exchanged a grin with Lynette and slouched deeper into the couch. Lynette shook her head, refusing to rescue Kat, and calmly went on with the sewing.

~~~~~

The sewing machine, already an antique when Lynette inherited it in high school, decided to play stubborn. Between the four of them and Bekka's considerable tech skills learned in years of backstage work, they got one panel of curtains reworked and hung. In between pizza and two silly movies and banana splits. Then the sewing machine dug in its heels and refused to cooperate. By quarter of midnight, Lynette was tired, her back hurt from bending over the machine, and her fingers had too many pinpricks to be counted. Besides, she had plans to spend the day at the zoo with Daniel on Saturday, and she needed her rest.

She went home with the news un-spilled and Kat still trying to remember who she had a date with the next day. Lynette knew Daniel would laugh when she told him.

It felt good, she realized, to share her life with someone who really cared. Someone who valued her for all her various facets, and not just as a trophy.

Maybe that was why she was so slow to tell Kat about her relationship with Daniel. Maybe she was afraid of becoming a trophy again, when they could become public with their relationship.

"Don't be stupid," she scolded herself in the privacy of her car. "Daniel's not like that. If anything, you should be eager to show him off as *your* trophy." The idea made her giggle; a sure sign of just how tired she was.
~~~~~

That piece of humor, however, she wouldn't share with him.

Saturday, May 31

"Morgan!" Max Randolph darted out of the doorway of Stay-a-While and snatched at his arm.

"Nice to see you, too, Max," he said, chuckling. "Where's the fire?"

"Are you busy? Can you sit with us? Just ten minutes?" She pulled on his arm hard enough to dislocate it.

Whatever Max wanted, Daniel could see with one glance that she was excited, not worried or upset or afraid. Whatever she wanted from him meant a lot to her. Besides, he didn't have anything pressing. He wanted to walk down the street to Blooming Miracles and see how soon Lynette was getting off work, so they could go to Lodi for some shopping at the outlet stores, but no hurry for anything. Nodding, Daniel let her lead him into the coffee shop.

Steve Coheny, one of the new technicians at Homespun sat in a booth with Tony Martin. Daniel was a little surprised to see the two young men together. During the production of *Shrew,* and afterward, Steve's interest in Max had brought out some latent jealousy in Tony. Daniel had approved of the jealousy and hoped it would lead to another step upward in Max and Tony's relationship.

"Morgan, this is... well, you know Steve," Max said as they approached the booth. "And this is—"

"Daniel, it's been a long time," Carlo Vincente said, leaning out from behind Steve. He held out a hand, which Daniel gladly shook.

Carlo Vincente had been a romantic lead in Hollywood thirty years ago. He had starred in half a dozen movies with Emily Keeler-Randolph. One of the elder statesmen of Hollywood, he worked behind the scenes nowadays, promoting education and charitable efforts and bringing dignity to an increasingly hedonistic profession.

"You know each other?" Max, Tony and Steve said almost in unison.

"Yes. Daniel was stage manager when I worked that summer stock production in Long Island... oh, sixteen years ago, wasn't it?" Carlo smiled and nudged Steve. "Get a chair for him, would you? You can stay and talk a while, can't you?"

"I'd love to," Daniel said, and snagged a chair from the table behind him before Steve could get up. "It's been a long time. What are you doing in Tabor? It's great to see you again."

"Now you've gone and spoiled all my fun," Max grumbled.

"Fun?" Daniel looked at the four at the table and felt that odd little shiver up his spine, warning him that he had walked into something extremely interesting.

"Well, it's kind of complicated," she began.

"Tell me about it," Tony grumbled. "I'm in the middle of it, and I'm still twisted around sometimes."

"Okay." She glanced at Carlo, who winked at her. Max blushed, which she didn't do very often. "You know that Dad—I mean, Joel Randolph isn't my real father. He didn't marry Mom until I was five."

Daniel felt like the entire balcony of Homespun Theater had fallen on his head. He rested his elbows on the end of the table and looked back and forth between Carlo and Max. The idea that burst into his mind made too much sense.

"Carlo is my father and Steve is my brother. I have *five* brothers all of a sudden. It's just disgusting," Max added with a snort of laughter.

"As soon as things settle down after *Our Town* is over, and Joel and Emily are both up to full strength, we're trying to talk Max and Tony into coming out for a visit," Carlo said. "Her stepmother and her other two brothers are very eager to get to know her. And her fiancé," he added, nodding to Tony.

"This is a dream, right?" Daniel said. From the grins on Tony and Max's faces, he knew it was too real, but he couldn't resist teasing them. "I thought you two would never figure it out. I even have a bet with the General, to see how many years it'd take you two to wake up."

"I hope you lost," Max growled. That earned laughter from Steve and Carlo.

"Congratulations. I bet your parents are ecstatic." Daniel held out a hand to shake theirs.

"With everything that's been going on," Steve muttered, "I think maybe they don't know yet."

That earned more laughter from the others at the table. Daniel excused himself to step over to the counter and order something to drink. He could just tell it was going to take quite a long time to hear the full story behind these sudden changes, revelations and discoveries, and he wanted to hear every word of it.

~~~~~

Two hours later, he finally tore himself away from the quartet to hurry down the street to Blooming Miracles. Daniel could only shake his head in wonder at the story he had heard. Of secrets kept, families divided, and the revelations and forgiveness that had come as a result of Joel and Emily's accident a month before.

Tony had come home from his writer-in-residence stint in California, finally aware of how much Max meant to him, and walked straight into the middle of the catastrophe that had surrounded the Randolph household. He had proved his love by being there for Max every step of the way.
~~~~~

News of the accident and the amazing rediscovery of Emily Keeler after twenty-five years of silence had reached all the way to Hollywood. Steve had come looking for his half-sister, after piecing together clues. He had used his mother's maiden name to keep his identity as Carlo Vincente's prodigal son hidden. At the same time, Carlo trying to learn whether a talented new writer in Hollywood was not only Emily's child, but his. The family reunion had been rocky, complicated by someone trying to steal Max's identity and a major writing cash prize. Judging by the growing ease between Carlo and his children, Daniel knew God had been bringing healing there, too.

He couldn't wait to see Joel and Emily and chew them out for keeping him in the dark.

If only he could hope for such a happy ending for Lynette, Kat and himself. The similarities between Carlo and Emily's story and his own separation from Lynette gave him hope.

Daniel wished he could tell Lynette, but he just didn't know how she would take the news. Would she take hope from Carlo's joyful reaction to learning he had a daughter? Would she decide to tell Kat her father's identity?

"Probably not," Daniel whispered as he crossed the street and glimpsed Lynette in the window of Blooming Miracles. "She can't even tell our daughter we're dating. How can she handle something bigger?"

He sighed and left it in God's hands once again.

Chapter Twelve

Thursday, June 12

"Shane again?"

Daniel leaned back and watched Bekka search through his library. There weren't many students he trusted enough to loan any of his precious, sometimes irreplaceable textbooks and research books. Bekka was one of the few. As a writer herself, she could be trusted to treat every book as a treasure. Daniel put his sneaker-clad feet up on his desk and prepared himself for whatever lonely hearts advice Bekka might need.

It was good practice for whenever Kat came to him, if she ever did. Two weeks into June, and Lynette still hadn't told her the truth. Daniel felt like a nag and a heel every time he brought up the subject, because she always seemed to give him those deer-in-the-headlights looks.

What Lynette could be afraid of, simply telling Kat they were dating, he couldn't quite comprehend. To keep her in his life, he was willing to let her take her time. Up to a point.

"What about him?" he finally asked.

"Kat got caught between Shane and that Roger Alcott jerk who runs around with the beret and phony French accent."

"What do you mean, 'caught'?" His feet came down from the desk with a thud. Not easy to do with sneakers on carpeting.

"She set up a date with both of them for the same time, same day."

"Oh, great." Still, he had to grin. Lynette had told him of Kat's occasional goofs in scheduling her dates.

"They both decided she was a ditz and dumped her." Bekka took a deep breath. Let it out. Took another one. "Then Shane came back later that evening and asked me out."

"Hate to say it, but it sounds like rebound to me."

"He said it wasn't. He said he even wanted to ask me before he asked Kat, but someone told him I was dating, almost engaged... I don't want to know who. I don't even want to guess, but out there in the world is someone who knew a guy was interested in me and got in the way." She let out a mock growl, prompting a snort of laughter from Daniel. "Anyway, we hit a silent film festival at the Cinematique. Did you know he rides a motorcycle? And he never takes off that cowboy hat of his." From Bekka's grin, Daniel decided that didn't bother her at all. "But that's not the weird part. When he dropped me off, he said he'd look for me in church in the morning. He goes to *our* church!"

"At least you don't have to worry about that part," he offered.

"Yeah, I know. But going to church isn't the same as being a Christian. I figured, you have to know more about him than me."

"Isn't it a little early to start worrying about getting that serious?"

"Well..." Bekka grinned. "It's more like a month now, and we have at least two dates a week."

"Moving fast." Daniel whistled. To his delight, she blushed.

"I really need to find out, before I go any further. You know?" She settled on the edge of his desk. "You had Shane in a couple of classes, and you mentioned Dr. Holwood talked about him. What do you think?"

"What do I think of him?" Daniel sat back, making his swivel chair creak. He stared at a point on his unusually clean desk — always a little too clean at the beginning of summer break — and tapped the end of his pen against his teeth as he thought.

Bekka sighed, a grin breaking the serious cast of her face. After years as his assistant, she knew better than to hover so close and wait while he thought. She shook her head and got up off her perch. She wandered around the corner of the office where Daniel had recently shelved all the new books he had accumulated over the past semester.

Bekka and Shane Hopkins? Daniel liked the idea more every time he considered it. They suited each other. Shane was another one of those perpetual students. Despite his motorcycle cowboy appearance, he was a solid, intelligent young man, and worked as many part-time jobs as Bekka. Most recently, he had started working at the Gold Tone Gym, and Vic Thomas spoke highly of him. Shane attended the *Bible in History* class Daniel now taught on Sunday, and his questions as well as his answers showed deep thought and insight. Daniel nodded, satisfied. He could trust Shane to take good care of Bekka.

It was high time she had someone in her life, looking after her.

"Dr. Morgan?" Marco asked, coming into the office with his shoulders hunched and his hands jammed into his back pockets.

"Well, I haven't seen you around here for a while." Daniel glanced over his shoulder at Bekka.

She shook her head and darted back into hiding.

"I don't—"

"Usually, you're following Kat around like a lovesick puppy. It's kind of cute, I suppose, as long as you don't turn into a stalker." Daniel thought of what Bekka had just told him about Shane and Roger and Kat's date debacle. What that girl needed was someone steady.

Come to think of it, Marco certainly fit the bill.

"I need to talk to you about Kat," the young man blurted.

"Advice? I haven't been too successful in the romance area myself."

"Until recently," Bekka muttered, just loudly enough Daniel heard.

He sat up straight, stifling an urge to pick up a stray book and heave it at her before she burst out laughing. She was probably hidden around the corner, out of reach, anyway. The last thing poor Marco needed was to know he had an audience.

"What's with you and Kat?" Marco demanded. His voice cracked. "I mean, are you two—"

"Not that it's any of your business, but I'm seeing someone about twenty years older right now."

"Yeah?" The relief that made Marco's eyes glow reminded Daniel of himself, in those first uncertain days of his college relationship with Lynette.

"You think Kat dumped you for me? Flattering, but... I'm not that kind of guy. Kat's been hurt. She doesn't trust men very easily."

"She trusts you."

"Maybe I'm the father figure she needs," Daniel drawled. He grinned, knowing Lynette would wallop him if she had heard him.

"Nah. You're not that old."

"Thanks. I think."

"But what do I do about Kat? She's—I mean, I really—I knew she was the one I wanted, the first time I saw her."

"Then don't give up. Be there when she needs you. Keep trying. She'll finally notice you're always there and you'll get your chance."

"You think so?"

"It worked for me. The right lady is worth waiting for. No matter how long it takes."

"Thanks. You have no idea how much better that makes me feel."

"Hey, I've been in the same boat. But I'll tell you something, Kat really likes Cedar Point. If you wave some tickets under her nose..." Daniel chuckled and Marco joined him a few seconds later.

He waited until Marco's footsteps vanished up the stairs out of the faculty dungeon before he turned to face the corner as Bekka emerged from hiding. She had that crooked little smile he had learned to draw from his students, when they weren't sure if he was going to praise them for brilliance or put them in their place for displaying undeserved arrogance.

He knew, as if he had been watching over her shoulder, that she had indeed seen him with Lynette on the ferry from Put-in-Bay. She had probably seen Lynette with him and the General at the Guardians game. But for some reason, Bekka had chosen to keep silent about it. He appreciated it, even as some truly nasty, cranky part of him wished she had spilled the beans long ago. He wouldn't break his promise to Lynette that he'd wait for her to tell Kat, but that didn't mean he couldn't pray someone else would do it first.

"So, that's why you think suddenly I'm an expert in dating," Daniel drawled, breaking the silence when the tension in the room rose a few more notches. "When did you guess?"

"I didn't guess, I've seen you and Kat's mom together a few times. So, about Shane—"

"He's attending my class on biblical history. He seems sincere enough. Ask him yourself." Daniel winked. "I suppose it would be out of line to ask what you think Kat's reaction will be when she finds out?"

"Depends on what she finds out."

"Uh oh." His smile faltered. "What's going on in that amazing brain of yours, Rebekah Sanderson?"

"I kind of put some things together at Thanksgiving. You two seemed to know each other a whole lot better than people who just met, and you both studied theater at Northwestern at the same time and..."

"We're picking up an old romance. Yes."

"I haven't said anything to Kat or Amy. Swear. I figure it's your business *when* she finds out. And *what* she finds out."

"You're subtle. And thanks for not asking."

"Sure." Bekka took a deep breath. "So, how—"

"Are things going between Lynette and me? Well, I've got her coming to church fairly regularly. We see each other at least once a week, besides church." Daniel let out a deep breath that could have been a sigh. "Some prayers would be a big help."

"Okay. But I wasn't asking about that." She tried for a grin. "I meant to ask, how about the four of us double-dating some time?"

If there was ever a time he wished he could hug one of his students, it was now. Daniel thanked God for Bekka in his and Kat's and Lynette's lives, even as their shared laughter echoed out to the stairwell.

Thursday, July 3

"We're being silly." Lynette slid down the wall under the phone until she rested on the floor with her heels against her bottom and her knees almost in her ears. "Look at the time! We should both be fast asleep. And it's not like we didn't see each other at all today, or we won't be together all day tomorrow."

"Bright and early," Daniel said over the phone, sounding too chipper for eleven at night, after a long day helping at Homespun Theater.

"You're sure I can't bring anything?"

"Well—"

"Ah hah! I knew it. The General is a wonderful host and I'm sure we're going to have a perfect day cruising on the Goodtime, but I know he can't think of all the details."

"Potato salad."

"What?" She was sure she hadn't heard Daniel correctly.

"Potato salad. He hates it, so he never orders it, but what's a picnic at the lake without potato salad?"

Anyone else, she would have accused him of making it up, but Lynette knew the General well enough by now to believe anything Daniel said about the man's eccentricities. And Daniel did love potato salad. Sometimes it had been the only edible food on the cafeteria's alleged salad bar in school, and he had always been delighted to take it.

"All right, but I am not starting a batch of potato salad at this time of night. Is deli salad all right with you?"

"Only kind I eat."

"What time are you picking me up?"

"How about ten?"

Later, she laughed at how easily that went. She had been avoiding Daniel coming to the house for so long, and he didn't even react when she specifically asked him to pick her up.

"Maybe at this rate, we'll be ready to tell Kat we're dating... by Christmas," she told her too-quiet kitchen after Daniel hung up.

In answer, the phone rang. Kat wanted to borrow her picnic basket. Lynette held her breath, waiting for her daughter to babble about her current swain, and then ask what her mother was doing for Fourth of July. Maybe she could say something like, "A picnic with Morgan and the General and the Randolphs, it's late, I'm going to bed, see you in the morning, love you," and hang up the phone?

Lynette was almost disappointed when her daughter did none of the expected. The conversation ended before she could brace herself. The house was too quiet when she turned off the lights and got ready for bed.

Friday, July 4

Lynette overslept the next morning and had to rush. She forgot the picnic basket, had to go back, and nearly forgot to stop at Heinke's for the potato salad before going to Kat's apartment to drop off the basket. Then she worried about her outfit as she hurried to the deli counter.

Did she look infantile, or too youthful, or just plain silly or overdressed in her floppy brimmed hat and snappy pale green outfit? She had thought it looked perfect for a picnic at Huntington Beach and then a cruise up the Cuyahoga River and along the shores of Lake Erie, because it had a nautical look with its square collar and the little gold anchors embroidered on all the pockets and seams.

Don't be ridiculous. You look fine, and it's too late to change.

The way her morning was going, Daniel would be waiting in the driveway by the time she got back from dropping the basket off with Kat.

Lynette heard voices through the apartment door before she rang the bell. Male voices, as well as the girls. That probably meant Kat's date was there, along with Amy's Joe. If she was lucky, the boys had just arrived.

Bekka opened the door, and there was something about her grin when she let Lynette in that made her wonder what was up. Sure enough, Amy and Joe, and Kat and a boy who looked vaguely familiar stood in the living room, looking ready to take off in their various directions for the day. Lynette breathed a sigh of relief. Now, if she could just get this over with and away so she wouldn't make Daniel wait, the day would be salvaged.

"Here you are, honey. Sorry I'm late, but I had to run through Heinke's and get some potato salad for my picnic." Lynette held out the basket to Kat and started to turn to leave.

There, that wasn't so bad. Break it to her in little pieces that I have a social life she doesn't know about.

The thought made her want to giggle.

"Are you going out today, Mom?" Kat blurted, staring.

"Oh, don't sound so surprised. I still have a few good years left in me."

"You look great, Mrs. Tyler," Amy said.

"Sorry, Amy. It's Lynette Teague, now. I finally got rid of Mike's name."

"And there was much rejoicing..." Kat murmured.

"Well, what do we call you now?" Amy asked.

"Lynette is fine with me." A response which made her daughter choke a little.

"We can't—I mean, you're Kat's mom," Bekka said.

"Then call me Mom. I always wanted a lot of daughters." Lynette spread her arms as if to embrace all three roommates.

"I don't know," Amy murmured.

"Can I call you Mom?" Joe asked, pasting a smarmy smile onto his face.

"Only if you marry one of my daughters." Lynette winked at Amy. Joe froze, eyes widening, which brought laughter from the others.

Then the doorbell rang.

"This place is like Grand Central Station," the somewhat familiar young man said as he reached to open the door just a step ahead of Bekka.

No, Lynette did recognize him. He was Marco, the boy Kat had over for Thanksgiving dinner. Didn't Daniel tell her how Marco was turning into a stalker, and he had actually advised the young man not to give up on Kat? Lynette smothered a giggle, delighted to find the advice had been taken, and her daughter had actually broken her "no more than two dates" rule. Maybe things were changing. She certainly hoped so.

"Kat, I just came to tell you —" Daniel stopped short, one foot still in the hallway. "Oh, hi, Lyn." He grinned at her. Judging by that shine in Daniel's eyes, she had chosen a good outfit.

It was all going to come out now, she realized. Maybe it was the best way. With plenty of witnesses, Kat couldn't go too ballistic. Or could she?

"Lyn?" Kat echoed.

"Uh — my friends at ABC liked your synopses and want to see a few scripts, Kat," he continued. Daniel raised one eyebrow in question and Lynette smiled.

"Really?" Her daughter froze, but the delight was evident.

"Oh, that's wonderful, Daniel!" Lynette said. "So you still think Kat should try to get into their summer intern program next year?"

"It's a step in the right direction," Daniel said. He grinned, and she heard echoes of all their discussions of Kat's future spread over many of their dates. What else were two proud parents to talk about, but their little girl? It had felt so right, and she had been able to share so much of Kat's childhood with him during those times, too.

"Still?" Amy squeaked.

"Write for the soaps? No way!" Kat broke her paralysis and nearly dropped the picnic basket clutched in her arms.

"What is wrong with that?" Lynette said. "You'd be closer to the industry than if you stayed here in Cleveland, writing your fingers off."

"It's the soaps, for goodness' sake! They're full of neurotics who can't keep a promise and gullible idiots who don't know a lie when they hear it. A kid goes from diapers to high school in three years and a woman with five grown children and six husbands gets pregnant. Or maybe you should wonder why a woman with six husbands and ten lovers hasn't gotten pregnant yet. It's not real!"

"If you want reality," Bekka offered, "go work at the Mission in the senior center or with the abused women, or work with snotty sixth graders in a summer drama program. That's reality."

"Excuse me," Amy said in a very soft voice, "but I'm wondering about this 'still' remark. You two talk about Kat a lot?"

"Well, not a lot... We talk about other things, too," Lynette said, her face warming as she met Daniel's gaze. He just grinned wider. It was the moment of truth, and she hoped he was fully prepared not to let anyone steamroller them.

"I didn't know you were talking at all," Kat said.

"Your mother is a grown woman and your advisor's romantic life is none of your business, young lady," Daniel responded with just a little too much smile.

"Get ready for the explosion," Marco murmured.

"Explosion?" Kat whispered. She tried to smile and only got a stiff grimace. "So, you two are—like—dating?"

"We certainly are. In fact, I was on my way over to your mother's house to pick her up. The General is taking all of us on the Goodtime's holiday cruise." Daniel grinned at Lynette and offered his arm. "Since we're both here, why don't you just go with me now?"

"That sounds good." Lynette's face felt definitely warmer as she slid her arm into Daniel's. "See you girls later. Have a good time."

The five left behind in the apartment were utterly silent as the door closed. Lynette listened, but she heard nothing as she and Daniel went to the elevator. They didn't say anything until the doors had closed safely between them and Kat.

"Well, that went extremely well," Daniel muttered, and he slumped back against the wall of the elevator with exaggerated relief.

Lynette snorted, trying to muffle a totally undignified giggle. Daniel grinned. Before the doors opened two floors later, they were both leaning on each other, laughing quietly with tears in their eyes. The apartment building and the parking lot were fairly deserted, which was a relief. They kept their arms linked as they hurried to the parking lot. Lynette glanced back once to see if anyone was watching, even though she knew Kat's balcony looked out over the Metroparks behind the building, not the parking lot and the street.

"Did you notice Marco in there?" Daniel said, after they retrieved her potato salad from her car and got into his car. He pulled out his keys.

"I think it's a good sign. For both of them."

"He's a good kid."

"And you trust him with Kat?" She muffled another chuckle when Daniel had the grace to color a little and look sheepish. "Danny, you're acting and sounding like a father. I like it."

"Yeah, I kind of like it myself." He winked at her as he turned the key in the ignition.

"You're good with kids," she said, after they had stopped at her house to pick up her bag packed for the day. "If you had gone to Hollywood, you would have missed your true calling."

Daniel nodded. He smiled, but there were shadows in his eyes that made Lynette wonder if her words had dredged up too many painful memories.

~~~~~

Daniel remembered Lynette's words that evening as they made the return trip to the docks in Cleveland. Most of the cruise ship's passengers were staying out until the fireworks had ended or were so worn out from picnicking all day in the hot sun, they didn't have the energy to wander
~~~~~

the deck or make much noise. It felt like he and Lynette had the whole upper deck to themselves. Just them, the sunset, a few early sparklers being waved along the shore, and the lake.

Lynette had been more right than she knew. There was so much he would have missed if he had followed his first dreams and pursued fame and fortune. He might have found his niche immediately, risen to stardom — and then fallen away to obscurity. Look at Emily Randolph, for example. She had been a rising star, then left Hollywood to raise her daughter alone. The accident in April had brought Emily to the public's attention again, and none of the Randolph family particularly seemed to enjoy it. Some good had come of that rough time in their lives, such as Joel's reconciliation with part of his family, and Carlo Vincente finally discovering he had a daughter. Daniel firmly believed there were more disadvantages than advantages to having dreams of glory and fame and riches come true.

He liked teaching. He enjoyed watching his students bloom into their potential and dream their dreams. In a lot of ways, Lynette was responsible for his mostly satisfactory life. He wouldn't be here if she hadn't pushed him away. Daniel knew he could never tell her that, though, because she would only feel the guilt. She would never see his gratitude. She might never see the peace he had found in his life.

Instead of trying to speak what filled his heart, Daniel put his arms around her. When she leaned into his embrace with a sleepy, happy little smile, he dared to brush a kiss against her cheek. Lynette melted a little more against him. She was soft and warm, and she blushed in the shadows cast by the setting sun behind the ship when he cupped her other cheek in his hand and turned her face enough to find her lips. She tipped her head back, leaned a little closer, and met him halfway.

Their first kiss in more than twenty years didn't have the sparks and buzz and the hungry, roller coaster satisfaction Daniel remembered. He wasn't the hot-blooded, impatient young man he was back then, either. The kiss was just the way he wanted their relationship to be for the rest of their lives. It was deep and warm and rich and gentle. It promised more and sweeter in the future. Lynette kept her eyes closed when they finished. Daniel tucked her head under his chin, looked out at the sunset-streaked water, and blinked away a few ridiculous tears.

He wouldn't go back to that hot, fumbling, rushed college romance for anything in the world.

Monday, July 7

Kat didn't call on Saturday, as Lynette expected and dreaded. She didn't stop by the house or the shop when she knew her mother would be at work.

"I don't know if she's giving me the silent treatment or if she's still in shock," Lynette confessed, when she and Daniel met for lunch at Stay-A-While two days later.

"Maybe she doesn't know what to say," he offered. "Just like we weren't quite sure how to tell her we were together."

"Together." A tiny smile relaxed some of the tension that threatened to crack her skull like a walnut. "And it wasn't *us*, it was me. Nervous and feeling guilty, which is ridiculous, because I wasn't doing anything wrong or betraying anybody."

"Maybe we were scared she'd be mad that *I* was dating someone, even her mother."

"You." Lynette stared for several long moments, then blinked and looked away across the little restaurant. A chuckle escaped her. "I remember having crushes on several professors in school. What will she do when she finds out—" The words caught in her throat.

"Who I really am?" Daniel shrugged, and this time he had to look away. Down into his coffee, as if it held the secrets of the universe.

Lynette appreciated it that he didn't say "That I'm her father" here, even though there was no one in the shop but the girl at the counter and another couple tucked away in the opposite corner booth. Certainly no one close enough to overhear and report their conversation. It still made her feel jittery, itchy inside, when she considered Kat's possible reaction to that news. She would be delighted—who wouldn't want Daniel for a father?—but that would have to wait until she got over her shock, and most likely fury. At Lynette. For years of silence and secrets and lies.

"Why don't we wait until she gets over this before we take the big step?" he continued, finally meeting her eyes again. "How about we... oh, I don't know. Take a drive along the lake on Sunday. Pack a picnic lunch and drive until we find a nice spot and just sit and talk."

"A family picnic." Why did just saying the words put such a huge, suffocating lump in her throat?

"Let's see how the three of us do together, before we think about dumping another big shock on her. I mean, it's a little late to start into the Mommy and Daddy and Baby makes three routine." Daniel tried to grin, but his mouth didn't seem to want to stay where he put it. The corners trembled enough to make Lynette want to throw herself across the booth and hold him until the ache went away.

She had done this to him. To Kat. Daniel had a right to be more than just a favorite teacher to their daughter. He had every right to confront Kat with the truth months ago. But he had held his silence in respect for Lynette's wishes.

When would she stop hurting him?

"That sounds good," she finally said. She took a deep breath. "After church? We'll have the picnic all ready, and pick up Kat straight from church, all right?"

"Sounds good." He took a deep breath, and some of the ache that caused wrinkles around his eyes eased a little. "Let's hope Kat thinks so. Do you want to call her, or should I?"

As it turned out, Lynette didn't have to call Kat. She found her daughter sitting on the front step of the condo, reading a bound sheaf of papers. Lynette suspected it was the bundle of synopses Daniel had sent to his friends in New York, which had been returned with comments written all through it. She decided to take it as a good sign that Kat looked at it, instead of throwing it out and rejecting the entire idea.

And a good sign her daughter was here, waiting for her. Wanting to talk.

At least, Lynette hoped that was what Kat wanted to do.

"So..." Kat followed her mother into the kitchen after a silent, smiled greeting at the front door. "How long have you and Morgan been dating?"

"Well, we started in college."

"Mo—om!" She sank down into the nearest chair and propped her elbows on the table, her head in her hands.

"Believe me, Kat, it was as hard getting up the courage to tell you as it was for you to finally hear it."

"You didn't tell me. It kind of popped out at everybody." Her daughter groaned and slouched back in the chair. "So, how long since you two got back together?"

"Well, Daniel helped me move."

"Does he know? You didn't tell him what that slime bag tried to do to me, did you?"

"Sweetheart." Lynette sat down in the chair opposite her and reached across the table to take her daughter's hands. "Daniel suspected there was something wrong with Mike, just like Bekka did. He was praying for you, too. When he learned about the divorce, he came to see me. I was so ashamed, and so scared he'd be angry with me."

"Angry with you? For what? You didn't do anything wrong."

"And neither did you. Remember that. You have nothing to be ashamed of. Mike was the one in the wrong, and he's the villain here. I was scared Daniel would be angry with me because I didn't take care of you, I didn't protect you. I mean, you're all grown up, but I'm still your mother."

"Yeah, but... Okay, you've been dating since March. How come you didn't tell me? Mom, it's July, for Heaven's sake!" Despite her anguished wail, which was half acting, a tiny smile caught one corner of Kat's mouth.

"How come it took you so long to catch on?" Lynette returned with a grin of her own.

"Sheesh, you'd think you two were doing something wrong."

"Maybe we slipped back to our college days. You know, sneaking around behind our parents' backs."

"You haven't been necking in the park, have you?" Kat shook her head, hurrying on before her mother could react. "No, Morgan's got too much class. He's not that kind of guy."

He used to be. Lynette sighed, wondering how much Kat's opinion of and respect for Daniel would change when she learned the whole truth.

"Has he at least tried to kiss you?"

"Kat!"

"Mom, I'm twenty years old."

"Yes, and I hope you haven't been necking in the park, either. How are you and Marco doing?" Lynette added, glad to turn the tables on her daughter, and maybe change the track of the conversation. To her delight, Kat blushed. The next half hour sped by, as Kat told her mother about Marco's persistence, his sweetness, the flowers he bought for her for no reason at all, just a single carnation or daisy. They had gone on a record five dates since they got back together. He was always there to help her with chores for Daniel.

"Uh huh. And have you had the guts to face Daniel since the Fourth?" Lynette asked.

"No. But I have to work this afternoon." Kat looked around the kitchen. "Maybe I came over here to kind of delay things?"

"No more delays. You have to face him sooner or later or lose your work-study funding. Besides, we want you to come with us on Sunday."

"Sunday? Like—to church?"

Lynette stopped for nearly three heartbeats. She had never expected her daughter to equate Sunday with church. That had to be Bekka's doing, and suddenly Lynette knew she could never do enough to express her gratitude to the older girl.

"Maybe later. Daniel was thinking the three of us should spend some time together. Go on a picnic. Along the lake somewhere. What do you think?"

"A picnic." Kat sat very still, looking at her mother, her eyes a little dazed. Abruptly, she shook herself as if waking from a dream, nodded, managed a smile. "Sure. Why not?"

Chapter Thirteen

Lynette called Daniel to warn him and give him the good news, as soon as Kat left, still promising to head over to the theater to get to work. He laughed and promised he wouldn't push things.

"It's going to work out, Lyn. You just relax and trust God and see how it works out."

"Just because you've been praying about it?" she retorted, half-laughing herself.

"That, too. But it's going to work out because we both love Kat and she knows it. And I love you, too," Daniel added, his voice suddenly so soft, Lynette could hardly hear it.

Despite that, his voice cut through her like a cannon blast.

"Danny—" She choked.

"It's okay. I'm patient. We'll just take this one step at a time. All right?"

"All right," she whispered.

Her heart was still racing, and she felt she would burst into tears, long after they said their good-byes and she hung up.

Sunday, July 13

The picnic didn't start out as smoothly as Lynette could have hoped. Kat sat silent and stiff in the back seat of Daniel's car, answering in monosyllables until they had driven halfway to Sandusky.

"Hey, I've got a great idea." Daniel took his eyes off the highway long enough to glance into the back seat. It took all Lynette's willpower not to look and see Kat's reaction. "Why don't you get hold of Marco and the four of us can go to Cedar Point in another week or so, when summer classes close down? The General has a handful of discount tickets left and he's been up there enough times already this summer. He's trying to get rid of the rest so they don't go to waste."

"The General goes to Cedar Point?" Kat squeaked. A giggle burst out of her and the stiffness in the atmosphere shattered like a soap bubble. "Somehow, I just can't see him at an amusement park, much less on rides."

"He belongs to the Roller Coaster Fans of America," Daniel said, shaking his head. "The man's a lunatic, that's all I can say." He glanced at Lynette and slightly cocked his head toward Kat in the back seat. "What do you say? I swear, you two won't have to hang around with us old folks for the entire day."

"Old folks?" Lynette spluttered.

That set Kat off laughing. Daniel waggled his eyebrows at her. How could she resist? With all three of them laughing, she knew the picnic was going to be a success.

The wonder of it was, most of the conversation centered around the year-and-a-half she and Daniel had been together at Northwestern. The plays they were in together, classmates they had lost track of, classes they shared, professors they remembered. And Kat wasn't bored. She kept coming up with more questions, her eyes gleaming with interest.

Lynette fought tears several times, knowing this was how it could have been all their daughter's growing years, if she hadn't been so proud, so sure she knew best.

"Do you have any yearbooks from Northwestern?" Kat asked, when they had eaten the last cookie and gathered up their paper plates and wrappers to throw away.

"A few." Daniel nodded and glanced at Lynette. She didn't quite understand the question in his glance, and she didn't know why Kat had asked that question, so she just widened her eyes and shrugged.

"Mom doesn't have any."

"Yes, I do," Lynette corrected. "I just... left them in Chicago with your grandmother. There wasn't much room for moving things, when we first came to Ohio. Most of the car was filled with your toys and books." That earned a groan and a grin from Kat.

"Could I maybe borrow them?" their daughter persisted.

"Why?" Daniel paused in closing the cap on the apple juice.

"I want to look through them, that's all."

When Kat shrugged like that and her voice dropped away at the end of a sentence and she wouldn't meet anyone's eyes — that was a sure sign she was up to something and trying to hide it. Lynette had always been grateful her daughter wasn't a very good liar, though she could act any part without trouble, otherwise.

"Who are you looking for?" Daniel asked, his voice softening, too.

"My dad," Kat nearly whispered.

"Kat—"

"I don't even know his name. Mom won't tell me. She says it hurts too much," she hurried on. "She said not to ask you about back then, about my dad, because she said it'd hurt you, too. So I won't. But I can at least look, can't I?"

"You look like your mother," Daniel said with that crooked smile that always hurt Lynette worse than tears from anyone else. "Even if your father was standing here in front of you, there's no way you'd recognize him."

Oh, yes she would, Lynette cried silently. She had seen Daniel in their daughter's face every day since she had been born. But she knew Daniel was right. Only someone who knew the identity of Kat's father could see his features in her. Kat did look too much like her mother.

"I can at least try, can't I?" Kat asked. "Please?"

Daniel looked at Lynette for a long moment, and she realized he waited for her permission. She knew he wanted to do that for their daughter. What would it hurt? She nodded.

"Sure. Remind me, if I don't remember to bring them to school tomorrow," he said.

Kat's grin and the delight that sparkled around her were all the thanks Daniel needed. Lynette knew, if circumstances had been different, Kat would have thrown her arms around him. He would have loved that.

But they wouldn't have been having that conversation at all, if circumstances had been different, would they?

It was hard to pretend everything was wonderful, as they cleaned up their picnic and got back in the car and started the long, leisurely drive back to Tabor Heights. Lynette let Daniel and Kat carry most of the conversation as they stopped at tourist attractions and roadside stands to buy cheese and fruit, beef jerky, scented candles, and flowers. She kept her smile strong and pleasant and answered when they asked her questions, and even pointed out places along the way that she would have liked to investigate, if she hadn't been aching so deeply inside.

Kat would hate her when she found out the truth. Daniel said he forgave her and Lynette almost believed him. But if Kat exploded with hurt and anger when she learned about her mother's lie, what she had done to her father before she was born, what were the chances she would push her mother away and cling to her newfound father? What were the chances Daniel would grab hold of his long-denied daughter and let Lynette, the villain in this piece, fade out of their lives?

Half her heart knew Daniel would never do that. He wanted so much for them to be a family, he would give everything he had to heal the rift between them and keep mother and daughter together. But he was only a man, still healing after years of hurt. Who was to say he would do the noble and right thing?

Kat can't ever know, Lynette told herself a dozen times, and just as many times told herself not to be ridiculous. She had all but promised Daniel they would work up to telling Kat the truth sooner or later.

Not if we're not together anymore, that quiet, terrified part of her offered. *Let him go. You did it before. Let him slide out of your life or push him out. Kat's done fine without him all these years, and so have you. Why let him ruin things?*

And though Lynette fought the argument inside her heart and head all the way home, it still hung on after they dropped Kat off at her apartment and Daniel left her at her condo. The shouting voices had dropped to whispers, but they remained audible. Even in her dreams.

Sunday, July 27

Despite her misgivings, Lynette invited Kat to join them at church. She refused the first Sunday but agreed the last Sunday in July. Lynette didn't know whether to be relieved or afraid. She knew they looked very much like a family as they walked down the right-hand aisle toward the front of the church.

Why the front? Why couldn't they sit in the back row, where only their neighbors would see them? The Randolph clan waited for them and Emily winked as she slid over to make room for Lynette to sit next to her. Lynette was in the seat, then Kat and then Daniel on the end, before she quite knew it.

Had the Randolphs been saving the remainder of the row for them, meaning Daniel had asked them? What would they say and think of her, when they learned the truth about her and Daniel and Kat?

Don't be stupid, Lynette silently scolded herself.

She had been invited to a barbecue at the Randolphs' house just a few weeks ago, to formally announce Max and Tony's engagement. Because of her help with rehearsals and costumes, she was considered part of the family at Homespun now, and it felt good to be included.

Carlo Vincente had been there, too. Before Lynette could quite recover from the shock of meeting him, and the further shock of learning Daniel knew him, she heard the story of how he and Emily had been in love, how they had argued and separated and he went to Europe before she was certain she was pregnant with their daughter. Hearing about the long years of silence and how Carlo believed God had healed them and brought them back together, so their daughter wasn't torn between them, made Lynette shiver and think hard. It could have been her and Daniel, with very few alterations to the details.

Joel and Emily were still recovering from their near-fatal collision with a drunk in a truck. Joel would probably use that cane for the rest of his life. Emily still walked slowly and talked with the slightest hesitation, as if it took longer for words to get from her mind to her tongue. Yet they both radiated a joy in life that Lynette seriously doubted came from their close brush with death. Was it church? She was still impressed with how the entire congregation had rallied around the Randolph family during the time of the accident, and long afterward. Would her mother's old church in Chicago have done that?

Probably not, she decided after just a moment of thought. Those Old

Money families had plenty of servants and employees to take up the slack, so why inconvenience their friends and members of their congregation? Lynette knew her mother's former pastor certainly wouldn't have rolled up his sleeves to help finish building a set or hang lights for dress rehearsal, like Pastor Glenn had done. He also wouldn't have been caught dead helping to landscape the church or hold a drug addict as the skeletal girl vomited all over him at the Mission, which Tabor Christian operated. Pastor Glenn did all that and more. He seemed to enjoy the dirty jobs more than teaching from the pulpit.

They were a world's worth of difference from the so-called Christians she had grown up among. Could God be so different in Tabor than in Chicago? They were certainly more active here in Tabor, with meetings and classes and activities that emphasized families every day of the week. The Mission had a daycare and senior center, a food and clothes donation center, where people who fell short could come for help anonymously. Lynette appreciated that people's pride was protected here.

She had only found out by accident that Daniel was involved in a group that helped find homes and jobs for unwed mothers. He never would have told her if she hadn't seen the notes on his desk, of tasks to accomplish before the next meeting. How many unwed mothers in Chicago would have dared go to her mother's former church for help? None, Lynette knew. If they would be so brutal to one of their own, what chance did strangers have?

Please, God, she prayed. And stopped there. She didn't know what she wanted to say. She wasn't quite sure what she was thinking.

Lynette only knew that by the time she worked through her questions and tried to straighten out some of the confusion that made her want to burst into tears at least twice a day, the sermon had ended already. She turned to smile at her daughter, but Kat was already on her feet, gathering up her purse and tugging her skirt straight, visibly eager to leave.

Lynette smiled and introduced her daughter to her new friends, who all welcomed her just as warmly as Lynette had been when she first started attending with Daniel. It helped that Kat knew the Randolphs, and the Holwoods, who sat two pews behind them. Still, by the time the three of them made it to the parking lot, Kat seemed to have shrunk into herself. Almost as if she was ashamed to be there? Or just praying nobody she knew would see her there? She was non-committal when Daniel asked her how she liked the service. She blamed a late date with Marco, saying she was tired and hadn't really been able to follow anything. Lynette kept quiet. Who was she to be critical, when she had been somewhere else entirely during the whole service?

"I don't think this little experiment worked," she murmured, watching Kat go into the lobby of her apartment building. Lynette knew it was a bad sign that Kat had turned down lunch with them. Maybe they had been forcing the family togetherness?

"We should have suggested she sit with Bekka and Shane," Daniel said, nodding. "Even the high school kids are allowed to sit with their friends, instead of with Mommy and Daddy."

"Bekka and Shane?" Lynette chose to ignore the *Mommy and Daddy* reference. It made her squirm; made her fear Daniel was going to ask her to start preparing Kat for the big announcement.

"This is Bekka's home church."

"I knew that. But Shane?"

"They're pretty serious."

"It seems to be a contagious disease." She tried to turn the shiver inside her into a joke. "I mean, Amy and Joe haven't had a real fight in weeks, and Kat seems to have settled on Marco, and now even Bekka has someone."

"The kids are growing up." He shrugged and smiled at her before pulling out of the parking lot.

Yes, she acknowledged, and she had forced her daughter to grow up without a father. Would she ever be able to go a day without feeling some level of guilt or shame?

Daniel kept insisting that everything had worked out, that he was grateful, that he liked the man he had become. He insisted God had given them all a second chance.

Second chances were fine, Lynette knew. But they had both changed. Maybe this was a second chance to reinforce her first choice, made before Kat was born. She wished she could ask Daniel to step back and give her some breathing room, some time to think, but she knew he would take it the wrong way.

Or would he?

Either way, she couldn't do that. They were going to Cedar Point for the day tomorrow. Like a family. She wasn't going to ruin it for Daniel or for Kat. They deserved some fun, some good memories, no matter what decision she had to make in the future.

Monday, July 28

Something bothered Lynette, Daniel knew. It took a while to pick up on it, but he noticed her smile dimmed a little and she didn't chatter as easily or laugh as freely each time Kat and Marco met up with them during the day.

It wasn't like they made a conscious effort to find the younger couple during their day at Cedar Point. After all, the amusement park was huge, and they likely never would have found Kat and Marco if they had tried. Every time the couples did meet up with each other, they were heading toward the same ride, or one set was getting off while the other was getting into line. They ate lunch together at the Red Garter Saloon and watched the Old West-style song and dance show. Daniel wondered if they would run into any of his students who had managed to obtain summer jobs at Cedar Point. After all, he had helped at least a dozen put together their audition tapes or write up their resumes for the performance venues. And then of course there were the students who were simply content to work the many rides and games and concession stands. After considering the possibility a few times, Daniel told himself not to try to find anyone, and if he did notice anyone, he wouldn't make contact. Today he was here to have fun, not play teacher. He was here with his family.

That thought reminded him of his cousins, and he talked about them with Lynette and Kat. Kat's interest was piqued when she learned Abby had her own small plane. She gave flying lessons out of the little Stoughton airport and ran a courier service. She helped her brother raise Chad and Candy, standing in for their dead mother.

That might change very soon, Daniel hoped. Tyler Sloane, the new director of the Royal Community Theater, had been showing more than casual interest in Abby.

Daniel told Kat about his cousins, playing on the relationship with Tyler, since Kat knew him also. The Royal Community Theater regularly shared scripts, equipment, and costumes with the university theater department.

Talking about the rest of his family gave Daniel the clue he needed to Lynette's discomfort. She grew too quiet and stopped eating and fidgeted with the straw of her cream soda. He suspected he talked about family too much, and she thought he was pushing again.

Maybe he was, but didn't Kat have a right to know about her family? The Morgans were a small clan, all he had left in the world, and Kat's Grandmother Teague didn't have any other relatives, no cousins for Kat to depend on. Daniel knew quite thoroughly how important family was. If he thought he could get away with it, he would invite Al and his kids, Abby, and Tyler over to his house for a barbeque to meet Kat and Lynette. But he knew he couldn't get away with it. Not without starting a lot of awkward questions in Kat's mind.

Lynette might get angry enough to leave him again. He couldn't take that.

So Daniel let the subject die out and switched the conversation to the other entertainment venues scattered through the park. There was the I-Max Theater, with a screen several football fields wide and tall. Kat said they had already seen it and they sat so close she got motion sickness. That got a chuckle even out of Lynette. They compared notes on what they had seen and done so far, and when lunch was over, split up to go their separate ways again.

Daniel talked Lynette into posing for an Old-Time Photo in costume, he as a riverboat gambler, and she as one of the dancers, complete with feathers in her hair and lots of ruffles in her skirt. He splurged and got double prints in plastic frames. Lynette teased him that she would treasure it forever. If such a photo didn't get him thrown off every committee at church and maybe get his membership revoked for good measure.

"I'd like to see them try," Daniel said, laughing. He could just imagine the consternation that would go around the church if he stopped participating. He didn't think he did that much, but he helped in so many areas, it might make a dent.

Besides, Joel Randolph had posed right here for a far worse picture with Emily last summer, and it had been Pastor Glenn's idea. He and his wife, Rita, had been delighted to be in the picture with them, as far as Daniel knew.

They bought saltwater taffy and made sure they bought the thick slabs of fries sprinkled with coarse salt and malt vinegar. And corn dogs. And SnoCones. They grumbled together that the Pirate Ride, which had been labeled a historical structure, had been closed down. They rode the Antique Cars and the Octopus and the Witch's Wheel, and Lynette snuggled closer when Daniel wrapped his arms around her to brace them both against the spinning, twisting, upside-down rides.

He let himself believe her too-quiet moments had been just that, moments, and she was fine again.

Kat and Marco fell asleep in the back seat of the car on the way home. All four of them were sweaty, gritty, sunburned and too full of sugar and grease to be comfortable. Daniel hadn't had so much fun in years.

If only he hadn't been afraid to relax completely and share all his plans for the future with Lynette, as each one popped into his head. It felt so right to think about and plan things they could do together as a family. Christmas Eve with the Randolphs. Opening night dinners with the cast of each BWU production. Participating in the all-community garage sale in Tabor Heights next spring. The list went on and on. But that would only happen when Kat finally knew the truth and accepted it.

Kat knew they were dating, that they had resumed a college romance. When would it be the right time to tell her the whole truth? Daniel knew the longer they waited, the harder she would take the revelation. Kat had tried to laugh about the months of secrecy. Would she be able to laugh when she knew he was her father?

When would it be too late to tell Kat, without her being hurt and feeling betrayed by them, and creating a rift that would make the twenty years of silence from Lynette seem like spring break?

Marco was the difficult one to wake up, when Daniel dropped the younger couple at Kat's apartment. He and Lynette laughed softly at the way the young man stumbled over to his car, with Kat guiding him. Daniel thought about making a joke about getting the kids tucked safely into bed, then decided now wasn't the right time. A flicker of irritation shot through the drowsy, comfortable feeling. He was trying to be patient, but Lynette's reluctance to bring the truth out in the open did wear on him. He had to be honest about that.

Maybe that's the problem? I want honesty, and she's still hiding behind half-truths. Please, God, there's going to be a breaking point, and a day of reckoning. Don't let Kat get hurt when it comes. Please don't let me lose Lynette again.

When he dropped Lynette off at her condo, she scooted over on the seat and kissed him, almost before he could turn to her. A warm, soft kiss on the cheek. Not quite what Daniel had been looking forward to. He forced a smile and let her slide out of the car and hurry up to her door, her arms full of two costumed bears they had won at the guessing booth, her framed photo, a box of taffy, and half a bag-full of squashed, partially melted cotton candy. He waited until she had the door open, then turned and waved to him, smiling, before she stepped inside.

"What's wrong, Lyn? I thought everything was getting better." Daniel sighed and put the car into gear and pulled away from the curb. "Lord, please..." He didn't know quite what to say, he only knew he felt helpless and unable to stop a cloud from taking away the brightness in his life.

Tuesday, July 29

Tuesday morning, Daniel returned to his office from an unscheduled meeting with Dr. Holwood to find Bekka waiting. She hadn't taken a seat—which made sense, because the only empty seat in sight was his desk chair. No one took his desk chair, even when he wasn't there.

He paused in the doorway, watching her inspect the souvenirs from yesterday's trip. An orange sports bottle marked with the logo of the Millennium Force. A little neon green stuffed bear, maybe three inches tall, which was his share of the loot from outwitting the college girl manning the guessing booth. The only bear that wasn't in an embarrassing, ridiculously poofy costume.

Bekka grinned and bent to get a closer look at the picture from the old-fashioned photo booth. Daniel had dressed up like Maverick, with the topcoat and flat-topped hat, a tumbler of some liquid in one hand and a fan of cards in the other. Lynette leaned against his shoulder, dressed in feathers and flounces, and reaching around him to take a card from his hand. They stared into the camera, stone-faced, but Daniel remembered how they had fought not to fall down laughing.

"A picture like that could get me thrown out of church," Daniel said, coming in behind Bekka. He grinned at her as he slid into his seat.

"Good time yesterday?" She shoved aside a couple books he had been planning to review, for possible inclusion in the fall syllabus.

"Didn't Kat tell you anything?"

"She was still in bed when I left for work." She settled down on the corner of the desk. "Everything okay?"

"Sure. Why?"

"Well, she's a little bugged by going to church."

"She doesn't have to go if she doesn't want to." Daniel winced, remembering how stiff and quiet Kat had been on Sunday. He thought it was because she had to sit with them, when she was used to sitting with Bekka when she did attend. If Bekka was worried, then it was more than just the seating arrangements that bothered her. "Though I would be very happy if she'd get into the habit," he admitted, a moment later.

"Kat does a lot of things to make people happy and she's afraid to speak up when she's uncomfortable. Look what happened with Chef Creepo," Bekka hurried to add when Daniel opened his mouth to deny her words. That stopped him short.

"That's the last thing I want," he murmured, and slouched further into his seat. He nodded, frowning, and thought for a few moments. "I guess I should talk to Lynette. Maybe she could give me some ideas."

"That's part of the problem." Bekka took a deep breath and studied her clasped fingers as she hurried on. "Kat thinks her mother is going just to please you, and she's afraid it'll break you two up if she doesn't go with you. She thinks church makes her mother uncomfortable."

"Of course it would. Those hypocrites at her home church in Chicago—" Daniel shook his head. Was that the problem? He was trying to force her into a mold and he didn't realize it? How could he have been so insensitive?

Yet at the same time, another part of him grumbled in pure frustration. What was wrong with Lynette, that she couldn't see the difference between her mother's church and the people here in Tabor Heights? Couldn't she see they were real, alive, giving and caring? In Chicago, they had only cared about appearances. It was hard to believe that Moody Bible Institute was only a few blocks away from such a cold, indifferent place. At Tabor Christian, a healthy percentage of the church concentrated on pleasing God rather than people. They had a ministry to unwed mothers, among other ministries to the downtrodden and untouchables that the Chicago church would have consigned to the lower reaches of Hell before they would even admit they existed.

What was wrong with Lynette? Was she deliberately blind? Or was her hurt too deep to ever let her trust religious people again?

"They made it hard on her because she was an unwed mother who wouldn't identify the father," Bekka said slowly. "Somebody probably found out she refused to marry you, and used that against her, too."

'Marry *me*?" Daniel felt like the chair had vanished underneath him. And the floor and most of the room. He forced himself to meet Bekka's gaze and smile. "What makes you say that?"

'Because Kat looks like the two of you put together and it makes a whole lot more sense, the way you look after Kat, if she's your kid. I doubt you were ever the kind of guy who would walk away from his kid, so her mom made you go away, didn't she?"

Daniel took a deep, long, shuddering breath. It felt so good, and yet so terrifying, to realize someone had guessed the truth. He was glad Bekka had guessed; other than the Randolphs and Pastor Glenn, Daniel couldn't think of anyone he *wanted* to know the truth. Bekka would be there for Kat when the news broke. She would help Kat if the unthinkable happened and she pushed both her parents out of her life.

"She wanted me to keep going, onward and upward," he whispered, "make my mark on Hollywood, and then come back for them. I got a job and cut back on my classes and got an apartment so I could take care of her. When I wouldn't stop asking her to marry me, she left town." Daniel blinked hard against the tears that burned his eyes. The ache of those memories was as deep and crushing now as it had been twenty years ago.

"You can't imagine how Kat's face haunted me, the first couple of weeks of her freshman year. And when I was convinced that it was just a coincidence, I went to Thanksgiving at your place, and there Lynette was, Kat's mother." He let out a loud, aching sigh. "All the praying I did, all the bargains I made with God for years, until I finally gave up. Please, just give me back Lyn and our baby. I didn't even know if she had a boy or girl until that day."

"I just love *coincidences*, don't you?" Bekka drawled.

Daniel grinned, and it felt a little more natural now. He wished he could get away with hugging Bekka, just to express what couldn't be said, how much he appreciated her being there. Maybe he had made Bekka his surrogate daughter, thinking he would never find Lynette and their child.

A dropping sensation cut through the warmth slowly seeping back through his heart and body. He hadn't shoved Bekka out of his life once his flesh-and-blood child appeared, had he? He prayed he would never be that kind of shallow, narrow-focused person.

"I guess I've just been taking it for granted that God's given us a second chance," he said, opening up to the sympathy in her big brown eyes, "and nothing is going to go wrong this time." He let out another long, loud sigh and felt as if the pressure inside him deflated a little. "Thanks for not saying anything. Lyn doesn't want Kat to know just yet."

"If you're not careful, she'll never know. Kat really needs a dad. Her mom needs a knight in shining armor."

"Slightly dented armor," Daniel said with a crooked smile. "Thanks, Bekka. I thought I was supposed to be *your* advisor."

"Hey, summer break." She shrugged and slid off the corner of the desk. "Now that I've totally disrupted your day, I should get to my class."

"Pray for us today, okay? I'm meeting Lyn for lunch, and I think it's time we talk."

"Sure."

The phone rang just after Bekka's footsteps on the stairs faded away. It was his sometime writing partner Sam, calling about renewed interest in a speculative script for an in-production TV series he and Daniel had collaborated on nearly a year ago.

"Whoa. Back up. What was that about going to New York?" he said, after Sam had talked almost non-stop for more than four minutes. Daniel clocked him, as he always did, looking for a new speed record, intelligible words per second.

"Not *going* to New York—*living* in New York." His friend and partner chuckled. "We could be a breath away from finally hitting the big time."

"We've talked about this before, Sam—"

"Yeah, yeah, I know. You have commitments. Whatever happened to sabbaticals? Taking a leave of absence?"

"This is my career. I love teaching. My home is here. One script does not a career make." Daniel shook his head, hearing in his own voice an echo of wiser and older heads who warned him when he was first charting his course for fame and fortune.

"Three, four months max. Come on, Danny-boy. What are you afraid of?"

Blowing my chance to finally have a family, Daniel almost answered.

Chapter Fourteen

Daniel had plenty of time coming to him, and the administration had granted sabbaticals before with little more than a week's notice before the start of the term. It was unorthodox, but the administration of Butler-Williams University liked to keep its faculty happy. As long as the classes were covered by competent substitutes and student teachers, of course.

With a little less than a month until the fall semester started, Daniel knew he would have no trouble asking for time off. But he didn't want to. Kat was here, and Lynette. Sometimes he had nightmares where he went away for just a few days and when he returned, they were both gone. Lynette had vanished that easily before

What if he asked Lynette to go with him?

Daniel sat up, slamming his sneakers down onto the floor. He stared at the picture of himself and Lynette in Old West garb and barely heard Sam continue his persuasive spiel that could convince a used car salesman to buy an Edsel.

What if they went to New York together? They could lay a firm foundation in a place where no one knew them, with no memories, no mutual friends, no distractions to get in the way.

"Okay, you win, you snake oil salesman," he said, and burst out laughing when Sam stopped talking for an unprecedented seven seconds. Daniel timed him.

"You mean it?"

"Find out what's involved, what they want, how much of a commitment I have to make. Find out if I can cut loose if it's not for me." Daniel bit his tongue against asking if he could bring a friend. Sam was a great guy and understood his spiritual commitment and values, but he would automatically assume shared quarters. In the old days, straight from college, Daniel wouldn't have hesitated. This time, he and Lynette were doing it right; nothing more passionate than good night kisses until he put that ring on her finger.

Fortunately, Kat wasn't working today. She wouldn't be working for two whole weeks, during the break between the end of summer term and preparing for fall semester. Daniel knew it would be nearly impossible to hold back the good news if she were around. He wanted Lynette to know before anyone else.

He left half an hour early for lunch, to stop at the administration building and pick up the paperwork to request his leave of absence. Just in case.

Daniel worked on the paperwork while he waited for Lynette to join him at the Whistle Stop for lunch. He read through it once before putting pen to paper, then checked his watch. It was now five minutes after she was due, and no Lynette in sight. He started filling out the paperwork, expecting to be interrupted at any moment, and was surprised to get to the signature and date line on the very last page, and still no one sitting across from him in their usual corner booth. According to his watch, Lynette was more than twenty minutes late now. Was something wrong?

"Ready to order now, Doc?" Dexter, their usual waiter asked as he refilled Daniel's iced tea for the second time.

"Maybe I should. Ah... my usual." Daniel glanced around the restaurant, built in an old railroad depot, with boxcars added on three sides to expand the seating. No sign of Lynette. "Where's the phone?" One of these days, he told himself, he would invest in a cell phone. If only he didn't hate technology so much.

He called Blooming Miracles. Lynette hadn't come to work today. He called her condo and got the answering machine. Daniel forced himself to hang up the phone and go back to his table before he called Kat, too. No sense in worrying her.

Daniel barely tasted his Reuben deluxe with spicy fries. He took half of it back to the office. Pounds of tension dropped off his shoulders when he stepped into his office and found his answering machine light blinking.

"Daniel? I'm sorry, I have to cancel. Just not feeling well, I guess. Maybe I'm getting old, and all that fun yesterday is taking its toll." Lynette's breathy little laugh did sound weak. "I have a neighborhood meeting tomorrow night, and I'm working every day for the rest of the week. Maybe we should just wait until Sunday, all right? Talk to you then."

Daniel settled into his chair, smiling, silently kicking himself for being so worried. It was just a mix-up in timing. If he hadn't left his office early, he would have been able to talk to her.

Then the time and date stamp played at the end of Lynette's message and his smile froze.

She had called *after* he would have left the office to go to the Whistle Stop. He hadn't missed her call to cancel by leaving early.

What little Daniel had eaten for lunch turned heavy in his stomach as a chill worked through him that had nothing to do with the year-round coolness of the theater basement. Lynette had played the same trick, calling just after he had left to meet her, a dozen times during those last few miserable weeks of their relationship in school. Just before she told him she was pregnant. Just before she shoved him out of her life.

"No." Daniel flinched at the harshness in his voice. "She's not going to do that to me — to us — again."

Lynette just wasn't feeling well, that was all. Sunburned and headachy and probably a touch of indigestion from all that junk food they had indulged in yesterday. She certainly sounded uncomfortable and weak when she called.

He would just keep his good news for Sunday. They would go out for lunch after the service and he would tell her then. She would be happy for him. Their relationship would grow stronger and closer.

Daniel had himself convinced by the time Bekka came back that afternoon to check with him. He was on the phone, trying to verify an order of textbooks he needed. The university bookstore had placed the order correctly — he had verified the paperwork — but the acknowledgement from the publishing house made absolutely no sense.

When Bekka peeked into his office, he had run out of paper, with no more in plain sight, and had started making notes in the blank margins of his unused calendar desk pad. The nasal-toned man on the other end rattled off numbers that made no sense to Daniel. He scribbled with one hand, tucked the phone between shoulder and ear, and reached with his free hand for the catalogue sitting in the middle of a stack of catalogues. Then he caught sight of Bekka's face. She grinned and waved to gesture *never mind*, but he shook his head.

"She never showed up," he whispered loudly, then flinched. It figured — the irritating little man on the other end had ignored everything Daniel told him, but heard every word when he spoke to someone else. "Yeah, I heard you," he said, and rolled his eyes in total frustration.

Bekka shrugged, offered a sympathetic smile, and left. Daniel sighed and wished he could just hang up. Unfortunately, that company carried over 70 percent of the books the BWU faculty chose to use. Daniel knew better than to irritate the company's obnoxious, oblivious representative and cause trouble for his fellow teachers.

When Sam called back, just before quitting time, Daniel almost told him to cancel all arrangements for this career-changing, short-term venture in New York. Taking a deep breath, he agreed to everything Sam proposed. After all, why should he put his entire life on hold? If this was meant to be, it would all work out for the best.

Wouldn't it?

The question was, he couldn't be sure if he applied those words to his relationship with Lynette or advancing his career. Or maybe it was his teaching career at BWU that felt so tenuous right now?

Please, Lord, I'm stepping out on the waves right now, and the storm is about to break. Please don't let me be like Peter and take my eyes off You any time soon. Keep me from taking the wrong step and sinking. And please, let Lynette and Kat be in the boat when I climb back in, okay?

Sunday, August 3

Lynette called just before Daniel left to pick her up for their usual breakfast arrangements, and said she was running late and she would drive herself. Then she accepted an invitation to join three other couples for lunch after the service. Daniel swallowed a grumble and pushed aside his irritation that they wouldn't have any time alone together. He wanted Lynette to make friends at Tabor Christian, didn't he? It was good that she felt comfortable enough in their renewed relationship to accept invitations without checking with him, first.

After all, they weren't married, were they? Not even engaged. And he certainly wasn't the kind of man who would demand such slavish obedience from his wife. At least, he hoped not.

Such thoughts wiped away the lingering gloom of resentment that had stayed with him since that missed lunch date and the badly timed cancellation call. Daniel enjoyed the long, leisurely lunch, and when Lynette volunteered to help Lanie McGrath finalize her decision about wallpaper and tile and countertops for her kitchen remodeling project, he didn't protest. Even when it meant Lynette followed the McGraths home instead of spending the afternoon with him. He wasn't able to talk with her as he planned, but that was all right. He might have even better, more solid news for her when they did talk.

Friday, August 8

Lynette missed their lunch date on Tuesday, and this time she didn't even call to cancel. Daniel stopped at Blooming Miracles and found she had just left on a delivery run. She would be gone for at least two hours, with a van-full of arrangements and bouquets. It was hard to frown in the face of the owner's delight in the growing success of her shop, which she was glad to attribute to Lynette's talent and her wonderful way of making friends of all their customers.

Still, Daniel grumbled on the drive back to his office. He called her house, asking her to meet him for dinner.

Lynette didn't call back.

Daniel waited until Friday, then went to her condo when he knew she should be home. The garage had no windows, so he couldn't look inside to see if her car was there. He walked along the front of the house, trying to look in the windows, but all the shades were drawn against the hot afternoon sunshine.

Fighting a churning inside that threatened to come out as either fury or paralyzing fear and hurt, Daniel stomped up to the front door and rang the doorbell. He stared at the front door, willing it to open.

No response.

He took a few deep breaths, silently urging himself into calm before ringing the bell again.

Daniel waited through three more tries of the doorbell, pausing between rings to listen to the sounds in the house, the neighborhood. The laughter of children at play somewhere mixed with the clatter of dogs barking and the drone of an airplane passing by on its way to Cleveland Hopkins Airport, but no movement from inside Lynette's house. Daniel clenched his fist, raising it to pound on the door.

Then he stopped himself, shoulders slumping a little, and left the tiny porch.

No matter how hard he tried, he couldn't keep his mind from replaying those miserable weeks after learning Lynette had simply vanished and wasn't coming back to school, and her mother wouldn't give him a clue to where she had gone. Daniel knew he could ask Kat to help him find her mother, but he didn't want to admit to anyone that they were having problems.

Not yet, anyway. He needed to talk to Lynette, first. Weren't there guidelines in Scripture about handling problems between two people? It wasn't time to bring in outside mediators. Not yet. He hoped.

When he got back to his car, he slouched in front of the steering wheel for several moments, silently praying for patience. For understanding. For strength. For God to take this ache away before he did or said something they would all regret. A single tear escaped his left eye, but he ignored it as he yanked the key in the ignition and started the engine.

Long after the neighborhood was quiet again, the front door creaked open and Lynette peered outside. Dark smears of sleeplessness marked her eyes. She was pale and blinked rapidly in the half-light of the porch. She tried to smile, looking at the two tiny oil spots Daniel's car left in her driveway. Shrugging, she went back into the house and slowly, softly closed the door.

Half an hour later, the garage door opened and Lynette drove out. She looked in both directions several times, and she laughed at herself as she realized she fully expected Daniel to be waiting around a corner, prepared to ambush her.

He hadn't ambushed her in college when she avoided him, so why did she expect him to resort to such tactics now?

Still, she almost turned around four times between her house and the parking lot at Tabor Christian, and it was little more than a mile in distance.

Dr. Harris was just heading for her office with a fresh cup of tea when

Lynette walked up to the front desk in the church office to sign in for her appointment. The church's professional counselor smiled and walked up to the desk, waving for the three church secretaries, who were all answering phones, to let her take care of it.

"Hi, Lynette. I've seen you with Morgan, so I know who you are even if we haven't been introduced." The silver-haired woman held out her hand to shake Lynette's. Her skin felt cool and smooth, and her neat, pale gray summer suit combined with her warm smile to give Lynette a sense of comfort.

Maybe, for the first time in weeks, she had made a smart decision.

"Would you like some tea before we go to my office? Apple juice? Ice water?" she continued when Lynette shook her head. "All right. Come right on back this way." She inclined her head and led the way down the long hallway lined with doors.

Please, God, I'm not very good at listening to You, but could You tell her what I'm supposed to hear? What am I supposed to do? I'm scared to death. Lynette swallowed a gasping little laugh, when she realized she had just prayed her first coherent prayer in what felt like years.

"Let's just get everything out in the open from the start," she blurted, almost before Dr. Harris had shut the door.

Lynette debated half a second whether to stay standing, pace, or accept the seat in the easy chair with thick, pale green cushions. Her legs trembled almost as much as her hands, so that settled that. She dropped into the chair and let the words spill out.

"Daniel and I had a child when we were in school. I threw him out of my life, even though he wanted to marry me and take care of us. I've made some bad choices, and now we've come back together, twenty years later."

"And you're scared to death you're going to totally ruin what could be a wonderful gift of God's mercy and grace?" Dr. Harris nodded as she settled down in the chair directly opposite Lynette's. "If you *weren't* scared, then I'd be worried."

Lynette burst into tears. It felt perfectly natural to let the other woman reach across the gap between their chairs and wrap both arms around her.

Thursday, August 14

"Want me to get that?" Bekka asked, when the phone rang. Daniel crouched in front of his bookshelves at the opposite end of the office, digging through layers of dust and cracked bindings.

"No. What do you think an answering machine is for?" He sighed and twisted around enough to see her over his shoulder. "Sorry. Shouldn't be taking things out on you."

Daniel wished he could blame the countdown until classes started for his frazzled state of mind. Sam called every three hours with a roller coaster of news about their possible sale in New York. First, they had lost the deal, then they were the answer to the prayers of three different producers who wanted to pick up the now-scrapped project, then they had become dog meat, then only two soaps wanted to take them on as temporary staff to "prove themselves," then their contribution to the project had been altered and turned into its own concept, and was predicted to be the next mega-million-dollar hit. Add to that the pressure of trying to decide when to hand in his leave of absence request forms and not being able to talk to Lynette since the Sunday before last. It was a miracle he could get dressed in the morning.

If it weren't for Kat, he probably would have starved. Since settling down with Marco as her nearly constant companion, she had doubled her efficiency and her caring spirit extended to everyone around her. She brought him coffee and bagels or an egg sandwich for breakfast, even though she was only supposed to do that on days he had a first period class, and classes hadn't started yet. She usually ordered something for lunch without telling him, plunking a carton of Chinese or slices of pizza down in front of him with a grin and a wink. Daniel ate and continued with his work and wondered how such a wonderful girl could come from two such totally messed-up people.

It had to be Bekka's influence, he decided in that moment. He wasn't much good to anyone lately, and it was hard to have any charitable or complimentary thoughts about Lynette.

His guilty feelings over that situation only made things worse.

"Anything I can do? Besides stop pestering you for advice on my career?" Bekka added with a lopsided smile.

"How about some advice on my career? My friend at ABC wants me to consider a writing slot at—" He stopped as his answering machine finally clicked on.

"I'm not here," Daniel's message said, with slightly hollow tones. "If I'm not in class, I don't know where I am. When I figure that out, I'll call you back. Leave a message."

That was the stupidest message he had ever put on the machine. What made him think it was clever and witty? If those studio execs in New York ever heard it, they would break off the deal immediately.

Somehow, though, he couldn't get up the energy to change the outgoing message. Maybe because he remembered so vividly Lynette smothering giggles until she was red in the face, the day he recorded it. She sat right there in that corner chair now piled six feet high with books. He just didn't have the gumption to erase even one good memory.

"Cute," Bekka muttered, earning a grimace from him.

"Daniel?" Lynette sounded a little breathless and tinny through the machine's speaker. "It's Lyn. Please pick up the phone. You have to be there. Look, I know I forgot about our date. Again. Okay, for the sixth time. And I'm never home when you come by. I'm sorry. Please, don't act like a spoiled little boy and give me the silent treatment. It didn't work when we were in college—all right, so it did work, when I used it on you. But it won't work now. You have to be there, because I just called your house and—"

The answering machine squealed as the space available for the message came to an end. Daniel held very still, staring at but not seeing the book clutched in his hands. He wanted Bekka to be discrete and sympathetic and leave. He wanted her to stay and offer more of that amazing wisdom that had been so perfectly timed when he needed it.

"How are things going with you and Shane?" Daniel asked, still not turning around.

"Fine. Kat and Amy nearly had heart attacks when he picked me up last night. It's like they think I'm supposed to be a nun or something."

"Still ragging on you about keeping secrets from them?" He levered himself up from the floor and came back to his chair. He moved stiffly, shoulders hunched, not really looking at anything as he navigated the cluttered floor of his office.

He knew all about secrets. He wanted to walk out into the lobby right now and tell Kat she was his daughter. Lynette would accuse him of doing it to punish her, and she might be right.

What about all this good news that turned sour on him? What was the use of a giant step in his career if he didn't have anyone to share it with? He knew it was childish, but Al and Abby, Chad and Candy just didn't count anymore. He had told them two weeks ago. Of course, Abby had to throw a celebration dinner for him, and she invited Tyler, and Daniel had threatened an extremely uncomfortable, lingering death if Tyler told anyone in the theater community. It had been fun, it had been silly and relaxing. Until he left to go home and Lyn wasn't there in the car with him, sharing memories of the celebration. Al and his kids, Abby and now even Tyler were his family, but they weren't enough for him. Not after a taste of what it could have been like for the past twenty years.

Daniel knew how bitter secrets could be if they were kept unwillingly. He wished Bekka all the happiness in the world with her secrets and her career and her long-overdue romance with Shane Hopkins.

At least someone was happy in this world, today.

"It's not like I kept Shane a secret. They were never around, or too busy with their own problems when I wanted to talk, or when he came by and..." Bekka shrugged.

"You two go to church together?"

"Every Sunday he doesn't have to work. He really wants to switch to full-time at the gym, so he has a better schedule. His other boss makes him work every other Sunday, but Vic doesn't open up Gold Tone until after lunch, so everybody can go to church."

"Don't ever date someone who doesn't believe as you do, Bekka. It's not worth the heartache. You get pulled in two directions."

Daniel almost laughed at his words. Who was he to give such advice? He was the one who hadn't gone to church that Sunday. If Lynette had showed up and waited in vain for him, he had no idea. He had left the house and took a long drive, not really paying attention to where he was going. He also unplugged the answering machine at home, so he wouldn't have to hear her voice, leaving another excuse message, when he came in. Or worse, see there wasn't a single message, because she didn't care where he was.

"She wants you to choose between her and God?" Bekka whispered.

"If only it were that simple. I could fight against that. I could persuade her to see—"

Daniel sighed. There was so much he didn't understand. So much that was only theory. Half the time, he raged that Lynette avoided him. The other half of the time, he avoided her because he knew he'd dredge up all those years of hurt and loneliness and batter her with the bitter accumulation.

He didn't hate her. He simply didn't want to find out he no longer loved her. Silence was easier. Silence and trying not to think. Or feel.

"She's pretty much made up her mind already that I'll choose God over her, so why continue things?" he finally said.

"I'm the last person to give advice on romance, but it sure sounded like she wanted to work things out when she called just now."

"We've already tried talking things out. Several times. I relax and think it's all cleared up, then something happens, and I find out she understood one way and I understood another. I just don't want to go through what Amy and Joe do all the time." Daniel shook his head. "You'd think I'd have learned by now."

"You never loved anybody but her, have you?" Bekka waited. Daniel refused to look at her. He wasn't the kind of man who fell down crying, especially not on the shoulder of his daughter's best friend. No matter how much a surrogate daughter she had become. "Maybe you should tell Kat—"

"No! I'm her friend. Maybe a better friend than if she knew I was her father. I've already ruined things with Lyn. I don't want to lose Kat."

The phone rang.

"If that's her, I'd answer it," Bekka offered.

"You're not me." Daniel shook his head and finally looked at her. "I'm sorry, Bekka. I know you care. I know you want to help, but—I think that book you need is at home. Let me look for it tonight, all right?"

"Sure. Thanks. Um... see you tomorrow, then."

Bekka waited for his response, little more than a nod, before she slid off the edge of the desk and hurried out of the office. Daniel listened to his answering machine message and decided he would change it. He just didn't know when.

"Danny?" Sam crowed. "Look, I have to talk to you right away. The bigwigs want you here yesterday. It's a little step, but that's smart. We have to prove ourselves, show them we can be team players, then you can go on back to school and work long-distance. It's smooth sailing from there. We are on our way to the big time!"

The machine squealed as Daniel snatched up the phone. For the first time in days, his heart pounded with excitement. There was a bitter taste in his mouth as he made his decision.

"I'm here," he said, and reached for those leave of absence papers he had put in the bottom of his in-basket. "What's the deal?"

He glanced at his open office door and caught movement. Kat was busy chattering and giggling with Marco as they copied and sorted papers, but that could come to an awkward end at the worst possible time and they would hear what he said. Daniel wanted this all settled before he made his announcement. Listening to Sam spill all the glorious, long-awaited details, he caught the door with the instep of his shoe and kicked it closed.

As soon as he got off the phone with Sam, he ran to the administration building to turn in his application papers. The proper authorities knew they were going to be filed weeks ago, so it was only a matter of formality. When Daniel returned an hour later, Kat and Marco were gone and the book Bekka had been looking for sat in plain view on a shelf at eye-level. Daniel shook his head, wondering if he should apply for medical rest leave instead of his leave of absence.

This had to be God's will, right? When he filed his request papers, Dean Jacobson and Dean Foley were both coming back from an early lunch and took the papers as Daniel handed the stack to their shared secretary. Both elderly women smiled like saints and told Daniel it was about time he took some time off. Then they went into Dean Jacobson's office and shut the door.

His leave of absence was the next best thing to approved. So why didn't he feel any better?

When he went into his office, the phone rang before he could even sit down, put his feet up and get comfortable for some serious thinking and soul-searching. It was Lynette again. She sounded angry instead of pleading this time.

Daniel snatched up their Old West photo and flung it across the office. The frame came apart at two corners and the thin plastic sheet that protected the photo tore. Daniel let out a snort of bitter satisfaction when the dented photo did a double somersault, bounced off a stack of books and ended up in the wastebasket.

He stayed standing, staring at the big black plastic wastebasket long after Lynette ran out of message space and the machine cut her off. Then, moving like arthritis had settled into every joint, Daniel crossed his office and reached into the wastebasket.

Friday, August 15

The next afternoon, when he left to talk with Dean Jacobson about final arrangements for his approved leave of absence, Daniel had already cleaned his office in preparation for the graduate students and temporary teachers who would be using it. His books were filed according to the notated list he kept trying to use every year. All his sticky notes to remind him to do things — which he had done months ago — and the tear sheets to remind him of lesson plans were removed from his desk, computer, tack board, and the sides of his bookshelves. He tore the June and July calendar pages off his desk pad, bringing his unusually clean desk up to date. Last of all, before dragging his overflowing wastebasket out into the lobby for the night crew to empty, he put the book Bekka wanted in the middle of his desk. There was no way she could miss it.

Daniel looked at the shattered and barely repaired photo of himself and Lynette. He looked a long time. There was no way he could miss it, being one of the few things on his clean desk.

What was he doing? School started next week when the freshmen came in on Friday for orientation. He would be free to take off for New York once he had turned over his notes and lesson plans to the General and Joel Randolph and the graduate students who were eager to "get their feet wet," according to Dean Jacobson. Daniel was free to follow his dreams until Christmas break ended.

But was he?

He had yet to tell Kat or Lynette. Or anyone not involved in the transfer of his responsibilities. In some ways, this big break of his was as secret as the identity of Kat's father.

"Am I running away?" Daniel whispered, as he looked into Lynette's eyes in the photograph. "Did I do something wrong, to frighten her, and now I'm punishing her for something *I* did?"

The photo blurred in his sight. Daniel wiped his eyes with the heel of his hand and reached for the doorknob with the other hand. He couldn't waste any more time. He couldn't afford to be late.

But what if he was hurrying to make the worst mistake of his life?

He barely got a reaction out of Kat and Marco when he told them he was going to be out, probably for the rest of the day. They nodded and Kat waved as he hurried up the steps, and went back to their laughing and talking, planning what they would do on their first day back to classes. All the innocent, fun college activities Daniel could barely remember.

"Just the man I needed to see," Joel Randolph called, as Daniel headed down the sidewalk away from the theater. He waved his cane and picked up his pace.

"Should you be moving around like that?" Daniel asked, as he waited for his co-teacher to catch up with him.

"Only way I'm going to get stronger is to push myself. Stretch my wings and take some chances."

"What's got you in such a good mood?"

"Miracles happen every day, my friend." Joel chuckled and clapped Daniel on the shoulder, trying to muffle the sound of his heavy breathing.

Daniel had to agree. Joel might have lost his leg. Emily might never have awakened from her coma. If they could have such drastic, blatant miracles in their lives, was it so wrong to hope for some small ones in his?

"Just got back from a very long lunch," Joel continued as they started down the sidewalk again.

"Considering it's three? Yeah, I'd say that's long."

"Hey, it's not every day your little girl picks up her engagement ring. We had to celebrate."

"That's progress. I thought it'd take them until Christmas to get the ring. When's the wedding? Have they set the date?"

"Don't push it." Joel winked. "God only gives out so many miracles per family." He leaned heavily on his cane when they came to a stop at the intersection. They had to cross Sackley Road and walk two more blocks to get to the administration building. "Final interview with the Dynamic Deans Duo?" He waited for Daniel to nod. "You need to get away. It'll do you good."

"Will it?"

"Haven't seen Lyn in church lately. Except when she's there during the week, talking to Gwen Harris."

Daniel glanced sharply at his friend, but Joel just gave him an innocent look. Why would Lynette be talking to the church's counselor?

He didn't see when the light turned green and Joel started across the street. For a moment, Daniel couldn't see or feel anything except an expanding lightness in his chest. If that was hope, he might just die of it.

Chapter Fifteen

Lynette called the theater to talk to Kat. It was time she called in her daughter's help to track down Daniel.

But Kat had left and Marco was there, finishing up her work for her.

"I don't know where she was going," the young man said. Something hummed and rattled in the background, and Lynette suspected it was the copy machine. Her daughter had said something about Daniel working overtime on his lesson plans, far ahead of schedule, and being ten times more organized this year than last year.

"Is Dr. Morgan there?" she made herself ask. If she could let her answering machine take message after message from him, he had every right to ignore her calls, too. Still, it hurt to keep calling and get nothing but the hissing of bad phone wires.

"Nope. And he won't be here much longer, either. Something weird's going on," Marco hurried to add before Lynette could ask. "He got a bunch of papers today from administration, and he's been having interviews and setting things up with a bunch of grad students from Case and John Carroll. Kat said it's just a bunch of stupid rumors, but what if it's true?"

"What rumors?" Lynette slid into her kitchen chair and held onto the edge of the table. This was no time for her relaxed, tucked-against-the-wall, phone talking position.

"Well, I guess Dr. Morgan's finally taking a break. The scuttlebutt is he has a job in New York or Hollywood or somewhere waiting for him, and he's going away in a week. I think Kat's out running around trying to find out what the truth is." Marco paused. Lynette heard him swallow. Hard. Like she had heard Daniel swallow when he had fought not to cry in those days when she had hurt him so badly. "She's scared. And ticked."

"I know exactly how she feels," Lynette said between clenched teeth. "Thanks, Marco. I'll... I think I'll check the apartment to see if she's there. Talk to you later."

She hung up before he could respond and ran for her purse and her keys.

Maybe it would have been faster if she had run to the girls' apartment building, Lynette thought. The traffic this late in the afternoon was thicker than molasses in December. The slow pace gave her plenty of time to fume, shifting from blaming herself for Daniel's silence, to raging at him for acting like a spoiled brat, to sniffling and blinking rapidly to fight tears as she mentally scolded herself again. All the good gained from her four sessions with Dr. Harris seemed to melt away like ice on a July sidewalk.

Lynette had just about decided she'd like to grill Daniel on the same scalding sidewalk—just who did he think he was, leaving town without telling her?—when she reached the apartment building. She saw Kat's car pull in at the other driveway entrance, and nearly ran into the Tabor Heights PD squad car in front of her when the officer stopped to make a left turn into the city hall parking lot.

"Get hold of yourself," she said between clenched teeth, and prayed the officer ahead of her wasn't looking in the rearview mirror and couldn't read lips backwards.

It only took her another two minutes to find a parking spot, but it felt like hours. Kat was already inside. Lynette told herself to be grateful she knew where her daughter was. Maybe Kat had news, solid facts instead of rumor.

But what if Daniel really was leaving? Marco certainly sounded sure of himself.

Why was he leaving without telling her? It wasn't like she hadn't tried to contact him for nearly a week now.

All right, so she had avoided and ignored him for twice as long, but she was trying to fix things, wasn't she? What gave him the right to treat her like that? He was supposed to be the leader in their relationship, wasn't he? The strong one? The mature one? The spiritually stable and understanding one?

Maybe it was time she grew up, Lynette admitted, as she hurried to the door into the lobby.

"Lyn!" Daniel called.

In the glass door to the apartment building, she saw a dim reflection of Daniel hurrying down Span Street, waving to get her attention.

"I'll start growing up tomorrow," she muttered, and reached for the door handle.

"Lyn, wait up! I know you can hear me!" Daniel shouted.

Lynette's hand shook so hard her fingers slipped off the handle. She was never going to get inside before Daniel caught up with her. Then another resident came to the door and opened it to leave. She flashed the silver-haired man a smile and slipped inside. The reflection in the tinted glass door into the lobby showed Daniel running across the parking lot. Lynette let out a tiny hysterical laugh when the elevator doors magically slid open before she had crossed the lobby.

On the way up to the third floor, Lynette feared the elevator would get stuck between floors. Or Daniel would push the call button for the elevator and it would go down to fetch him before it let her off at her destination. She checked the floor numbers twice when the doors opened before she stepped off, then she ran down the hall to the girls' apartment.

The door hung open and she could hear Kat talking with Bekka and Shane.

"Morgan's leaving town!" Kat squealed. "Some geek graduate student is teaching his classes this semester."

"Where's he going?" Bekka asked.

"He didn't get fired, did he? Morgan's the greatest. You should have heard him explaining Shakespeare my junior year," Shane added.

"You'd think he'd at least tell me," Kat snarled. "I mean, he's my advisor. I'm his assistant, for Heaven's sake. He's dating—"

"Kat, do you have any idea what that rat fink is doing?" Lynette demanded, bursting through the door. She slammed it shut. That felt good.

"I just heard myself. I was hoping you'd know."

"Why should I expect him to tell me anything? He can criticize my life, but I can't tell him anything about his!"

At the back of her mind, Lynette knew she should keep her mouth shut, but it felt so good to let loose to someone besides Dr. Harris. And anyway, why shouldn't her daughter know what her father was doing to drive her crazy?

"I think I hear some ice cream calling," Bekka muttered. She scrambled to her feet and into the kitchen, with Shane close behind.

"I'm going to kill him," Lynette continued, barely noticing them leave. "This is worse than the last time he left. At least I told him to go away forever. He should have listened to me. *I* should have listened to me!" She grabbed handfuls of her hair and yanked.

The pain shocked her. What was she doing? Her throat tried to close up and she sniffled, feeling a tidal wave of tears threatening to burst forth.

"Mom?" Kat reached for Lynette's arm to lead her to the couch. "Are you okay?"

"You know what's crazy? I wanted to push him out of my life, and then I thought, I shouldn't just walk away like last time. There were so many loose ends, and I've been getting help and trying to call him but now he's giving *me* the silent treatment."

"Sounds like you were doing it to him, first," she muttered.

"Whose side are you on?" her mother demanded.

The doorbell rang, cutting off Kat before she could answer. They both jerked and turned to stare at the door.

The doorbell rang again. Kat took a step to go open it. Lynette snatched at her arm to stop her. As if she had x-ray vision, she knew Daniel stood there, leaning against the door, one fist raised to pound it down if he had to.

"Don't," Lynette whispered. "It's him."

A third ring. After two seconds of waiting. Daniel pounded on the door, hard enough to make it rattle in its frame.

"Lyn, I know you're in there!" Daniel called. "Kat, open the door, will you?"

Lynette muffled a shriek when Kat again reached for the door. She caught her daughter by the arm and pulled her back two steps.

"Mom, don't you want to know what's going on?" Kat twisted her arm free and lunged for the door, yanking it open before her mother could stop her.

Daniel hurried through, holding out a hand to stop it from being slammed in his face. Sweat beaded his face and stained his shirt and he breathed rapidly, as if he had run up the stairs from the lobby instead of waiting for the elevator.

"Don't you ever listen when someone shouts your name across an entire parking lot?" he demanded, stomping over to Lynette. She backed away from him several steps.

He was furious—but at least he was talking to her again.

Would it do them any good?

Right then, she didn't really care. Let him feel as hurt as she had been for what seemed like months.

"I don't want to talk to you. Ever," she added, with a little hiccup as a sob tried to work its way up her throat. No. She refused to cry. Not where Daniel could see her.

She honestly thought she could save this relationship? Who did she think she was kidding? She was a complete failure when it came to men. She should push Daniel out of her life once and for all.

"That's what you said the last time," Daniel said, with ice in his eyes.

Lynette let out a little shriek and raced for the bathroom. She slammed the door and fumbled with the lock. Burying her face in a towel, she waited for the sobs to erupt.

But of course, now that she had a way to salvage her pride, the need to cry a flood trickled away. She could hear every word coming through the bathroom door.

"That's pretty definite," Kat said. She let out a shaky laugh. "At least she didn't call the police."

"She wouldn't, would she?" Daniel said.

"I might. What's going on?"

"I came to say goodbye—"

"That's real late-breaking news."

A hint of a snarl in Kat's voice made Lynette flinch. Her daughter sounded so much like her, and she had hoped to protect Kat from that kind of tearing anger and hurt. Where had she gone wrong?

"It all just started coming together the last few days. I wanted to tell you what's going on before some idiot in Administration leaks the news."

"Too late."

"You and your mother have a right to hear it from me rather than rumors. Right now... can you explain it to your mother for me, since she won't listen?"

"Explain what?" Kat almost shouted.

"I'm going to New York."

"How long? For what? Why didn't you tell me before?"

"I already told you. It just started coming together. I'm lucky I could get my sabbatical at such short notice. I'm going to write —" He paused, and when he spoke again, there was a thickness to his voice that could have been laughter or shock. "—for the soaps. A totally new show, new concept, but still the soaps."

New York. Daniel was going to New York. Finally.

Without her. Without a word. Not even a good-bye.

"What about me? What about us?" Lynette demanded, bursting from the bathroom.

"If you'd give me time to explain —"

"Can I take notes?" Kat snarled, the angry hurt in her eyes spearing them both. "You could probably use this for one of your scripts!"

"You wanted Kat to explain to me a minute ago. You weren't going to tell me, were you? You love Kat more than me!" Lynette reached both hands for Daniel, uncertain if she wanted to shake him, strangle him, or wrap her arms around him and keep him from leaving.

"Why not?" He advanced a step on her and she jerked back without thinking. "She doesn't forget dates and then sulk when I can't rearrange my schedule to suit her every whim."

"Whim? I do not have whims!"

"And then ignore every phone call I make," Daniel barreled on. "How many calls did I leave you today, Lyn? I lost count at ten. I dare you to say I haven't tried to tell you. I wanted to talk to you, and then we'd tell Kat together. But there isn't going to be any together for us, is there? Just like last time. If you can't have what you want, then the rest of the world can just take a flying leap!"

"I haven't been home all day," Lynette nearly whispered, offering a trembling smile in the face of his red-faced, simmering fury.

Why hadn't she checked her answering machine when she got home? Instead, she had called Kat from the kitchen and let the rumors Marco repeated send her flying out of the house again. When was she going to learn?

"Sometimes I think you haven't been home your whole life." Daniel turned, stomping away from the two, who stared at him in perfect unity of wide-eyed, stunned expressions. He slumped, then pulled himself up straight again. She could almost hear the agonized groan he wouldn't release.

"I'm sorry," he said after a moment, his voice softer. "You're the only person in the world who can rile me like that, Lyn. I wanted so much for it to work for us this time. I guess I just have to accept that it's not meant to be. You won't give me any more of a chance now than you did when we were kids. All right, so I'm out of your life. I can live with that. I've had practice." He took a deep breath and finally turned around to face them again. "But I won't let you lock me out of Kat's life anymore."

"Daniel—no!" She wanted to plead, to convince him that she hadn't given up, but the resolution in his stony face terrified her. Now was not the time or the place. He couldn't really mean to tell Kat the truth now, when they were all furious with each other, could he?

"What are you afraid of, Lyn? Kat's got more talent than both of us rolled up together. She deserves every chance she can get, and I'm going to do everything I can to make sure she gets them. I won't let you stand in her way."

"You have to stay out of her life," Lynette insisted.

"Mom!" Kat yelped.

"For Heaven's sake, Lynette—" Daniel sighed, but she cut him off from saying more.

"When you get back to Tabor, I want her to be assigned to someone else as her advisor. I don't want you to talk to her, don't write to her, and keep your hands out of her career."

"Hey!" Kat's protest turned into a whine.

"Kat's an adult," Daniel said, dropping into a low, reasonable voice that made Lynette want to relax and listen and trust him. She muffled a sob when she realized it was all acting. "She deserves every chance she can get. Every chance I can find for her. You have no right—"

"No, you're the one with no rights," Lynette said. She knew that was the wrong track to take, the wrong words to speak, but she couldn't help herself.

Was he going to take her daughter away from her? Was he planning on punishing her? She had Kat for the first twenty years of her life, so now it was her father's turn? Lynette refused to let that happen, even if that aching down deep inside cried out that he *did* have the right.

"I gave up thinking of my own rights a long time ago. Kat *is* my responsibility, no matter what you say. I should have taken that responsibility a long time ago. You have no right getting in her way!"

"I have every right. I'm her mother!"

"What is wrong with you two?" Kat shrieked, stumbling forward to stand between them. She held up both hands like a traffic cop, to stop them. "I don't know what your problem is, but don't make me some prize in this stupid fight you're having."

"Tell her, Lyn." Daniel took a step back and unclenched his fists.

"No." Lynette took a deep breath that broke a little. She refused to break down crying, even though she suspected tears would probably go a long way toward healing the situation. "I can't. Everything was just fine until you came back into our lives. Why did you have to come to Cleveland?"

"Why did you leave Chicago? I've been here fifteen years!"

"What are you talking about?" Kat demanded.

"They're too stubborn to tell you," Bekka said, shocking all three of them as she came through the curtain from the kitchen. Shane stayed in the doorway, watching wide-eyed. "If someone doesn't tell you what the big deal is, I will."

"You told her?" Lynette gasped. Something went numb inside, as if she had just stepped beyond the point of being vulnerable to hurt and shock.

"She figured it out for herself," Daniel said. "Bekka's the only one with any brains around here." He nodded to Shane, offering a limp smile. "Sorry. Didn't see you there at first."

"It's okay." Shane glanced around the room and strategically ducked back into the kitchen.

"What are they talking about?" Kat nearly wailed and stumbled across the living room to Bekka.

"Better sit down," Bekka said. She glanced back and forth between Daniel and Lynette. Both just stared at her. "No takers?" She shrugged when neither one moved and offered an apologetic little smile to Kat. "Morgan is your father, that's all. And your mother doesn't want you to know."

"Mom?" Kat whispered, turning to face Lynette as she went white beneath her summer tan. "Is this true?" She barely waited for her mother to nod. "When were you going to tell me?"

"Never." Lynette sighed, feeling suddenly empty with the numbness that crept through her. In a way, it was a welcome sensation. "I sent him out of my life before you were born. I never dreamed he'd be your advisor. Or that you'd inherit his writing ability."

"I thought Cleveland was the last place you'd ever come," Daniel offered with a crooked smile.

"Mom, you said my father died before he could marry you," Kat said.

"Not exactly." A tiny laugh escaped Lynette.

"Gee, that's an understatement. Morgan? Or should I start calling you *Daddy*? How could you agree to just ignore me? You're not that kind of guy—are you?"

It tore through Lynette like a knife with a rusty edge, that her daughter could stand there, so still and pale, so much hurt turning her voice to an icy razor, and yet she didn't fall apart. That was likely her fault, after putting her through years of suffering with Mike.

There had to be something wrong with her. She was an unfit mother. Her daughter hadn't felt able to trust her with the truth of what her stepfather did to her, and now Lynette couldn't cross five feet of carpeting to comfort Kat as she went through likely the most traumatic shock of her young life.

"Your mother didn't want me in your life." Daniel sounded more tired than anything now. "I was too scared to fight her on it."

"Fight?" Lynette choked, wanting to laugh. "You kept showing up at my dormitory with a ring and roses, until the RA threatened to have you thrown out of school."

"He wanted to marry you, and you didn't?" Kat staggered back a step. "Mom, you married *Mike*. What's wrong with Morgan that made Mike a better choice?"

"He wanted to give up his future... so we could be together. I wanted him to make something of himself, instead. I thought my way was smarter. Better for all of us." Lynette closed her eyes, hating the sound of such stupid reasoning, spoken with her own voice.

Had she really believed herself noble and sensible and showing real love, when she made that choice so long ago? It was a miracle Daniel hadn't hated her.

He didn't hate her. He couldn't hate her. If she didn't realize that truth by now, there truly was something wrong with her.

How could she have made herself believe he was going to just walk away from her? Where had she been for the last few months, when every word he said, every action he took, proved how precious she was to him?

How could she say she ever loved him when she kept hurting him?

"What's wrong with that?" Kat spat. "Mike never gave up anything for you."

"Would you stop shoving him in my face?"

"Why not? You shoved him in my face for years!"

"Don't talk to your mother like that," Daniel said.

"Oh, now you're going to start sounding like a father?" Kat snapped. She staggered away another step, looking startled at the viciousness that made Lynette sick to her stomach. "Mom, didn't you love Morgan? Ever?"

"Kat, honey, it takes more than love..." Lynette shook her head. She smiled tremulously and her voice wavered a little. *Please, God, everything I've got is Yours, if You'll just fix this. I'm sorry. Please, don't make us all suffer for my stupidity.* "I wanted him to become a star and come back for us," she whispered, silently begging Kat to understand. "Instead, he got silly part-time jobs and stayed in school and became a teacher."

"Morgan's a great teacher."

"He could be a great actor and an even greater writer."

"There are more important things in life than fame and money," Daniel began.

"Like being a religious fanatic?" Lynette winced as those words left her lips. Yes, it had been a fear of hers, as Dr. Harris had helped her discover in their talks. But she thought she had put that fear to bed once and for all.

Or did she need to say it to Daniel before she could let go?

"Will you two stop it?" Kat snarled. "I can't believe how stupid I was, wanting you to get together. I thought you would be great together. All you do is fight and argue. How did you ever make nice long enough to make me?"

"Kat—" Lynette gasped.

"This has nothing to do with you," Daniel began.

"It has everything to do with me! You're playing tug of war with me and I won't let you do it! Go on back to Mike the jerk, Mom. You only want a brainless jerk anyway. And you go on to New York and play with those morons in the soaps—*Daddy*!" Kat added on a sugary sweet snarl. "Both of you, just get out of my life!"

Both her parents reached for her at the same moment. Kat let out a shriek and ran to her bedroom. The door slammed shut and locked half a second later. Her shriek cut off instantly.

"She buries her head under a bunch of pillows and stuffed animals when she's really ticked," Bekka offered. She flinched when both of them jerked and turned to her.

For an eternal moment, the three stared at each other. Then Daniel sighed and held out his hand to Lynette.

"I swear, Lyn. I'm just going away for a little while. Then I'm coming back for you and Kat."

"I know." She gave her hand to him. Tears she could no longer resist welled up in her eyes and when she started shaking, Daniel wrapped his arms tight around her. "I ruined it for all of us, didn't I?" she blurted between sobs.

"No, sshhh. This big a mess takes at least two."

"I was jealous. That's all."

"Jealous?" He let go of her enough to move her to arm's length and see her face. "Jealous of what?"

"You're so happy. You've given up all your dreams, but you're happy."

"It's not what you know. It's who you know."

"More church stuff, huh?" Lynette whispered.

"Sorry—"

"No. I'm ready to listen now." She took a tighter grip on his shirt, determined to stay there in his arms forever if that was what it took to fix things.

Daniel said something to Bekka, then led Lynette out of the apartment. She clung to him, not caring what it looked like as they rode the elevator down and crossed the lobby. Daniel led her to one of the benches set up in the shade of the trees between the apartment building and the slope down into the Metroparks. The tears came back in full force then and she let them come.

Maybe if she had cried more and fought a little less fiercely to be strong and independent back in college, things might have turned out differently.

Daniel took her back to his house when she had cried herself into a sleepwalking numb state. He kept his arm around her shoulders and took most of her weight on himself, and that sensation of warmth and support and safety was the most wonderful feeling Lynette had ever experienced. She knew Daniel still loved her.

You loved me all along too, didn't You, God? I was pretty stupid, wasn't I?

It was a liberating feeling to admit that.

They stayed up past 1am, talking and crying, confessing and apologizing. Daniel never let go of her, except when he scrounged through his cupboards for the last box of tissues in the house, and to get a wet washcloth and put ice cubes in it for her swollen eyes and feverish face. Lynette didn't know whether to laugh or cry at these evidences of prolonged bachelorhood. She wanted to take care of Daniel, as she had never wanted to take care of Mike. He deserved someone who thought of all the little things that made life comfortable, like extra tissue boxes and matching towels and cream instead of powdered creamer for coffee, because he would appreciate it and never consider such treatment his due.

She made Daniel tell her everything about his opportunity to go to New York and work for a major network and promote his writing, finally. Lynette was surprised at how happy and excited she was for him, even as the knowledge that she was being left behind scoured another sore spot in her aching soul.

"No, you have to go," she insisted, when Daniel started making noises about still being able to cancel everything. "It's only for a few months."

"But I'm leaving you behind," he whispered, reaching out to cup her cheek, as he had done so many times through the long, tear-filled evening.

"You're not really *leaving*, are you? I know you'll be back. And it isn't that far to New York."

She forced a smile that didn't feel half bad when she finally got it on her unsteady lips. "Commuter flights aren't that expensive. I could come up to visit every other weekend, if there's room for me."

"There'll always be room for you, Lyn. You know that." Daniel gathered her close, pulling her up onto his lap, as he had done to comfort her several times already that evening. This time, there were no tears, though their kiss had a salty flavor. The contrast made the sweetness all the more distinct.

Thursday, August 28

Kat was never available when Lynette called the apartment. Daniel reported that she never came into the theater office when he was due to be there. They communicated by messages left taped to his office door, or on each other's answering machines, for nearly an entire week.

Daniel's arrangements came together as smoothly as if guided by an invisible angelic hand. An efficiency apartment in a hotel in a good neighborhood became available a month sooner than anticipated, and Daniel's name somehow was at the top of the waiting list instead of the bottom. As a resident, he could have guests stay at the hotel at a discount, making it even easier, and more convenient, for Lynette to come for regular visits and have her own room. They made plans for what they would do and see as she helped him clean up his house and pack everything into storage, so it could be rented while he was away. They never talked about Kat, except to report to each other that they hadn't been able to get through to her.

She met his cousins, Al and his two children, his sister Abby and Tyler Sloane. She would have to wait to meet the elder Morgans until they came back from their latest cross-country excursion. Lynette had insisted on meeting his family. No more hiding what they were to each other. She let herself hope and plan for the day Kat would meet her cousins. The welcome the Morgan family gave her made her cry with relief and renewed regrets. What had she deprived herself of all these years, for the sake of pride, misguided nobility, and warped love?

Lynette and Daniel attended two more counseling sessions with Dr. Harris before he had to fly to New York. Pastor Glenn attended the second one, and Lynette found she felt none of the discomfort, shame, and anger she had anticipated.

She was finally able to put aside the guilt and righteous fury and pride she had worn like armor all these years. In Pastor Glenn, she found she was able to forgive the self-righteous people who had wounded her in her hour of need.

Everything, Lynette daily reminded herself, would be all right. It would just take time.

If only Kat would talk to them.

Finally, the day came to take Daniel to the airport. She called to leave one last message for Kat before she went to pick him up. If there was one thing Lynette had learned through all this, it was never to give up.

"Kat, honey?" Lynette said.

She closed her eyes, envisioning her daughter listening to the answering machine. For all she knew, Kat was there in the apartment, simply refusing to pick up the phone. Her voice wavered a little but she forged on. This was important.

"I'm taking Daniel—no, I'm taking your *father* to the airport. He really wants to see you before he leaves. He won't be back until Christmas. Kat, this is mostly my fault. Danny wanted to take care of us both from the beginning. He's always loved you. I hurt him and I locked him out of our lives. He would have told you the truth from the beginning, but I wouldn't let him. Don't punish him for what I did, please? Come to the airport to at least see him off, won't you?"

She waited, praying her daughter would pick up. When there was only silence, Lynette gave the flight details before hanging up.

She had done what she could.

At the airport, Daniel and Lynette stood a long, painful while in front of the last security checkpoint, watching the other passengers stream down the concourse. They held hands and she leaned against his shoulder. Neither looked at the other.

"Well, I guess this is it," Daniel said, when the line had gone down and there was no more excuse for delaying.

"I'm sorry."

"For what?" He smiled a little, just a flicker of his lips leaving their usual flat position.

"I called Kat. I told her to come say goodbye. What if their answering machine is broken again?"

"It's not the machine, Lyn. It's us. We gave up on our dreams and then we tried to live them through Kat."

"You didn't give up. I'm the one who messed up everything. Afraid and jealous and trying to make you live the way I wanted."

"That's part of being human. I'm glad things worked out like they did. I'd rather stay teaching at BWU for the rest of my life and have peace in my soul than be a success in Hollywood or Broadway." He finally looked at her. "But it's kind of hard doing any of it without you."

"I'm here now. It took me a while, but—" Lynette's voice broke. Daniel let his computer case slide to the floor and wrapped both arms around her.

She still had a few tears in her eyes, but she managed to smile without trembling by the time he finished with having his computer checked and walked through the metal detector and got his shoes and wallet off the other end of the conveyor belt. Daniel turned around once to smile and wave at her before he went down the long concourse to the gates.

Lynette breathed a sigh of relief when she heard the first announcement for Daniel's flight, meaning he hadn't made a mistake, delaying until the last minute. She waved to him and tried to smile, and walked to the far wall, where she could still see him before the slope of the concourse took him out of sight. She waited, leaning against the wall, ignoring the curious looks the armed guard gave her. Did he think she had a gun or a bomb in her purse? It was barely big enough for her sunglasses and wallet.

"Mom!" Kat's shout startled her.

Lynette automatically turned to look for Daniel, though he had vanished and was probably on his plane already. She rubbed her eyes, refusing to cry now, then turned to weave through the stream of people heading down into the security checkpoint. Kat crossed the current and stumbled through to meet her.

"You just missed him." Lynette wiped the last tear from her eyes and hugged Kat. "He'll be so glad to know you tried."

"I'm sorry, Mom."

"So am I. We have a lot of making up to do, sweetheart."

Thursday, September 4

Daniel groaned in weariness as he came through the door into his dark apartment. If this tiny square of living space with Chinese screens to designate bedroom separate from living room separate from dinette and kitchen could actually be called an apartment.

His schedule at BWU had spoiled him. He wasn't used to heading for work in the dark to avoid traffic, and getting home from work in the dark every single day. Even after four days at the network, he still forgot to leave a light on when he left in the morning. He left the hall door open to give him some light as he crossed the room, trying to aim for the torch lamp set up between his desk and his sofa.

The phone rang. Daniel changed direction and fumbled the cardboard divider tray with his dinner. French onion soup sloshed, threatening the foil-coated paper that slowly let his corned beef on rye get cold. He had to get to that phone. It was probably Lynette, calling to let him know if she could come up to visit this weekend.

Daniel stumbled over the case for his notebook computer, which he had left sitting in the middle of the tiny square of Berber carpet that laughingly passed for his living room. His foot slipped on the slick, padded nylon. He bit his tongue against spilling the curses he had heard around him all day, which seemed to soak into his subconscious and soul like filthy rain on his clothes. He definitely needed some time away from the office. Lynette's presence for the weekend would be his salvation.

The answering machine clicked on as he fought to keep from falling or spilling his dinner. He caught his balance and thought that tall, thin shadow directly in front of him was the torch lamp.

"Uh... hi."

Daniel paused, his heart stopping for several painful seconds as his brain raced to identify that strained, young, female voice. The click of the switch was loud as the torch lamp spilled light across the room.

"Um... this is Kat. Mom gave me your number. Um, I just wanted to — I hope everything's going okay with your new job. Everybody misses you. They sent us a bunch of geeks to fill in for you."

Daniel flung away the tray with his dinner as he lunged for the phone. It hit the wall with a splat and a splash.

"Kat?"

"Hi, Morgan." Her voice cracked with broken laughter. "I mean — uh — Dad?"

Tears blinded him. "I miss you."

"Is it okay if I call you — "

"Whatever you want, Kat."

"I'm sorry," she whispered.

"It's okay. Everything's going to be okay. I promise."

Thursday, October 30

Lynette came up every other weekend to visit. Kat accompanied her during mid-term break and they made like tourists. She had fun visiting the souvenir shops, finding gifts for Candy and Chad. Daniel was more than relieved that she had fallen in love with her cousins from the start. Kat enjoyed her visit to the studio more than any of them expected and was suitably impressed by how much work went into the daily filming.

"Even if it is the soaps," she said, with only a trace of her former scorn.

The three of them laughed together over the change in her attitude. The merriment continued over their dinner, which they had made together in the handkerchief-sized kitchenette in Daniel's apartment.

Still, the flying visits and phone calls every other night weren't enough. Daniel waited and prayed and thought about it and prayed some more. The day before Halloween, he called Lynette in the middle of the day to ask the question that had been waiting for a yes for twenty-one years.

She wasn't home.

Daniel laughed and asked her anyway.

When he got home that night, his answering machine blinked, and he dared to hope there was an extra, jaunty rhythm to the tiny green spark in the semi-darkness of his depressing little apartment.

Depressing because Lynette wasn't there.

"I'm coming up on the afternoon shuttle," she announced, without identifying herself.

She gave the flight details three times, contradicting herself each time. Daniel laughed, knowing he would be able to find her in the enormous airport, no matter what.

"Oh, and if you haven't guessed, the answer to your question is yes. Of course. Forever. How long does it take to get a marriage license in New York, anyway?"

Daniel glanced at his watch. His laughter caught in his throat as he dashed for the door again. Now was definitely the wrong time to be late.

Hopefully, getting a license wouldn't take as long as the taxi would take, to get him to LaGuardia to meet Lynette's flight.

After all, even patience and faith could be overdone.

END

THANK YOU!

Thank you for reading this book from Mt. Zion Ridge Press.

If you enjoyed the experience, learned something, gained a new perspective, or made new friends through story, could you do us a favor and write a review on Goodreads or wherever you bought the book?

Thanks! We and our authors appreciate it.

We invite you to visit our website:

www.MtZionRidgePress.com

and explore other titles in fiction and non-fiction. We always have something coming up that's new and off the beaten path.

And please check out our podcast

Books on the Ridge

where we chat with our authors and give them a chance to share what was in their hearts while they wrote their book, as well as fun anecdotes and glimpses into their lives and experiences and the writing process. And we always discuss a very important topic: *Tea!*

You can listen to the podcast on our website or find it at most of the usual places where podcasts are available online. Please subscribe so you don't miss a single episode!

Thanks for reading. We hope to see you again soon!

About the Author

On the road to publication, Michelle fell into fandom in college and has 40+ stories in various SF and fantasy universes. She has a bunch of useless degrees in theater, English, film/communication, and writing. Even worse, she has over 100 books and novellas with multiple small presses, in science fiction and fantasy, YA, suspense, women's fiction, and sub-genres of romance.

Her official launch into publishing came with winning first place in the Writers of the Future contest in 1990. She was a finalist in the EPIC Awards competition multiple times, winning with *Lorien* in 2006 and *The Meruk Episodes, I-V,* in 2010, and was a finalist in the Realm Awards competition, in conjunction with the Realm Makers convention.

Her training includes the Institute for Children's Literature; proofreading at an advertising agency; and working at a community newspaper. She is a tea snob and freelance edits for a living (MichelleLevigne@gmail.com for info/rates), but only enough to give her time to write. Her newest crime against the literary world is to be co-managing editor at Mt. Zion Ridge Press and launching the publishing co-op, Ye Olde Dragon Books. Be afraid … be very afraid.

And please check out her newest venture: Ye Olde Dragon's Library, the storytelling podcast. Each week, listeners are invited to join Michelle on her blog to ask questions and give feedback and suggestions. Interspersed between the chapters will be interviews with authors of fantastical fiction. Listen to the podcast on your favorite podcast app or listen on the website: www.YeOldeDragonBooks.com, and click on the Ye Olde Dragon's Library link. Then go to her blog to interact: www.MichelleLevigne.blogspot.com

www.Mlevigne.com
www.MichelleLevigne.blogspot.com

www.YeOldeDragonBooks.com
www.MtZionRidgePress.com

Look for Michelle's Goodreads groups:
Guardians of Neighborlee
Voyages of the AFV Defender

NEWSLETTER:
Want to learn about upcoming books, book launch parties, inside information, and cover reveals?
Go to Michelle's website or blog to sign up.

Thanks for reading!
If you enjoyed this book, would you help Michelle by posting a review on Goodreads?

Are you a member of Book Bub? If so, please follow Michelle on Book Bub, and you'll get alerts when new books are coming out.

As a way of saying thanks, Michelle invites you to the Goodies page on her website. It will change regularly, offering you a free short story, a sample audiobook chapter, sneak peeks at new cover art, inside information on discounts and new release dates, etc.

Please go to: Mlevigne.com/good-stuff.html

Also by Michelle L. Levigne

Guardians of the Time Stream: 4-book Steampunk series
The Match Girls: Humorous inspirational romance series starting with **A Match (Not) Made in Heaven**
Sarai's Journey: A 2-book biblical fiction series
Tabor Heights: 18-book inspirational small town romance series.
Quarry Hall: 11-book women's fiction/suspense series
For Sale: Wedding Dress. Never Used: inspirational romance

Crooked Creek: Fun Fables About Critters and Kids: Children's short stories.

Do Yourself a Favor: Tips and Quips on the Writing Life. A book of writing advice.

To Eternity (and beyond): *Writing Spec Fic Good for Your Soul.* A book defending speculative fiction.

Killing His Alter-Ego: contemporary romance/suspense, taking place in fandom.

The Commonwealth Universe: SF series, 25 books and growing

The Hunt: 5-book YA fantasy series

Faxinor: Fantasy series, 4 books and growing

Wildvine: Fantasy series, 14 books when all released

Neighborlee: Humorous fantasy series

Zygradon: 5-book Arthurian fantasy series

AFV Defender: SF adventure series

Young Defenders: Middle Grade SF series, spin-off of *AFV Defender*

Magic to Spare: Fantasy series

Book & Mug Mysteries: cozy mystery series

Quest for the Crescent Moon: fantasy series starting in 2023

Steward's World: fantasy series reboot and expansion, starting in 2023

Liars' Quest: fantasy, 1st book in the Ye Olde Dragon's Library storytelling podcast -- check it out!